Also by Tom Catalano:

THE EDGE OF IMAGINATION

TALL TALES & SHORT STORIES

FUNNY RHYMES ABOUT LIFE!

WITTY WORDS OF WISDOM

NICHOLAS, THE SANTA STORY

POEMS FOR HIS GLORY

RHYME & REASON

POETRY 'N MOTION

VERSE THINGS FIRST

I DIG MUD & YELLOW BLOOD

RHYMES FOR TEENS

JELLY IN MY BELLY

RHYMES FOR KIDS!

TALISMAN
A TIME TRAVEL MYSTERY

A NOVEL

tom catalano

ISBN 978-1-882646-14-2

Published by:
Wordsmith Books
P.O. Box 1608, Crossville, TN 38558 USA
tomcatalano.com

My heartfelt gratitude to **Liz Catalano** and **Peggy Catalano**. It was your help and encouragement that pushed me over the finish line with this project.

A special thanks to **Rod Serling**, **H.G. Wells**, **Jack Finney**, and **Ray Bradbury**. It was their imaginative views of reality that inspired me as an author.

Back cover photo credit:
Emma Louise Photography
@emmalouisemoments

Part One – The Discovery

1

JOHN STUCK THE ENTRENCHING TOOL into the sandy soil just beyond the stringed line at the base of the hill where the terrain started to rise. The tool went in with little resistance. It felt odd, for up until now the ground was compact. He pushed a little harder. The tool head disappeared under the soil with only the hilt above the surface.

He and Professor Rutherford looked at each other. Their eyes widened. It was probably nothing, but it was the first surprising thing that had happened since they arrived on that godforsaken island.

"Open it up my boy!" the professor shouted. Open it up!" He could hardly contain himself. His heart raced. They hadn't discovered anything in their ten days on the island and they were leaving tomorrow. The possibility of a discovery, *any* discovery, made him giddy.

John left the entrenching tool where it was for fear that if he removed it the sandy soil would backfill on itself. Instead, he knelt down and used his trowel to scrape away the soil up to that area.

"What do you think it is, Professor?" he asked, without looking up.

Rutherford scratched his chin. "Could just be pocket erosion. Covered up by sand drifts. Nothing more. An air pocket caused by a decomposed stump. Could be an animal hole."

John stopped and sat back on his heels. He was as excited as the professor not to go home empty-handed, but the thought of some hidden animal or snake lying in wait gave him pause.

"Keep going!" Rutherford ordered, ignoring whatever danger might be lurking under the soil.

John leaned over and continued to dig, pulling more earth away from where the entrenching tool was embedded. The soft sand pulled away easily.

Sand began falling inward. It was dropping slowly at first, like through an hourglass, then faster. It was, as the professor suspected, a hollow area beneath the surface. How large and from what cause was still unknown. John grabbed the entrenching tool before it fell into the hole and tossed it aside.

Using his bare hands now, John pulled the sand aside, opening the hollow area. The ground inclined from the dig site and the hole, which was enlarging by the second. It was becoming apparent that the hole extended under that sloped area by at least a few feet, perhaps more.

The professor pulled out a flashlight. He grabbed John by the shoulder and forcefully steered him away from the hole, causing the student to lose balance and land on his backside. Rutherford, a portly man with a barrel chest, eased himself down to his knees. With a bit of struggle, he leaned into the hole. His knees and back ached. The flashlight illuminated just enough to see that the hole was too large to be a pocket left from a decomposed tree stump.

"What is it, Professor? What do you see?"

Rutherford pushed himself upright and stepped back without answering. "Keep going! Keep digging!"

John ignored his fatigue, his hunger, and the sweat dripping off his face. The prospect of discovering something, anything, was exhilarating. He scooped more sand away. His eyes stung from the salty sweat that streamed off his forehead but he dared not wipe it away. His sandy hands and arms would have been more irritating to his eyes than the sweat.

The opening was now more than a yard wide, angled at the same thirty-degree pitch as the hillside. John's fingers stung as he clawed at the top of the opening along the hillside, but it was solid rock. He couldn't open it any higher than about eighteen inches. He turned his attention to the opening at ground level. It widened another two or three feet until he encountered solid rock there as well.

Rutherford, standing watch just behind John, could see that there would not be further progress at widening the hole. Quickly moving to the opening, he stuck the flashlight into the hole, almost bumping John in the process. Sensing the professor's intent and not wanting to get knocked over again, John moved aside.

"Remarkable," Rutherford said, smiling.

John was crouched, one knee on the ground. His hands rested on his thighs as he panted. The heat of the day and his frantic effort on the hole had drained what little energy he had left.

Fatigue could not squelch his enthusiasm, however. It had been a long, arduous nine days with little to show for it. "What do you see, Professor? Is it a tunnel?"

Rutherford, bent over and peering into the hole, was lost in his thoughts.

"Professor?"

Rutherford looked over to his smiling young protégé. "A tunnel? No. Not a tunnel. A natural rock-formed cavity. Beehive shaped. A hibernation spot, perhaps. A storage grotto. Maybe nothing more than a geographical anomaly created by wind and erosion."

John removed the bandana he was wearing, shook it, then wiped his face with it. The sun beat down on his uncovered head and he began to have a headache. He hurried to retie the bandana. Instantly, he felt cooler.

"Shall we tell the others?"

"No!" Rutherford answered sharply. Realizing he'd been noticeably curt, he cleared his throat and lowered his voice. "No, let's see what we have before we get anyone's hopes up. It may be nothing. Besides, they need time to make finds of their own."

John scratched the back of his neck and bit his lip. It took all the willpower he could muster not to question the professor's decision. With all that his fellow students had been subjected to over the past nine days, with all their disappointments, he couldn't understand why they all shouldn't partake in the joy of finding something, even if it was only an empty hole.

The professor must have his reasons, he thought. Reasons that only an esteemed professor from a major university could rationalize. Perhaps, he thought, it was simply because time was running out. It was their last day on the remote island of Antigua. Tomorrow they'd pack up their supplies and return the trucks and rented tools to the old man who ran the supply house in Saint William. It was the port town where they had first arrived and from where they would depart. From there they would begin the arduous journey back home to Chicago. First there would be the lengthy journey by ship to Puerto Rico and past the islands of the Bahamas until arriving at Cape Sable in Florida. From there, they would take the train to Chicago, which would no doubt seem like they were traveling in the lap of luxury after so many days on the water.

It was a long trip for so few days on the island, John thought. He hoped that it would be—in the professor's mind at least—worth it.

Rutherford stood in front of the newly discovered hole and pondered the possibility of his trying to squeeze through the opening to see what, if anything, the mysterious fissure might reveal. Shaking his head, he surrendered to the realization that it would be a tight fit.

"Well, in you go, my boy," he said, stepping

aside.

John swallowed and his eyebrows rose. He didn't relish the idea of crawling inside some dark, damp, hole that might be infested with snakes, mice, or one of a dozen varieties of bugs and crawling things native to the island.

"Inside, sir?"

Rutherford stuck the flashlight into John's hand while shoving him from behind. "Yes, yes! In you go. Take the flashlight."

John spread out on his stomach and peered into the hole. The sun was in its descent and past the treetops at the top of the hill. Harsh shadows started to blanket the ground, including the hole opening. There was no way of telling whether the hole was shallow or cavernous.

"I can't see anything."

Rutherford rapped John firmly on the shoulder. "The flashlight, boy! Use the flashlight and describe what you see."

John weighed the potential danger against facing a persistent, and increasingly irritated, professor and decided to proceed. He stuck the flashlight into the hole with his left hand. He pulled himself closer to the edge and deeper into the hole with his right.

With half his body into the hole, he felt the professor's grip on his belt, keeping him from falling in. It was a reassuring lifeline but only moderately comforting.

"What do you see?"

John panned the flashlight. Light filled the space,

bouncing shadows off the solid, irregularly shaped rock walls. It was a natural formation with the only opening the one he now occupied. It looked more like the inside of a stone egg than a beehive as the professor had described, but since he had never been in either, one analogy was as good as the other.

Rutherford scowled, tapped his foot. "For the love of everything holy, what do you see?!"

The air inside the mini cave was stale, malodorous. John coughed. His nasal cavities burned, and his stomach soured. Worse, it felt like disappointment.

"Nothing here professor," John said in the hollow surroundings. His muffled voice sounded as if he were speaking into a glass.

Rutherford's breath quickened, he leaned over. "Keep looking! There must be something. An arrowhead, a fossil, a … ."

Suddenly, John spotted something. He redirected the flashlight to the sandy floor. There, among the twigs and dried plant roots, was a tiny speck of something that reflected the light. It was not much larger than a small pebble, and he'd almost missed it. It was probably nothing more than a mineral deposit catching the light just right, but if there was one thing he learned from Professor Rutherford's archaeology class, it was to take nothing for granted.

"Wait a minute, I see something!"

He reached for the glittering speck but could not reach the bottom of the hole.

"I need a brush," he called up.

Rutherford grinned widely as he fumbled to

remove the brush from his utility belt while still holding onto John.

John reached behind him and took the brush. Being careful not to drop it, he let the brush slip through his fingers until he was holding the end of the handle. The six-inch handle was just long enough to reach the bottom of the hole. He carefully and gently brushed away the compacted sand around the sparkling dot. What he thought was a tiny mineral deposit did not get brushed away with the sand. Instead, it got larger, to the size of a fingernail then the size of a coin.

He continued brushing away the sand despite the pain around his midsection from laying over the stone opening. Sweat dripped off the tip of his nose. He thought he might vomit from the dank smell.

The shape of the object began to reveal itself. Cylindrical, gold metallic, about the size of his palm with various bumps, like half spheres, on the surface.

"There's definitely something here, Professor," he called up, his voice strained from the pressure on his chest. "Round and shiny. It's not a rock, but I don't know what it is. Could be man-made."

Rutherford beamed. His heart raced, and he could hardly stand still. Finally, a discovery! It would have been better if they'd found it several days ago, but better late than never. "Can you reach it?"

"There's something else."

John continued to brush away the area around the shiny cylindrical object. Gently at first. Then with quick flicks. Something started to appear. What at first looked like bent slightly brown twigs soon revealed themselves to be thin bony fingers from a human skeleton encircling the object.

John gasped and his head jerked back. Just as quickly he composed himself and returned to the task with a renewed and frantic resolve. Sweep, sweep … the radius and ulna bones from an arm. Sweep, sweep … a rib cage, spine, skull. All perfectly intact.

"Bingo, Professor!" John shouted, the excitement almost too much. He was out of breath from being upside down, his chest burned, and his stomach ached, but his adrenaline was pumping out of control.

"What?! What did you discover?!"

"A human skeleton, sir! And it's holding the shiny object."

Rutherford was smiling and bouncing on his toes. "What else? Pottery? Tooling? Weapons? What else?!"

John shook his head, even though the professor couldn't see. "No, sir. Just the shiny thing."

"Bring up the object."

John wasn't sure that he had heard correctly. Removing something from a dig site without first cataloging it, detailing the depth of the find, measuring it from all angles, and taking photographs was not normal operating procedure. The professor had always been a stickler for the smallest details. He stressed that in class and insisted on that in the field.

"I beg your pardon, sir?"

Rutherford's jaw clenched. "Bring it up, I said. Bring it up!"

From inside the hole John shook his head. It didn't seem right. But not wishing to question his respected mentor, John used the brush to carefully slide the object out of the clenched bony fingers of the skeleton.

"A little lower, Professor. Six inches or so."

Rutherford, his back already aching from being hunched over supporting the weight of his young protégé, took a half step closer toward the entrance of the hole. Now using both hands, he lowered John just enough to reach the object.

John grabbed the puck-like object and clutched it tightly. He didn't want to risk dropping it and having to go in for it again. It was weighty, four or five pounds, and cold. A stab of pain shot up his arm. His fingers tingled. He gasped and his hand shook. His chest hurt and it was difficult to catch his breath. He was tempted to drop the brush and flashlight and use both hands to hold the object but didn't.

He couldn't tell if Professor Rutherford was still holding on to him. He felt like he was floating, trapped in a vacuum and being sucked down. His entire body ached, and he was panting. The excitement of a discovery had quickly morphed into an ominous feeling of foreboding and panic. For what reason, he didn't know. Whatever the shiny object was, it held danger. He didn't know how he would know that, but something about it didn't feel right. As if he had desecrated a sacred burial ground.

The brownish bony skeletal fingers at the bottom of the hole were still curled. They looked strange sticking out of the sandy bottom holding nothing. As if they were reaching out to grab him. He started hyperventilating. He squeezed his eyes shut for a moment to calm what he told himself was an irrational fear.

"Are you all right, boy?"

The professor's voice was like a life ring buoy thrown to him at just the right time. He drew a deep breath and exhaled slowly.

"Yes sir. I just … need a moment."

Whoever was at the bottom of that hole on that remote West Indies island appeared to have died lying on their side with the object closely guarded. It must have held great value to them, as it appeared to be the only thing in the mini cave. If there were artifacts, pottery, tools, or weapons, perhaps they were buried deeper. Further digging would be necessary.

John couldn't help wondering what the circumstances were that drove this person underground. Or why they appeared to take only one object with them. And the biggest question of them all—what *was* that thing? After nine days of finding nothing, this was a huge discovery. The professor and the university would be ecstatic. He, however, was in pain.

His chest was raw from rubbing against the rock edge of the hole and blood was rushing to his head. He felt lightheaded. Between the pressure on his stomach and breathing the stale musty air, he wanted to gag. The churning in his stomach had him feeling nauseous.

"Pull me up please, sir."

With a mighty heave, Rutherford pulled John up and out of the hole. He rolled to his back, rubbing his chest and trying to catch his breath.

"Hand it here!" Rutherford ordered.

John, still recumbent, handed the object up and the professor snatched it.

Rutherford cradled the object in both hands, staring and holding his breath. He turned it over and around to get a true sense of its size and weight. Its diameter and shape were similar to, yet slightly thinner than, a hockey puck. Roughly three inches in diameter and ¾ inches thick. It was smooth along the circumference and along the chamfered edge. One side was flat, the other was bumpy with raised nodules of various sizes. There were no latches, hinges, or clasps. From the weight of it, it seemed solid. In the natural light, now dimming by the setting sun, it had a gold tint, top, bottom, and sides. The surface was coated with a dull film from the sand and powdery rock sediment. He rubbed it with his sleeve, grinning, half expecting a genie to emerge like from Aladdin's lamp. Nothing emerged, nor were there any openings from which a genie could appear, if one did exist.

Rubbing the surface caused the object to shine brighter. In all likelihood, by its luster and weight, the object was solid gold. If so, it would be worth a great deal of money. The larger question, he realized, was its purpose. And why it was at the bottom of a hole with a human skeleton. In the tropical climate of Antigua, skeletonization would only take weeks, but only forensic investigation could tell for certain. According to John, the skeleton did not have clothing, which indicates that it had probably been there for many decades if not hundreds of years. Maybe longer.

There were only a few more hours of sunlight

left. Harsh shadows surrounded them. The day was ending quickly, as was their stay on the island. Refusing to take his eyes off the golden object, Rutherford shook his head and cursed under his breath. If only this find had been discovered three days earlier. No matter. There was one thing he had learned years ago. If luck wasn't volunteered, it was your right to make it. Or *take* it. He hadn't gotten as far as he had in his career and position in life by waiting for the planets to align or … .

"Professor?"

Rutherford took a step back, almost stumbling. His head snapped toward John, who was staring and looking bewildered. He cupped his cheek and shook his head. Inexplicably, he drew the golden object to his chest.

"Professor, we're losing our light."

Rutherford swallowed and nodded. "Yes…light."

John stood, brushing off his shirt and trousers. "Do you want me to put the object back now?"

"No!" Rutherford snapped. He clutched the object with both hands now, even tighter.

"So that we can catalog and document it, I mean," John explained. "You'll want it to be with the skeletal remains when we measure and describe, right?"

Rutherford turned his back on the boy and the hole. He stared at the sea, about 200 feet southward. A slight breeze was blowing. The temperature had dropped a degree or two but not enough to provide relief from the searing heat and thick humidity. Waves crashed against the rocky shore, the smell of saltwater in the air. He removed his white brim hat, set the newfound golden object in it, and wiped his brow with his sleeve.

Taking a deep breath, he turned back to John and smiled. "No, not this time. I'm afraid we've lost our window of opportunity. We came close, but not quite far enough. We'll get credit for the discovery, of course. We'll document the plot location of the hole and the skeleton but the next group from some other university will have to do the analysis. It will be *their* find. *Their* accolades."

John lowered his head and sighed. "And the object?"

The professor scowled. "That's ours."

"Won't the next group want to study the object as it was found in relation to the skeleton?"

Rutherford took a half step toward John. His eyes narrowed, brows furrowed. His jaw clenched and his cheeks reddened.

"You are not to mention this find to anyone. Do you understand? Not even to the other assistants. I need time to examine this. Study it. And I don't want to be disturbed with petty interruptions."

John felt a fluttering in his stomach. This did not at all seem like the methodical professor he had come to know and respect.

"Yes sir, but can't we at least let everyone know that we had found something? They've all worked so hard."

Rutherford held his breath for a moment, then exhaled slowly. His tight facial muscles eased, and he smiled.

"Of course. But *only* about the skeleton. Say

nothing about the object." He put his hand on John's shoulder. "Only the skeleton. Are we clear on this? Only the skeleton. Is that *clear*?"

"I don't understand why, professor. But I will do as you say."

Rutherford squeezed John's shoulder tightly. It hurt, but John did not grimace. "Very good! I knew I could count on you. You are my most prized assistant. You are certain to go far."

The compliment was as shallow as the hole they had just discovered, and John felt falsely placated by having received it. Still, he was only an assistant, and the professor was a well-respected, tenured professor from the University of Chicago. In time, he hoped, the mystery of secrecy would reveal itself. For the moment, however, he just needed to follow instructions and be patient.

2

WHILE THE OTHER ARCHAEOLOGY research students, Taylor, Harrison, Louis, and Hannah, knelt next to the opening taking turns peering into the hole with their flashlights, John watched the professor take the gold object back to his tent.

"From the size of the skull, it doesn't appear to be Paleolithic," the chubby, rosy-cheeked Harrison said. "Too small."

"Perhaps Mesolithic or Neolithic," Louis speculated, pushing on the bridge of his black horn-rimmed glasses.

Taylor rolled his eyes and scoffed. "You're both idiots. Look at the color of the bones. Light brown. Any bones from the Neolithic era or older would be much darker from having absorbed nutrients from the soil over a longer period. Everybody knows that."

"He's right," Hannah added. "It's not as old as that. Definitely post-medieval."

Taylor sat back, crossed his arms, and smirked. While the others continued to examine the remains in the hole, he winked at Hannah. To have her validation was, he hoped, a good first step in winning her affection, something he hadn't been able to do to this point.

"At least a few hundred years, no?" Harrison asked after taking his turn to peer into the hole. Unlike the others, he couldn't squeeze far enough into the hole to get a close look.

"Probably was walking along this path next to the hill, fell into this hole and died," Louis hypothesized. "Then a windstorm kicked up and covered the opening."

"Wrong again, Copernicus," Taylor mocked, standing. "There are no tools, no weapons, no artifacts. Nothing they might have if they were traveling." He scratched his chin. "No, he—or she—didn't wind up here by accident. It's like they were put here."

"Buried," Hannah added.

Taylor nodded. "That's *my* guess."

He smiled, sensing that he was finally making a connection with her. She was arguably the most sought-after girl on campus. Attractive, intelligent, and available, so far as he knew. And, because her father was the university president, she was influential. Probably wealthy too. He tried flirting with her back on campus, but she always rebuffed his advances. Once, she even called him arrogant, self-centered, and "a general pain in the ass." Probably playing hard to get, he reasoned. That, in itself, was a turn on. Perhaps, he thought, being the best-looking guy on the island improved his chances.

Hannah ignored him, as she usually did. She

didn't care for his bravado, vulgarity, and disrespectful demeanor. She had always been more interested in guys who were caring, sincere, and humble. Like John Shaw.

She couldn't deny that she was attracted to John. Had been for a while. He was smart and good looking, but in a cute, clean-cut way, not rugged like Taylor. He was a likeable, down-home, boy-next-door type. Approachable, and certainly not condescending or demeaning. If she wasn't the daughter of the university president, she might have made her interest in him known. Because too many boys might try to use her influence with her father to their selfish advantage, she deliberately kept herself from getting too close to anyone who attended the university.

"What do *you* think?" she asked John, intentionally turning her back on Taylor.

John had been standing off to the side listening and observing, his hands in his pockets. He had already seen everything that there was to see in that hole—and more.

"Yeah, how about it, plow-boy? Any speculations?" Taylor sneered. He'd seen the flirtatious way that Hannah looked at John during the trip, and he resented the competition.

John looked back toward the professor's tent and shook his head. "It's a mystery all right."

"What's a mystery is why you are even on this trip," Taylor muttered softly, but deliberately loud enough to be heard by all.

Harrison snickered.

Louis fidgeted. He didn't like confrontations and

felt one was brewing. "Should we begin measuring?" he asked, surveying each of his colleagues hoping for something resembling leadership in the absence of any coming from the professor.

"We're losing light," Taylor answered.

"Taylor's right," Hannah agreed. "There's no time. We still have to break down our sites, collect our equipment, and load the trucks."

"But the skeleton … ," Louis started to say, standing, pointing to the hole.

Hannah stood up and sighed heavily. "We have to leave it for the next group."

"We do the work, and they get the glory," Harrison grumbled, stomping the ground.

Louis shook his head. "It's not fair."

"That's life," Taylor said, running his hand through his hair. "Get used to it. We should cover up the bones so they don't find anything."

"Yeah, we should!" Harrison said.

Louis nodded. "I agree."

Hannah scowled and kicked a spray of gravel in their direction.

"Hey!"

"What gives?"

"How did you children ever wind up in archae-ology?" she asked sharply. "Don't you understand the concept? Discoveries are not meant for the discoverer. They are meant for humanity. Nothing can be gained by keeping it a secret."

John looked at her and smiled. His admiration for her rose higher than it was already. He agreed that nothing could be gained by keeping it a secret. His smile faded as he wondered why the professor didn't feel the same way.

26

3

DR. HENRI RUTHERFORD entered his tent and quickly zipped the flap shut. There was barely enough natural light to see what he was doing. He turned on the battery-powered lantern sitting on the small round table in the center of the tent and hung it on a hook overhead.

Removing the golden puck-like object from his pocket, he set it on the small wood table. It made a loud *clunk*, and he froze for a moment wondering if it would draw attention from the students. Not likely, as they were all at the hole examining the skeleton and lamenting that they couldn't stay longer to excavate it.

Next to the table was a short, unpadded stool that was functional but not comfortable. It didn't matter; he was too excited to sit anyway. He paced the tent like a caged mountain lion, never once taking his eyes off the object. The light from the lantern reflected off the different sized bumps and nodules, sending sprays of dots across the walls and ceiling like a miniature disco ball.

He stopped in front of the table and slowly rotated the object. The pinpoints of light rotated across the tent like a time-lapse photo of stars speeding though the heavens. An interesting effect that revealed nothing about the object.

He sat on the stool and leaned forward, staring at the puck without blinking. Without taking his eyes off the object, he reached into his breast pocket and removed a leather-bound notebook. The one with notations not meant for the university.

He quickly flipped pages until getting to the first blank one. In the top right corner he wrote the date and then proceeded to document the discovery. Since this was his private notebook, he did not hesitate to mention the involvement of John Shaw. When it came time to file his official report with the university, however, there would be no mention of either Shaw or the golden object. It would accurately describe an exhaustive search of the assigned area with skeletal remains being the only find. It would have been too late, he will write, to do anything other than document the location of the discovery, which was protocol.

It wasn't the first time that Rutherford withheld information or artifacts from the university. His tenured position afforded him considerable freedom with his research and documentation.

Since he always came back with valuable infor-mation, critical finds, and historical artifacts, the Board of Trustees never questioned his methods or integrity.

They had no reason. He was highly trusted and respected. Anything and everything that the professor discovered equated to noteworthy attention for the university, including publicity, higher enrollment, and prestige. Sending Rutherford and his students out to do research was no more than a fishing expedition. If they landed a whale, wonderful. If they came up empty, the students gained necessary field experience. For the university, it was a win either way, and they touted the effort. Rutherford, however, saw it for what it was—a one-sided poker game. The university always won. He'd often wondered if they weren't as self-centered and motivated by greed as he was.

After so many years as an archaeologist and as a prominent professor at one of the most prestigious universities in the country there were very few goals left to achieve. Unbeknownst to the university trustees, he'd amassed a small fortune over the years. Not from the salary he drew at the university—although it was more than adequate for just his wife and him—but from the sale of the artifacts he pilfered from the digs he'd been on. The university had no way of knowing exactly what was found at the dig sites and believed him when he turned in his report. They always got the best of the lot. He made a point of that. Whatever remained, a cooking utensil, a piece of jewelry, some coins, were his. A finder's fee of sorts.

Having participated in digs in many different countries, he had trustworthy dealers on several continents with whom to sell the items he now claimed as his own. Those people had connections with museum curators and private art collectors. They paid handsomely for the chance to own a previously undiscovered piece of history. Neither the middleman nor the final recipient asked any questions, which relieved them of all responsibility. Or so they believed. By skimming just a few artifacts at each dig site, Henri Rutherford became a very wealthy man.

Rutherford chose to live in a small two-bedroom bungalow on the south side of Chicago within walking distance of the university so as not to flaunt his wealth. He did not want to draw attention to himself or his money. He wasn't beyond enjoying his spoils, however. He adorned the inside of the modest home with lavish furniture, expensive art, and modern appliances. His wife, Irene, never suspected that the niceties that she'd become accustomed to came from something other than his salary.

It was one of his fencing contacts who had given Rutherford a tip that the island of Antigua had a history of unique discoveries. The professor doubted, however, that the items the fence alluded to were as strange as the one before him on the table.

If it was solid gold, as it appeared to be, it would certainly command a hefty price, even more if it was an ancient artifact. Collectors paid dearly for items that had historical significance. Such was the nature of the collector—to not just understand history, but to possess it.

He lifted the object and held it in front of him using both hands. He ran his fingertips over the smooth raised bumps. They were irregular in size and arranged in no particular pattern that he could ascertain. Each bump was smooth and perfectly shaped. Some were the size of a pea. Some were half that size. Others were smaller still, the size of pinheads or mustard seeds. He paused for a moment and marveled at the spray of dots covering the inside of the tent, dancing in different directions as he turned it in his hand, smiling.

There was no sharp edge or a handle. It did not appear likely to be a weapon or a tool. There was no opening. It certainly was not a domestic utensil or storage device, at least not one that he could identify. Its perfectly cylindrical shape and remarkably flat bottom—or top, whichever it was—had to have been manufactured using sophisticated technology. This, however, did not seem feasible. The skeleton was old. Just how old was still in question. But certainly there could not have been any technology available during that time period to make something so precise.

Rutherford set it on the table before him and then rubbed the ache from his wrists. Leaning over, he retrieved a silver flask of whiskey that he stored in his satchel at the foot of his cot and took two long sips.

The alcohol warmed his insides and made him feel lightheaded. Ordinarily he had a high tolerance for alcohol, but standing in the hot sun all day seemed to accentuate the effects. He closed his eyes and took a deep breath, grateful for the reprieve from the stress of the week and the aggravation of finding something too late to do much good. Damn the timing of it all.

On another day, another dig, he might have helped the students break down the camp and ready the trucks for their return journey. But the students all knew what needed to be done, and he needed to be alone. He scowled. If he didn't think the students would hear he would have pounded the table with his tightened fists. To leave Antigua with a skeleton still lodged in the ground and nothing but a gold puck thing to account for their efforts was disheartening.

If the Board of Trustees at the university thought that he would give up the only find of the trip to them, they would be sadly mistaken. Fortunately, they would never know. He would share the news of a skeletal discovery but the gold would be his. Reward for suffering a long trip, searing heat, and spitting out sand for a week.

John Shaw. His bright, enthusiastic, first year student research assistant. The only one who knew that something other than the skeleton was found in the hole. The question was whether the boy could keep a secret. In the past, other assistants knew what finds turned up at the digs, but once they got back to the university, no one ever knew what became of the objects. The students—young, naïve, and trusting had no reason to think that every item had not been accounted for, cataloged, and was being studied by someone somewhere. By the time they completed the school year, at least a few of the items had long since been sold on the black market. No one was ever the wiser.

This was different. There was only one item in question and his most astute student knew about it.

Rutherford took two more long gulps from his flask. He felt warm, relaxed. His thoughts were swimming in the euphoria of the alcohol. He lifted the object again to feel the weight and smiled. Whatever the historical significance, it would bring a healthy return. Perhaps enough to retire on. He laughed and stroked his bearded chin. How fortunate he was to belong to an organization that not only paid him well, but also offered him the opportunity to become rich. If they only knew.

The sudden knock on the pole at the entrance of the tent startled him, nearly causing him to drop the weighty object.

"Who is it?!"

"It's John, professor. May I talk to you please, sir?"

Rutherford gently set the object on the table and placed his hat over it.

"Come."

John tried to pull aside the canvas flap door, but it didn't budge.

"Excuse me, professor, but it seems to be secured from the inside."

Rutherford smiled. "Yes, so it is." He pushed himself up and the stool toppled backward. His legs felt rubbery and his balance was off. Fortunately, he only had to take a few steps to unzip the flap. After doing so, he stepped back to allow John to enter.

"John Shaw, my young protégé. What brings you out at this time of the evening? Why aren't you packing up your gear for the return journey tomorrow? You will need your rest, I assure you."

John stepped inside the tent. "Yes, sir, I'm sure we will. I'm all packed and the tools are loaded in the trucks."

Rutherford reset the stool and sat down, using the table to steady himself. "Then what is it, young Shaw?"

This was the first time that John had the privilege of being inside the professor's tent. It was significantly larger than his own, and he was able to walk around inside without bending over. Other than the lantern hanging from the ceiling, a cot in the corner, and the small round table and stool in the center, it was devoid of any creature comforts of home.

"I wanted to talk to you about our find today."

"Of course. What about it?"

"I couldn't help but wonder what was going to happen next?"

Rutherford nodded. "Ah! A very good question. We will submit our summary log along with the plot number to the university to receive credit for the skeletal discovery. And also to the Antiguan government for accreditation. The next archaeological group will find our observations useful when excavating the area. It is indeed unfortunate that we won't be able to complete the investigation … ."

John interrupted. "No, sir, I mean the other thing."

Rutherford looked away for a moment then scratched his head, feigning confusion. "And what thing might that be?"

John's eyebrows rose in surprise. He couldn't believe that the professor didn't know what he was talking about.

"Why, the round object we found in the skeleton's

hand."

Rutherford inadvertently looked at his hat on the table, reassuring himself that the object was concealed.

"Oh, that."

"Yes, sir," John said softly, taking another step deeper into the tent. "Forgive me for saying so, but we don't seem to be following standard operating procedure. At least not as I remember you teaching back at the university."

Rutherford stood quickly, his brow furrowed and teeth clenched. "And what do you know about 'standard operating procedure,' young Shaw? Hmm? How many digs have *you* been on? How long have *you* been studying archaeology? A *year*? I've been a professor for *twenty-five* years! How dare you lecture *me* on what is or isn't standard operating procedure!"

John's eyes widened and he took a half step backward. "I'm sorry, sir. It's just that in class you said … ."

The damned alcohol! Realizing that he'd probably overreacted, Rutherford closed his eyes and took a deep breath, exhaling slowly. He was drawing unnecessary attention to himself. He had to be careful with this one. It wouldn't be beyond this particular student to make trouble if he wanted. All it would take would be a comment or inquiry about the object to the university administrators, and his career would be over. Who knows, they might also press for prosecution if they believed the boy.

Rutherford smiled, forced as it was. "I know. I said that we need to be thorough. Diligent. And we *will* be. Because of the oddity of the object, I have taken a personal interest in it. As is my right. I will be documenting the find personally and it will be in my report to the Board of Trustees."

He put his hands on both of John's shoulders, as much to keep his balance as to keep the boy from moving to the table and uncovering the object.

"Rest assured that all will be handled properly," he lied.

John nodded and turned to leave the tent. Then he stopped and scratched his chin. "There's still one thing that I'm curious about."

Rutherford cleared his throat and rubbed the back of his neck. He wanted to escort Shaw out so he could get back to examining his prize. He straightened up, his hands in his pockets, tapping his foot. It took every bit of self-control that he could muster to ask calmly, "And what is that?"

"Why are we not sharing the discovery with the others?"

Although his thoughts were still fuzzy from the alcohol, Rutherford was well-practiced at being articulate while under the influence.

"There is precious little time before we must depart. Just look at how much time you and I have spent discussing it! I wouldn't have any time to contemplate or analyze. What little time I had left would be spent explaining myself and theorizing. No, it's better that we just keep this to ourselves."

From the blank look on John's face, Rutherford could tell that the boy hadn't completely accepted this rationale, but he didn't care. He didn't want to continue the conversation. There was much to learn about the object's composition, age, and of course, its resale value. He didn't want to waste time justifying himself to a *student*.

John stared at the professor, his mouth open slightly. He nodded, but clearly did not agree or understand.

Rutherford knew this wasn't over. Odds were good that the boy would not stay silent about it. Shaw was too moral, too questioning. He was likely to say something to the other students, if not the Board of Trustees. The university, the community, and the media will cry 'scandal.' An investigation will ensue. They will discover the cache of yet unfenced stolen artifacts in his home. They will demand an explanation, for which there would not be an acceptable answer. Further investigation will reveal that over the years he had stolen hundreds of artifacts that rightfully belonged to the university and sold them for his own profit. Of course, he will lose his position. Prison was almost a certainty. All because of a nosy, self-righteous, overly enthusiastic, know-it-all, do-gooder! No, this was not over. If anything, it was just the beginning.

At that precise moment, Dr. Henri Rutherford knew that John Shaw would never return to Chicago.

4

THE SUN SET, quickly swallowing the island in darkness. Waves could be heard crashing on the shore. The wind picked up, as it had every night since arriving on the island, whistling over the treetops, through the palm tree fronds, and past the row of tents. The flapping tent canvases were a cacophony of irregular high-pitched drum beats growing louder by the minute. If it weren't for the numbing effects of the alcohol, Rutherford knew he would get no sleep at all.

With very few belongings to pack for the next day's journey, he decided to take a walk. He wasn't ready to sleep, as if the wind would even let him, and he had to think. He had to go *now*, for soon the wind and accompanying sandstorm would make it prohibitive. Perhaps the fresh air would help him decide what to do about his overly inquisitive student.

He stepped out and zipped the tent flap shut.

There would be enough of that blasted sand over his satchel and cot by the morning without inviting it in. The air had cooled, but not much. He stretched his arms outward. It felt good to be up and about.

The three pickup trucks they had rented in the port town of Saint William were parked down the gravel road a hundred yards or so from their campsite to the east. He sauntered down the road to be sure that the students had correctly packed their tooling and equipment. It gave him something to do while formulating a plan. A quick look, he thought, and then back to the tent for some sleep. Or more whiskey, depending on his mood.

At the rear of one of the trucks was a dark silhouette of a lone figure. As Rutherford approached he could see that it was John Shaw. The boy was securing a tarp over the top of the stored gear in the open bed pickup. He was in the process of tying down the last corner and did not hear the approaching footsteps over the gusty wind and flapping tarp.

"Difficulty sleeping?"

John drew a quick breath and spun around. "Professor! You startled me."

"So I see. Everything seem to be in order?"

John nodded. "Yes, sir. With the exception of our tents and personal belongings, everything is in the trucks. We'll be ready to go tomorrow as soon as you give the word."

Rutherford, now next to John at the rear of the pickup, lifted the end of the tarp and peered in. "If it isn't too much trouble, can you reach in and retrieve one of the specimen crates? I'd like to make sure that we properly categorize and transport our gold object."

John's eyes widened. "Does that mean … ?"

"Yes, by all means, let's share this with the others before we leave. No reason they can't bask in the excitement that you and I have enjoyed. Wouldn't you agree?"

John beamed. His joy and relief were barely containable. "Professor, I am so pleased. The others will be too." He quickly turned and leaned over the tailgate to retrieve one of the wooden boxes that they had brought to the site intending to pack and transport any artifacts they might discover. Since they had come up empty until the last day, the boxes were beneath everything else.

It took several minutes to shift the tools and gear to get to the nearest rectangle wooden box, half the height of an orange crate. It scraped along the bottom of the bed, but the noise was barely audible over all the island sounds.

"Ah-ha! Found it."

Suddenly, the flat side of a shovel came down hard on the back of John's head. The pain burst through his skull like an exploding migraine. He was instantly dazed, his legs felt like rubber, and he dropped to his knees. Before John could regain his senses, another blow followed, and another. He collapsed face down on the ground, blood streaming from the back of his head.

When opportunity presents itself one must take advantage of it, Rutherford knew. He felt breathless, dizzy, but exhilarated.

There was no time to waste. He put his fingers to the boy's carotid artery. There was no pulse. Death was likely instantaneous. The final blows were more out of frustration than necessity. The howling wind had covered up the blows, another lucky break.

Still holding the shovel, the professor dragged John's lifeless body by the back of the collar to the nearest dig site, the one designated as A52-1D, which had been worked on by Louis, the spindly bookworm.

He turned the body over and laid it face up in the recessed site. When the others woke in the morning, they would discover the body and conclude that John had gone for an evening walk. Since the stakes and strings had been removed to prepare for their departure the next day, he must not have seen the recessed terrain. It will appear that he lost his footing, fell into the site area, hit his head on a rock, and died.

It wasn't planned, but Rutherford was pleased that it was Louis's site that he had come to first. Louis was credible. Taylor, on the other hand, was arrogant, self-serving, and openly antagonistic toward Shaw. Everyone on the expedition, including many on campus, knew that. The one thing Rutherford didn't need was a murder investigation. This had to look like an accident. Ironclad. Hannah, as the daughter of the university president, would draw too much attention just because of who her father was. Harrison was a bumbling buffoon. He might come across the body and falsely think that someone on the island was out to get them all. His skittish personality would almost certainly cause mockery and possibly raise suspicion. Louis, on the other hand, was studious, calm, and believable. Meticulously detailed and observant. Honest. If it appeared to him that John

Shaw's death was an accident, then everyone would believe it, including the Board of Trustees and law enforcement.

Rutherford dragged the flat side of the shovel in a serpentine pattern back to the pickup truck, smoothing away his footprints and the blood that had leaked from John's head. By the time he got back to the truck there was no blood left on the shovel or the surrounding area. Working quickly, he stored the tool, along with the wooden specimen box, in the truck bed under the tarp. After tying down the tarp, he leaned against the back of the truck, took a deep breath, and sighed heavily.

He then went back to his tent to contemplate his last remaining challenge—when and where to fence his treasure.

5

THROUGHOUT HIS ADULT LIFE Henri Rutherford could have been accused of being many things: a manipulator, a schemer, a liar, a thief, and perhaps even a conspirator, but until now, no one could have ever accused him of being a murderer.

He wasn't sure how he felt about that, but he chose to ignore the guilt and potential ramifications. It was just business. All he wanted to do was make a living, as was his right. Shaw got in the way, that's all. He had the potential of making trouble and had to die. Just business.

Rutherford removed the gold object from his pocket and set it on the table before him. He stopped pondering what it was and focused on what it would bring on the black market. It may or may not be enough to retire on, but it certainly would pad his savings.

Although his wife Irene didn't ask for much

and seemed to require little, he felt obligated to provide more, as was his role as income earner. Having grown up poor, she had learned early on not to ask where the money came from. She was just appreciative that it kept coming. If she ever suspected that the income was derived from illicit means, she never questioned it openly.

He picked up the thing, enjoying the weight of it. Weight meant volume; volume, profit. If only it had historical significance, he thought, the profit would double. Maybe triple. He rolled it around in his hands. Up and over, around, sideways, up and over again. There were no markings, no inscriptions. Not that he expected one, but he looked for a date or engraved initials of the craftsman who made it. There wasn't so much as a scratch. In all his years of study, he had never seen anything like it.

The wind was incessant. The tent sides were vibrating more than they had all evening. Unlike previous nights, tonight the noise was welcome. It meant that airborne sand would drift over his tracks and all hints of blood. By the time they discovered Shaw's body, it would be half covered in sand with no evidence of what really happened. He wanted to laugh.

Rutherford removed his hat, replacing it with a high intensity illuminated head magnifier. With his elbows resting on the table, he held the object sideways in front of his face. He squinted and his eyes watered at the strain. He wiped them dry with the back of his sleeve. At this angle, using the magnifier, he was able to detect a microscopic seam along the beveled edge, just below the bumps.

Perhaps it *was* a container, he thought. His hopes rose with anticipation that something even more valuable was inside. Diamonds, ancient coins in pristine condition, tiny scrolls of historical records from a society long since extinct. The possibilities were endless. His heart raced.

Using his fingernails, he tried to pry one side from the other. The seam was so slight that he couldn't get his nails in between. He removed a pocketknife from his jacket, opened the blade, and tried to force a wedge between the two halves, but with no success.

Perhaps it wasn't a seam separating one side from the other at all, but rather a thin, almost imperceptible, decorative engraving. He turned it flat, nodule side up, but was unable to see the thin line. It was only after the thing was turned sideways that the line could be seen, and only upon close examination with the magnifier.

Once again holding the puck sideways, his eyes still focused on the line, he tried to twist the halves. First left and then right. They held tight. If they were indeed halves, they seemed fused. Or maybe they weren't halves at all.

Pinching tighter, he tried again, his fingertips aching. The halves of the puck seemed to rotate. Just a little. An eighth of an inch. Maybe less.

Suddenly, the tent went completely dark. The wind stopped blowing. The tent sides no longer flapped against the support poles. There was an eerie stillness in the air that hung there for a second or two. He felt slightly lightheaded and gasped.

Then, just as suddenly, the inside of the tent was brighter than it had been since before sunset. But that was impossible. It was now past eleven o'clock. The sun had set hours earlier, but it was as bright as if lights were focused on the outside of his tent.

Of course, he thought! Shaw's body must have been discovered! Someone must have gone for a late night walk and found the boy. The students must now be surrounding his tent, each holding flashlights, ready to confront him and prevent his escape. But how could they have known that he was responsible? The boy was dead, he was quite sure of it. The only explanation was that someone must have seen or heard what happened.

His chest tightened and he had trouble catching his breath. His face reddened, and he felt feverish. What had seemed like the perfect crime just moments ago was now anything but.

He sat perfectly still, unblinking, the silence deafening. His heart rate increased. Beads of perspiration covered his brow. His mouth went dry, and his stomach soured.

He deeply regretted his actions. Why, he wondered, had he resorted to such a drastic solution? Maybe he could have tried bribing the boy first.

No, he reminded himself. The boy was too moral, righteous, and honest to be dissuaded. Murder was the only recourse. Or so it seemed. But now this!

The waiting seemed interminable. He wondered why they weren't barging in. Surely they wanted to confront him about the loss of their friend and colleague. Perhaps they were waiting for the authorities to arrive to make a formal arrest.

The nearest constable would be back in Saint William, the coastal port where they had rented the trucks and gear, nearly nine miles away. Even over the sound of the blowing wind, he certainly would have heard the roar of a truck engine or sirens. But he had heard nothing.

The tent was filled with ambient light, like waning daylight just before sunset. Not at all like focused beams coming from flashlights outside in the dead of night.

As a professional archaeologist, it was his nature to search for clues, scant though they might be, and put them together like a puzzle. And evidence was starting to indicate that no one was outside the tent. No one was waiting to confront him. And no one knew about John Shaw. Not yet anyway.

He stood up slowly, exhaling, careful not to knock over the stool—just in case anyone was waiting for him outside. The logical thing to do was peek out of the tent, if for no other reason than to be assured that no one was out there. But first, whiskey.

Rutherford sat back down. His nerves were shot. He closed his eyes and shook his head. Having to deal with a persistent do-gooder and disposing of his body was one thing. But now this full moon illumination, or solar flare, or … whatever the hell!

He could admit—to the right listener—that he was a thief, but adding 'murderer' to his list of infamous credentials wasn't without its level of anxiety. Now, it felt like more burden than he could bear.

Surprisingly, the flask wasn't nearly as empty as he thought it would be, and he stared at it for a moment.

Another oddity of the evening, he thought. He took a gulp. After breathing the dry air of the island day after day, the whiskey was harsh and stung his throat. Not that he minded. The irritation was a distraction. He took two more gulps. They went down easier.

As it had earlier, his head was swimming in the euphoria of the alcohol. He lifted the puck, admiring the weight of it, and tried to imagine what it would bring on the black market. He laughed and stroked his gray bearded chin.

After more contemplation and drinking, there was a knock on the pole at the entrance of the tent. It startled him, just as it had earlier in the evening.

"Who is it?!"

"It's John, professor," the familiar voice said.

Rutherford gasped. His jaw dropped open. John Shaw? Impossible!

He shook his head and rubbed his eyes. The alcohol was obviously clouding his thinking, distorting his judgment. It was not possible that Shaw could be alive. But there he was! Perhaps he crawled out from the shallow dig area, realized what had happened to him, and because of whom, and was now coming for retaliation. Maybe he didn't know *who* had beaten him and was now seeking help. Perhaps it wasn't Shaw at all.

"May I talk to you please, sir?"

The voice was unmistakably Shaw's.

Rutherford gently set the puck on the table and placed his hat over it, as much for discretion as for a weapon should he need it.

Realizing that he could not escape the inevitable

confrontation, he called, "Come."

John tried to pull aside the canvas flap door.

"Ah, excuse me, professor, but it seems to be secured from the inside."

His voice was calm and upbeat, not at all filled with anger, disappointment, or pain. If this was a young man bleeding profusely and hell-bent on revenge, he was managing to control his emotions superbly.

The thought flashed through the professor's mind that perhaps the alternative explanation he'd avoided thus far was that it *was* John Shaw, and he *was* dead. That this was some sort of a zombie, a being of the walking dead. He didn't even want to consider this alternative. He could fight or lie his way past some irate students, the authorities, and even an injured victim, but to fight the dead? That would be futile.

He expelled the air he'd been holding. Zombies? The walking dead? Nonsense. He didn't believe in such things. There had to be a logical explanation. A puzzle picture other than the one he had conjured up in his whiskey-distorted imagination. He was now anxious to find out what it was.

"Just a moment."

Leaning on the table, he pushed himself up and the stool toppled backward. His legs felt rubbery from either the alcohol or the mystery, or both. But he only had to take a few steps to unzip the flap, so he managed.

After running the zipper along the edge of the canvas flap, he stepped back quickly. He half expected a dead zombie to come barging in and beat him to death with a shovel.

No such thing happened.

John Shaw, bent over slightly, stepped into the tent. There was no blood. No nasty head wound. No evidence of death whatsoever. Not even a sign of a struggle or having been dragged a dozen yards face down along the ground to what was supposed to be his temporary, but quite dead, resting place.

It was temporary all right, for there he was, looking as full of life as he had earlier in the evening.

Something needed to be said. Rutherford tried to remain calm, but his words wanted to stick, crack. He took a deep breath.

"John, my young protégé. What brings you out at this time of the evening? Why aren't you packing up your gear for the return journey tomorrow? You will need your rest, I assure you."

Of all the things he might have said, he couldn't believe that those were the ones he managed to utter. It would have been so much more natural to ask, *"Why aren't you dead?"* or *"Funny seeing you on your feet when your head is so bashed in."*

John's voice was calm, controlled. He looked fatigued but not angry. Not at all like that of someone who had just been assaulted. Murdered, even. "I'm all packed and the tools are loaded in the trucks."

Rutherford reset the stool and sat down, using the table to steady himself. His equilibrium was off. His legs felt weak, his throat dry, and his thoughts confused. His eyes hurt and his temples throbbed. Anticipating the answer, he forced himself to ask, "Then what is it?"

"I wanted to talk to you about our find today."

Rutherford had to turn his head to hide his surprised expression. Had he heard correctly? *This* was what the boy had to say not an hour after he'd been bludgeoned with a shovel and left for dead? He wouldn't have been surprised if the boy had asked why he'd been attacked. Demanded to know why he had to die just so that the treasure wouldn't have to be shared or revealed.

Instead Shaw seemed oblivious to the incident. Was he being coy or just calculating? This casual tête-à-tête had to be a precursor to a demand of bribery, Rutherford reasoned. Or a claim to partnership. Opportunity for profit, when it presents itself, can often make a person focus on what *could* be, rather than what *has been*. No one knew that better than Rutherford, who had taken opportunity to a new level.

"Of course," the professor said, playing along. "What about it?"

"I couldn't help but wonder what was going to happen next?"

Ah, there it was, the precursor to discussing 'terms.'

Rutherford looked away. "I intend to submit our summary log along with the plot number to the university to receive credit for the skeletal discovery, and to the Antiguan government for accreditation."

"No, sir, I mean the other thing."

Rutherford stood, preparing for the altercation that he was sure would come, verbal or otherwise. "And what thing might that be?"

"The round gold object we found in the skeleton's hand."

Of course. Bribery. Partnership. Greed. Everyone was inherently greedy, Rutherford thought, even farm boys from rural downstate Illinois. The chance for quick money heals all wounds, even nasty gashes on the back of the skull. So what *was* the cost to remain silent about the gold puck and the attack, he wondered.

Rutherford glanced down at the table, reassuring himself that the object was concealed. "Oh that."

"Yes, sir," John said, taking another step deeper into the tent, closer toward the professor.

Rutherford took a half step backward, fully expecting his student to lunge at him at any moment. Although he was the larger man, older and likely stronger, Shaw had youth and agility on his side. While the whiskey would have a numbing effect on any blows received, it also would certainly hinder his reaction time should a fight ensue. He readied himself for the inevitable.

Shaw ran his fingers through his hair. "Forgive me for saying so, professor. But we don't seem to be following standard operating procedure. At least not as I remember you teaching back at the university."

Rutherford wondered if he had heard correctly. 'Standard operating procedure'? Within the hour, they had tread through secrecy, lies, deception, assault, and murder. No, they had left standard operating procedure behind long ago.

The professor felt his patience for this cat-and-mouse game depleted. His anger rose as his face tightened. His eyes narrowed and brow furrowed. The tone of his voice was sharp and cold. If a battle was to be waged here and now, then let it begin.

"And what do you know about 'standard operating procedure,' young Shaw? Hmm? How many digs have *you* been on? How long have *you* been studying archaeology? A *year*? I've been a professor for *twenty-five* years! How dare you lecture me on what is or isn't standard operating procedure!"

John, taken aback by the effrontery of his normally mild-mannered professor, took a step backward. "I'm sorry, it's just that in class you said … ."

Impossible! They were recreating the same conversation they had earlier in the evening. Before the confrontation at the back of the pickup truck. Before the murder! Shaw wasn't being coy, calculating, or even naïve. He was unaware that an altercation had even taken place. He wasn't aware because it never happened. That would explain his casual attitude, the innocent inquiries, and the lack of blood on his head, neck, and shoulders. Not to mention that he wasn't lying dead under an inch of windblown sand.

Rutherford shook his head slightly. So John Shaw *didn't* die. He *hadn't* been beaten with a shovel. They *never* met at the back of one of the trucks earlier in the evening. And it would appear that it wasn't even as late in the evening as he had thought.

The only remaining conclusion was that the whiskey had made him drowsy, and he had fallen asleep until just now being awakened. It must have all been a dream.

He drew a long cleansing breath and smiled, comfortable in the thought that he had solved the mystery.

"I know. I said that we need to be thorough. Diligent. And we *will* be. Because of the oddity of the object, I have taken a personal interest in it. I will be documenting the find personally and it will be in my report to the Board of Trustees."

He put his hands on both of John's shoulders. As much to confirm that the boy was solid, real, and not another dream, as to reassert his authority.

"Rest assured that all will be handled properly," he lied.

John nodded, turned to leave the tent, and stopped. He faced the professor. "Why are we not sharing the discovery with the others?"

The question was predictable. More than predictable, it was expected. Something more than intuition told him that Shaw would ask that. Even more eerie was the fact that he had heard himself repeat nearly word for word what he had said in the dream. Never before had a dream been so vivid, so accurate. Nor had he ever heard of someone's waking state emulating the elements of a dream, although the reverse was common.

"There is so little time before we have to depart," Rutherford answered. "I wouldn't have any time to contemplate or analyze the object. What time we have left would be spent explaining myself and theorizing. No, it's better that we just keep this to ourselves."

Rutherford recognized the look on John's face. It was one of capitulation, but not agreement or understanding. He'd seen it before. There was no mistaking it.

Without another word, John turned and left.

This wasn't over, Rutherford realized. Far from it. Just as he had envisioned in his dream, he was convinced that the boy was likely to say something to the others, if not to the university administration when they returned. John was too inquisitive, too virtuous. He would make trouble. There was little doubt about it. Fortunately, with the help of a predictive dream, or premonition, or whatever it was, he knew what he could do. What he *had* to do.

John Shaw had to die. This time for real.

6

SITTING ALONE IN HIS TENT, Rutherford couldn't decide what was more intriguing—the object before him or the predictive dream. They were equally odd, but for different reasons. It seemed that on some level they were related, although he couldn't fit them together to form a cohesive picture.

Refusing to let himself get drowsy from the whiskey and the long day, he stood and paced, never once taking his eyes off the object in the center of the table. Although it emitted no obvious magnetism or special power he was aware of, he was inexplicably drawn to it. They were connected, tied somehow to each other. Perhaps for no other reason than he had claimed ownership of it. But he didn't want to let it out of his sight. *Couldn't* let it out of his sight.

The sun was setting. The tent gradually grew darker, and Rutherford turned the lantern on. When he felt he had waited long enough, he checked his watch. A little after eleven. The students would be asleep. He planned to sneak over to Shaw's tent and smother the boy with a towel or blanket while he slept. Then he would drag the body over to Louis's dig site and deposit it there. Then, safely away from the tents, he would strike Shaw's head with a rock to make it look like he had fallen.

Thanks to the dream, he had a ready-made plan.

After dimming the lantern, he stepped out of the tent, zipping the flap closed behind him. There was no question of whether he should kill Shaw, or when, or even how. That had all been resolved in his subconscious while he slept. It would be easy.

Although it would be the first time that he would take a life, it didn't *feel* like the first time. The dream had felt real enough to make it seem like he had killed once before. He knew he could do what needed to be done.

He needed something thick to smother the boy, so he went to the truck to retrieve a blanket or burlap bag. It didn't matter, as long as it wasn't his hand. Although his large hands would have been more than adequate to seal both the boy's mouth and nostrils, he didn't want to risk getting scratched or bitten in the process. Perfect crimes left no evidence.

Not willing to take a flashlight with him and risk being seen, Rutherford made his way to the trucks in the dark. The sand and gravel crackled under his feet, but it was barely audible above the wind which had begun to kick up, as it routinely did at that time of evening.

As he approached the trucks parked side by side, he noticed movement at the rear of one of them. At first, he dismissed it as shadows caused by swaying palm trees.

The closer he got, the more he realized that it was not a shadow after all. It was the silhouette of a person leaning over the rear gate. John Shaw.

Rutherford was within ten feet of the tarped pickup before Shaw noticed someone approaching. The noise of the wind was adequate cover.

John spun around. "Professor, you startled me."

"So I see. Everything seem to be in order?"

He nodded. "Yes, sir. With the exception of our tents and personal belongings, everything is in the trucks. We'll be ready to go tomorrow as soon as you give the word."

It was unnecessary to plan for Shaw's demise in the tent, for the opportunity presented itself—again—at the truck, just like in the dream. It made sense. If his subconscious had sent him the blueprints for the perfect murder, who was he to deviate from them?

"If it isn't too much trouble, can you reach in and retrieve one of the specimen boxes? I'd like to make sure that we properly categorize and transport our newfound object."

John's eyebrows rose. "Does that mean … ?"

"Yes, by all means, let's share this with the others before we leave."

John beamed. His joy and relief were palpable. "Professor, I am so pleased. The others will be too."

He quickly turned and leaned over the tailgate to retrieve one of the wood boxes from under the tarp.

While the first blow to his head was excruciating,

he never felt the second. Or the third. By then, John Shaw was dead. Again.

7

RETURNING TO HIS TENT as stealthily as he could, Rutherford zipped himself in for the night. Taking a quick look around the interior, he noted that it was just as he had left it. Dimly lit with the soft yellow glow cast from the lantern above. He half expected something to be out of the ordinary, although he wasn't sure what. He sighed.

Had he been in a brick home with a chain lock, deadbolt, and pit bulls, he wouldn't have felt safer than he did at that moment. No one had seen his departure or return, and no one had seen him drag Shaw's lifeless body over to Louis's dig site.

First thing in the morning, he would notify the university of Shaw's unfortunate 'accident,' and someone would have to notify the family, but it wouldn't be him. Naturally, there would be some paperwork to fill out in Saint William, mainly authorizing the transportation of the body back to the United States. Otherwise, for him, the worst was over.

The wind was now thumping the canvas against the tent poles. It was a noise he knew that he wouldn't miss once they left. He was thankful it had muffled his attack on Shaw. Thanks to Mother Nature, his involvement would go unchallenged.

He almost pitied Hannah's father, Phillip Miller, the president of the university, who would have to break the news of John's death to his parents. Almost. But accidents do happen. A shame, too. The boy seemed nice enough. A bright student but too inquisitive. Too damned righteous for his own good.

Once again, lifting his hat off the table, Rutherford revealed the inspiration for his crime, the mysterious gold puck ... thing. The light from the lantern reflected off the bumps and nodules, spraying pinpoints of light of various sizes across the walls and ceiling. It looked like he was staring at the celestial heavens on a cloudless night. He could almost pick out constellations: Orion, Cassiopeia, the Big Dipper. He shook his head. It was nothing more than whiskey euphoria.

Whatever the thing is, or was, it seemed to be nothing more than an interesting conversation piece. Although Rutherford could not date it back to a particular period, its uniqueness *might* add to its value. If not, someone could just melt the damned thing down for the solid gold it appeared to be. Either way, he would command a pretty price.

With his elbows resting on the table, wearing his head magnifier, Rutherford lifted the puck and held it sideways in front of him. He ran his fingertips over the bumps. Just like in his peculiar dream, there seemed to be a thin, nearly imperceptible, seam that ran the circumference along the rim. It was amazing how detailed his dream had been and how closely reality seemed to be following it, he thought. No doubt some high-priced Michigan Avenue psychiatrist would have a field day analyzing him about this. None would be given the chance, however. Too many details would need to be omitted and what remained would be so vague as to be useless.

Following the lead from his dream, he tried to pry one side from the other using his fingernails but without any luck. His pocketknife proved just as useless. Remembering from his dream that neither effort worked, he tried twisting the halves. They moved. Just a little.

Then, just as it had about an hour ago, something felt different. The tent went completely dark for a moment then suddenly brightened. The wind stopped blowing. The tent sides ceased flapping. Just like in his dream, within seconds it seemed more like dusk than late evening. The grayness within the walls of the tent and the stillness of the air felt too real and eerie to be a coincidence.

His mind raced, and he tapped a fist against his lip. His thoughts were muddled. His fatigue and confrontation with John Shaw had left him spent. Maybe it was the earlier blast of whiskey. Whatever the reason, Rutherford felt his capacity for logical thought shutting down. Perhaps after sufficient rest he would wake with a clear mind, and everything would be copacetic. All anomalies explained.

As exhausted and confused as he felt, he was afraid that sleep wouldn't come easily. If nothing else, he was suffering from sensory overload. But he had a solution for *that*.

He unscrewed the top from the silver flask and took a long drink of the aged whiskey. It went down hard and burned his parched throat. Not that he minded all that much. The irritation was a distraction. He took two more swallows. They went down easier. He was becoming lightheaded. It was just what he needed to fall asleep, though there was no guarantee that it would be a restful slumber.

He lifted the puck and tried to picture his fence's expression when he set it on the mineral scale. He laughed and stroked his bearded chin.

Then, seconds before it happened, Rutherford knew what would ensue.

A sudden knock on the tent pole.

He bolted upright, flushed, his stomach nauseous. He closed his eyes and shook his head to clear the effects of the alcohol. He'd heard the knock earlier that evening and then again in his dream—if that is what it was. Now he wasn't so sure. He wasn't sure of anything. His orderly world of predictability was thrown into disarray.

Even archaeology, which by its very nature consisted primarily of broken and missing puzzle pieces, could be counted on to make sense once enough puzzle pieces were assembled. But now, nothing made sense. There were not enough puzzle pieces to form a picture—

Impressionist or otherwise.

These experiences, he now realized, were happening again just as they had earlier in the day. It had been no dream. Somehow, some way, everything had repeated.

The only explanation was that he was losing his mind. He was locked in some sort of a mental loop that rewound itself, giving him the illusion that time had passed and that it was happening again. It was a picture. Not a pretty one, but a picture, nevertheless.

Another knock on the tent pole.

He leaned forward and faced the entrance of the tent. Rutherford clenched his hands in his lap, rocked back and forth, and rubbed his fingers together. He did not want to answer it. Not this time. Not again. It would be John Shaw. He would want to talk about the object. About standard operating procedure. Later, Shaw would go out to the truck to check on his gear. There, Rutherford would engage him in small talk and beat him to death with the blunt end of a shovel. Again. He just knew it.

The heat of the day still saturated the tent, but Rutherford felt chilled. A bead of perspiration slithered over his forehead, and his temples throbbed. Even more than when he had killed Shaw—the first time. The first time, second time, how many times *had* he killed the boy?

None.

Shaw was still alive. He always was. The evidence of that was that he was now standing at the tent entrance no doubt wanting to talk about the object and procedure.

The whiskey, although warming and relaxing, had left him mentally impotent. Without his wits, nothing made sense. Worse, he felt paranoid. Afraid to think and afraid to act. He didn't want to answer the knock for fear that it would all begin again. And he was terrified to think of the reasons *why* it would be happening.

Insanity was the easiest explanation but certainly not the only one. Perhaps he was being punished by some deity for having lived a secret life of lies, deception, selfishness, and greed. A god, a demon, what did it matter? The end result was the same: punishment for a sinful life. This explanation was the most disturbing. It was the one he most feared, that there could be punishment inflicted beyond just this world.

Another knock on the tent pole, louder.

He would not answer. If he were stuck on a mental Möbius strip, then he had to do something to get off, to prevent the repetition. No, he would not go through it again. Not again.

Another knock, louder still.

"Professor? It's John, sir. I saw your light on. I hope I'm not disturbing you."

Rutherford, now perspiring profusely, rocked back and forth, holding his stomach. He shook his head.

"No. Go away. I'm not feeling well. Save yourself."

John wasn't sure what the professor meant by the last comment but dared not inquire further. This was a great man. He must have had his reasons. Who was he to question genius?

"Good night, professor. See you in the morning."

Yes, Rutherford thought, *I'll see you in the morning, because you won't stay dead!*

He didn't care to answer. No words would have formed anyway. His throat seemed frozen, his thoughts cloudy. All he wanted was to be left alone. More with his flask than his obscure thoughts. With any luck, he'd pass out without any additional pondering of this anomaly. Then wake up in the morning with little more than a bad headache. If he was *unlucky*, he'd wake up to another knock on his tent pole and the same exact thoughts.

8

AT FIRST LIGHT THE NEXT MORNING, Rutherford woke up still wearing clothes from the night before, the empty flask on his chest. There had been no more knocks, discussions, or altercations. It might have been possible to dismiss the events of the night before as nothing more than delusions created in a moment of alcoholic stupor, but he knew better. Something had happened, then didn't, then did again, then didn't. He knew all too well that whatever happened wasn't a dream. What remained was the question of his sanity.

He silently vowed never to discuss what had happened—or didn't happen. No one would understand or believe him. They would question the story, his motive for telling it, and of course his rational mind. Perhaps his stature as a respected professor at a leading research university would protect him, but maybe not.

It was just as likely that he would be referred

to the Chicago-Read Mental Health Center for further examination. Once there, they wouldn't be so quick to dismiss his story. They would question, probe, test, and prescribe a myriad of medications to find a root cause for such a breakdown. They would be relentless. Then, not being able to find an explanation, they might secure a court order and he would be required to remain there until he was 'cured.'

No, he realized, he must not tell anyone. Ever.

As he gathered the remainder of his belongings and shoved them into his satchel, he picked up the mysterious gold … talisman. Yes, he decided, that is what he would call it. A talisman with powers and influence beyond his understanding, but a talisman, nevertheless.

"You, my little friend, have somehow brought evil upon me. Until you appeared, I had never questioned my convictions or my sanity. Now I question both. What *are* you? And where did you come from?"

There was a knock on the tent pole.

Rutherford quickly shoved the talisman in his jacket pocket. It was starting again.

"Professor? Are you up?" the female voice asked. "We should probably get going if we are going to make it to Saint William before the tide."

Hannah Miller. Not John. Hannah.

"Yes, of course," he forced himself to say, his voice one octave short of cracking. "I'm coming."

Jumping to his feet, he hurried out of the tent, nearly bumping Hannah in the process. With satchel in hand, and the talisman hidden in his jacket, he started down the gravel path, then stopped. For a brief moment, he surveyed the excavation site where they'd spent the past nine days working. He was especially interested in the area worked by Louis. The stakes had been pulled and the windblown sand from the night before covered some of the dig area. More importantly, there was no body lying there.

With the exception of his, all the other tents had already been struck and stowed. The students hadn't waited for his direction, which was good because he felt unable to give any. He was no longer the person he was when they first arrived on the island. *Then*, he was a self-confident professor comfortable with his own life, corrupt though it might have been. He was directing the lives of others toward higher learning—and to assist him in his graft-induced treasure hunts, if he was honest about it. His life had changed over the past seven hours, however, and not for the better. Now, he questioned his own sanity.

Little did he realize that the worst was not over. Not by a long shot.

9

CLASSES RESUMED IN THE FALL at the University of Chicago. Professor Rutherford missed more of them than he led. Keith Fitzgerald, the capable but thoroughly uncharismatic teaching assistant, stepped the class through the lessons. He started each class by telling the students that the professor wasn't feeling well. No other explanation was offered. None was sought.

It was commonly known that the amount of time a professor was out of the classroom was in direct proportion to how noteworthy they were. The more advanced the degree they held, or the greater number of awards they received, the less they were in front of their students. Rutherford had earned enough points in that regard to put in nothing more than a perfunctory appearance once every couple of weeks, and no one questioned it.

John Shaw suspected that the professor's

absence was the result of something else. He had a strong feeling that there was something seriously wrong with the professor, and it wasn't illness. He wondered if it had something to do with the round gold object that they had found in the cave with the skeleton on Antigua.

The professor's aloof and reticent behavior started long before classes began in the fall, however. On the ferry from the port of Saint William in Antigua to Puerto Rico, then on the steamer from San Juan to Cape Sable in Florida, and then again on the train to Chicago, the professor didn't come within ten feet of the students or say fifteen words. He generally confined himself to his quarters. Periodically, however, he would take a walk along the deck, looking up to the heavens or across the waves, only to turn quickly and return to his cabin when one of the students spotted him.

The students discussed his erratic behavior a few times during the trip. Some speculated that their beloved mentor was physically ill. Others suspected he was disgruntled due to the uncharacteristic lack of success on the island. More than once, they wondered if he was disappointed in *them*.

Before they even returned home, however, the students grew tired of talking about their expedition. They'd been away from the comforts of home too long, living in cramped and dirty conditions, and were anxious to get back to their regular routines. Everything else was secondary, even the professor's capricious behavior.

Even now, back at the university, Taylor, Harrison, Hannah, Louis, and John avoided discussing their experiences on the island. They'd gone, experienced, and returned. The air had been hot, the food had been cold, and the sand had been a bitch. It seemed to take forever to get there and twice as long to get back. They found a skeleton that they couldn't research because they ran out of time and the professor had weirded out on them. It was over. End of story.

But for John, it wasn't. There was an element to the trip that the others didn't know about—the gold object. The subject never came up in any of the class lectures, and he didn't expect it to. Right or wrong, he would respect the professor's desire to keep the discovery of the object just between them. For now, anyway.

As he sat in Cobb Lecture Hall on the University of Chicago campus listening to a fourth-year teaching assistant drone on about sedimentary rock settlement, his mind drifted back to the professor and the object. Its uniqueness, the mystery of how it got in the hole, and the general secrecy surrounding it.

Whether in class, study hall, or his dorm room, he frequently found himself doodling round, flat symbols with lines like sun rays emitting from it. There had been a certain aura emanating from the thing. His fingers, hand, and arm had tingled when he had held it briefly. At the time, he thought it was just the uncomfortable position he was in while retrieving it. Or the natural excitement of finally finding something on the island. Now he wasn't so sure.

Since he was no longer in possession of the object, John was not affected by its physical influence, if in fact such a thing was possible. Nevertheless, it commanded his attention. Monopolized his thoughts. It was difficult to concentrate in class, and he feared the obsession would only get worse.

Whether he was developing into the inquisitive archaeologist that Rutherford would have admired, or simply suspicious of the professor's intentions, he knew that he was consumed with the mystery.

John's most difficult classes were yet to come. As if obtaining a degree from a prestigious learning institution like the University of Chicago wasn't difficult enough, a distraction of this magnitude would almost certainly impede that education. If he had any hope at all of completing the requirements of his degree, he had to get to the bottom of the mysteries—that of the object, *and* of his elusive professor.

In his dorm room, John paced, fiddled with the curtains, and straightened the bookshelf above his desk. He couldn't sit. Couldn't relax. It felt like every nerve in his body was electrified and his insides filled with effervescence. He knew that he should do something— *had* to do something—but didn't know what. The inactivity, the ignorance, was eating him alive.

The experience in Antigua affected him in ways that no one else could possibly understand. No one else, that is, except Professor Rutherford. The common experience inexplicably linked them. The professor should help him understand. That was his job, to help students learn and grow. Perhaps the professor was researching the object and would appreciate having an assistant. Surely he'd understand a student's insatiable need for unraveling a mystery. He knew what he must do.

This certainty should have provided him some measure of peace and tranquility. It didn't. Instead, John felt danger and apprehension.

He looked down and noticed his hand twitching slightly. His fingers were tingling, just like when he held the gold object.

10

PROFESSOR RUTHERFORD'S OFFICE and research lab were on the lower level of the Watkins building. Above the door was a brass nameplate with 'Archaeology Laboratory' engraved in black letters. After class, John went directly to the lab.

The lights were on, but the large, windowless room was empty. Two rows of black rectangle tables were pushed end-to-end. Along two walls were glass-enclosed curio cabinets with a variety of artifacts brought back from dozens of previous archaeological digs.

Each cabinet held articles of interest from specific time periods. Spearheads and hammers with stone heads, held together with fraying hemp twine. Clay pottery, some in pristine condition, and human bone fragments were showcased in one of the cabinets. Pieces of rusted iron breastplates, several inches of butted chainmail, a nearly complete coif, broken swords, and pieces of flint were in another. Fossilized plants and stone tablets with images of rudimentary art were in yet another cabinet.

Each item had an accompanying index card with a brief description, including the age, period of origin, location from where it was excavated, by whom, and a catalog number. It was an impressive collection, the likes of which were rarely found outside of museums or wealthy collectors.

John slowly walked the length of the room, past the long row of locked cabinets. He carefully noted the contents of each. The gold object that he and the professor found on Antigua was not in any of them. Just as he had suspected.

At the far end of the classroom was the professor's office. It had been added years after the initial construction. It was modular with windows along the top half and plywood painted pale green along the bottom. The windows were covered with half-inch horizontal blinds. John lightly rapped on the door. There was no answer. He tried the door, but it was locked. He peeked in the windows but the blinds were closed tightly. No lights were on. Wherever the professor was, it wasn't in his office.

On a campus the size of the University of Chicago, the professor could be anywhere. Or maybe he wasn't on campus at all. John was determined to find him. His peace of mind depended on it.

John paused after leaving the Watkins building. A passing breeze reminded him of their time on Antigua. It had been physically exhausting and mentally challenging.

Hope and optimism were in constant conflict with loneliness and disappointment. The heat, the sandstorm, the crappy food, the uncomfortable journey, would all have been worth it had they just come back with a discovery.

He reminded himself that they *had* made a discovery. A significant one at that. They had found an artifact of an unknown origin, worthy of significant investigation and discussion. Yet the professor had not mentioned it to the other research assistants or the students in the classroom. And it was not displayed in any of the glass cabinets with the other discoveries.

Perhaps, he thought, if he hadn't personally discovered the object, held it, or felt its weight, it wouldn't matter whether the professor showed up for class or dropped off the ends of the earth, for that matter. But the fact was, he *had* seen it, touched it, and had been sworn to secrecy about it.

Whether the object was the subject of a research paper, featured in Archaeology magazine, or placed under glass in the university laboratory, it didn't matter to him as much as finding out why the professor wanted to keep it a secret.

John hurried along the sidewalk leading to the main quad. He was anxious to go somewhere, although he was not sure where. Coming toward him down the path was Keith Fitzgerald, the tall and lanky senior teaching assistant who had conducted their class earlier in the day. His long-sleeve white shirt was buttoned all the way up. The stack of books he carried was clutched tightly to his chest, as if he were afraid someone would steal them.

Fitzgerald didn't recognize John. With an average class size of seventy-five in an auditorium setting, there was little chance that he knew, recognized, or took an interest in anyone in particular. Besides, he hadn't worked as hard as he did just to get into the university to make small talk. He had few friends and little time to make any.

"Hey, Keith," John said, stepping in front of Fitzgerald, now in full gait.

Fitzgerald, surprised that anyone was speaking to him outside the classroom, pulled up and stopped abruptly. "Are you addressing me?"

"I was wondering if you knew where I could find Professor Rutherford at this time of day."

Fitzgerald grimaced. That's what happened when you were friendless and humorless, he thought. People were always trying to get a rise out of you.

"Very funny," he said. He stepped around John and continued walking toward the building, anxious to get to the lab and prepare his lesson for the following day.

John looked away and scratched his head. He trotted after Fitzgerald, calling out, "I'm John Shaw. I'm in your class. Actually, it's Professor Rutherford's class. Earlier you said that he was out sick, but I was wondering if you knew how I could get in contact with him."

Fitzgerald stopped just before the double doors and turned; head tilted. "Fraternity initiation? A dare? A bet? Whatever it is, it doesn't matter. If you spent half as much time studying as you do thinking of ways to mess with the T.A., you'd ace the class."

He flung the door open and went inside.

John was stunned. He *was* acing the class, and he had no idea why Fitzgerald was being aloof. Whatever the reason, it annoyed him. A simple question warranted a simple answer. Or at least a respectful one. Not some self-righteous, defensive babble.

Out of principle, he reentered the building and hurried over to Fitzgerald just as the T.A. was about to descend the stairs to the lower level. He grabbed Fitzgerald by the upper arm to stop him.

Fitzgerald wheeled around. "What the … ?"

"Look, I don't know what you're thinking, and I really don't care. I just want to know if you know where I could find Professor Rutherford. I would like to talk to him."

Fitzgerald, a good six inches taller than John, yanked his arm away. "I don't know where he is. I don't *want* to know where he is. I hope I *never* find out where he is."

John's eyebrows rose. "I don't understand. Don't you get your direction from him?"

Fitzgerald scoffed. "You've got to be kidding. Rutherford was fired last year for stealing. He's been on the lam ever since. *Everybody* knows that. Where have *you* been?" He started down the stairs then stopped. "Not that I care much what you think, but I wouldn't take direction from that crook, no way no how."

Fitzgerald continued down the stairwell. His footsteps echoed until they faded completely once he entered the lab on the lower level.

John was slack-jawed. Surely there must be some mistake, he thought. Professor Rutherford fired for theft? When? He'd led the class as recently as a week earlier. He was seen in his office when John was in the lab doing research for homework assignments. He was with them a few months ago on the island of Antigua. Before that, he taught classes all through John's freshman year. The professor couldn't have been fired. It wasn't possible. Fitzgerald had to be mistaken.

John was more determined than ever to locate the professor. Any archaeologist worth his salt didn't come to a hasty conclusion based on flimsy evidence. He sure wasn't about to take someone's word for something. Especially when it sounded ludicrous.

The president of the university had his office on the second floor of the administration building, next to Watkins. On the first floor was the Registrar's office, where John knew he would find some answers.

"I'm a student of Professor Rutherford," he told the receptionist. "Can you tell me where I could find him?"

The gray-haired woman behind the counter only gave him a cursory look before returning to her typing.

He wasn't sure that she heard him over the click-clacking of the computer keyboard. "I need to discuss a homework assignment," he lied, thinking that he had better come up with a reason that seemed to require some urgency.

She quickly removed her reading glasses and looked up, sighing heavily.

"I was just hoping to … ."

"I know," she interrupted. "You're trying to get a story for the school paper. Or working on a thesis. Criminal justice, perhaps? Or maybe you just figure yourself smarter than the police and want a slice of that fat reward the university is offering. Am I right?"

John's jaw dropped, then he shook his head. "No! I really am one of his students. I just wanted to talk to him."

She turned back to her computer screen. "So do we. Ever since it was discovered that he had been taking artifacts that rightfully belonged to the university. The police would like to talk to him too. You must have been away a while."

First Fitzgerald and now the receptionist. Logic and common sense told him that they were wrong. They had to be. But an inexplicable feeling came over him. The thought swallowed him whole and made him question the obvious. It didn't make sense, but somehow he knew that what they said was the truth. The professor *had* been fired. He *was* missing. But this was not how he remembered the past three months.

The woman returned to her typing.

John turned away slowly, wondering what was happening. His thoughts felt like a jumble of jigsaw puzzle pieces. There was a familiar image there, but he couldn't fit it together. It felt like a dream vaguely remembered, or a suppressed memory.

Professor Rutherford was somehow part of that dream, of that puzzle picture. That much was clear. It was frustrating. Worse, it felt like the professor's life might be in danger.

John needed answers. He had to find the professor. Now, more than ever.

11

THE CAMPUS BOUNDARY of the university spilled out into the picturesque Hyde Park neighborhood of Chicago. Most of the professors lived in that area. It was quiet, tree-lined, and convenient to walk or ride a bicycle to campus.

Several blocks north of the campus, at the corner of 56th Street and Woodlawn, was a modest one-hundred-year-old, two-bedroom, wood slat bungalow with black shutters. It was the home of Henri and Irene Rutherford.

John Shaw had never been to the house before but had heard about it. The joke amongst archaeology upperclassmen was that it was the only house in the neighborhood that looked like a mummy lived there. Until now, he hadn't known what they meant.

The Rutherford residence was easy enough to pick out. It was the smallest, oldest, and least maintained house on the block. The paint on the white fence was peeling, and several pickets were missing. Dandelions overran the lawn, which was badly in need of a mow. The dark curtains in the windows were the only indication that the house had not been abandoned.

Seeing it now for the first time made John realize that if he were to earn his living with either archaeology or teaching—or both—he'd better be prepared to do it for the love of the profession and not financial gain.

He felt inexplicably drawn to the house, even knowing that the professor was not likely there. If Rutherford was truly on the lam, he could be anywhere.

John opened the gate, carefully latching it behind him. The concrete walk was cracked and uneven. Before he reached the steps, he heard a car coming slowly down the street. He turned to look, wondering if it was a neighbor who might be watching to see if the professor had returned or if a prowler was targeting an empty house.

It drove past and continued down the block. The driver never looked over.

John rang the doorbell, only half expecting someone to actually answer it. Then he rang again.

Surprisingly, the door swung open.

Standing before him was a graying, middle-aged woman holding a feather duster.

"Can I help you, young man?"

Not sure whether she was a hired cleaning lady trying to maintain the property while the professor was away or someone from a realtor's office readying the house for sale, he chose his words carefully.

"I'm John Shaw. Did Professor Rutherford live

here?"

The woman smiled. "Still does. I'm *Irene* Rutherford."

His eyebrows rose. If the professor was really on the lam, why hadn't his wife joined him?

"I'm sorry to disturb you. I'm a student in several of the professor's classes. I also joined him on the recent trip to Antigua."

He relaxed only slightly, wishing to reassure her that he was neither an investigator nor a stalker. Her smile never dimmed. She seemed unfazed and unsuspicious.

"I'd very much like to speak with him. Would you happen to know where he is?"

She looked at her wristwatch. "At this time of the day, he's probably in the lab. Have you tried there?"

"I did, but … he wasn't there."

John chose not to mention what he'd heard. There was no sense upsetting her with vicious rumors. It was obviously erroneous information, although he had no idea why he'd been given it.

"Perhaps he stepped out for a breath of air or tea," she said. "He likes to do his research after classes are over, before coming home. You might want to try back there."

John nodded. "Yes, thank you, I'll do that. I'm sorry I bothered you."

"No bother," she said. "Just doing a little straightening."

He looked past her into the house and saw a lavish interior. The walls were adorned with framed and spotlit oil paintings. Corner curio cabinets were filled with art and artifacts propped up on wire stands. On one wall was a set of swords in much better condition than any in the archaeology lab. Next to that was a floor-to-ceiling bookshelf with dozens of leather-bound books and even more artifacts.

This was the interior of a home more likely found in the upscale Evanston neighborhood where the president of the university lived. Certainly not one as dilapidated as this one looked from the outside. How could the professor, or his wife for that matter, live with such contradiction? There was no accounting for taste or tolerance, John thought.

12

THE SUN HAD NEARLY SET by the time John had walked the several blocks back to the Watkins building. Classes were done for the day, and resident students were settling in for the evening at their respective dorms or hunkered down at the Joseph Regenstein Library on the opposite side of campus.

The Watkins building was still unlocked but wouldn't be for much longer. Most of the buildings on campus were secured at eight o'clock. It was nearly seven.

John hurried into the building, anxious to see whether Mrs. Rutherford was correct about her husband and the others were wrong.

Other than John's footsteps, a vacuum cleaner humming from one of the upper levels was the only sound. He didn't see anyone. He trotted down the stairs, his heart racing. He found himself holding his breath.

Lights were on in the lab and noises were coming from the room. John opened the door.

Rutherford turned with a start and gasped. He had just closed and locked one of the glass cabinets when he heard the noise behind him.

"I should expect that by now," he said, drawing a breath and returning the set of keys to his pocket. He walked to his office on the opposite side of the room.

"Professor, I was hoping you had a minute." John said, crossing the room, trying not to sound surprised.

Now in his office, Rutherford leaned over his desk, hurriedly shoving papers into his brown leather shoulder bag.

"Professor?" John repeated at the office doorway. "I would appreciate a minute."

"I'm afraid I'm in quite a hurry," Rutherford answered, not bothering to look up. He straightened, turned, and started toward the door of the office clutching the bag.

John blocked the doorway. He had no intention of moving without at least an answer or two. "I need a minute," he insisted.

Rutherford dropped his head, then looked up. "Why are you doing this?" His voice was terse and gruff. "You know it's fruitless. Nothing you say or do is going to make a difference."

John didn't even pretend to understand what the professor meant. It really didn't matter. He was tired, frustrated, and confused. He hadn't trekked back and forth across campus to get brushed off so callously.

"I wasn't sure you would be here. Both Keith

Fitzgerald and the Registrar's office thought you didn't even work here anymore."

Rutherford froze. "You know about that?"

"That's what they said."

The professor shook his head and muttered, "Not in *this* timeline."

John wanted to ask what he was talking about but didn't. Something else was more pressing. "I would like to talk about the gold object we found in the cave on Antigua."

Rutherford dropped the shoulder bag to the floor but held onto the strap, his expression somber. His eyes glazed over. John noticed how poorly the professor had aged over the past few months. Although only in his mid-fifties, he was slightly bent. The wrinkles in his face and forehead were more pronounced. His cheeks and jowls sagged. He had more gray in his hair and beard. Worse, the sparkle of enthusiasm that had always been in his eyes was replaced with something else; angst, or perhaps exhaustion.

"So this is what it's come to then," the professor muttered softly, his eyes diverted.

"I beg your pardon?"

"How did you know where to find me?"

"I just came from your house. Your wife … ."

Rutherford looked up quickly, meeting John's eyes. "You met Irene?"

"Yes, sir. She told me where to find you."

"You've got to stop going there!" he said loudly, almost shouting. Then he pointed directly at John's face. "I've told you for the last time!"

He muscled his way through the doorway, bumping John in the process.

John wondered what the professor meant, as he had never been to their house before today.

Rutherford quickly exited the lab. He was halfway to the stairs when John, who was right behind, called out, "I would like to examine the object too, professor. I think the Board of Trustees would agree that as co-discoverer, I have a right."

Rutherford stopped. Without turning around he paused, shook his head, and swallowed hard. "Come by my house tomorrow night. We'll discuss it then."

John beamed. "Thank you, sir. I will look forward to it."

Rutherford wheeled around. "No you won't. You will regret it. You will regret it until the day you die."

13

RUTHERFORD HURRIED INTO HIS HOUSE, locking the front door behind him. He rushed in so quickly that he hardly slowed down to kiss Irene, who met him in the foyer. He was perspiring. After removing his coat and hat, he practically threw them onto the standing coat rack in the hall and headed straight for the liquor cabinet at the far end of the living room.

"Henri, you're in such a hurry this evening."

He removed a crystal tumbler from the cabinet and poured three fingers of Woodford Reserve bourbon whiskey, neat.

"A rough day," he answered without looking up, and then downed the drink. Almost immediately he was warm and lightheaded. It relaxed him but changed nothing. He poured an ounce more into the glass, set the bottle back into the cabinet, and plopped into the nearest chair.

Irene hated when he was so rough with the furniture, and the piece he threw himself into was her favorite. It was old, no doubt expensive, although he rarely discussed money with her. He was old-fashioned that way. None of their many beautiful and delicate souvenirs and artifacts would have lasted this long if he behaved like a bull in a china shop every day.

Usually, he was kind and sensitive, gentle and loving. Sometimes, after work, he would bring her flowers for no particular reason. Or he would reach across the table during dinner and hold her hand. She loved that. Occasionally, after their meal, they would sit together in the living room sipping cognac, talking about how wonderful their lives will be after retirement. He would put his arm around her and the world would feel perfect.

Every now and then, after a particularly rough day at work, he acted like he didn't seem to care that their possessions were fragile or irreplaceable. As if he could go out any time he wanted and get a Mexican Huastec terracotta head or a Valdivia limestone hacha like the ones they had on their mantel.

When he was in one of his 'moods,' Irene felt it best to just let him stew in his thoughts and drink his whiskey. She certainly didn't want to provoke him and chance that his attitude would morph into something abusive—verbal or physical.

"One of your students dropped by today," she said finally.

He closed his eyes for a moment. She thought he might have drifted off to sleep.

"John Shaw," he said.

She smiled. "He must have found you then."

Rutherford stared at the few drops remaining in the tumbler, swirling them around. "Yes, he found me," he answered softly without looking up. "He always does. Right after he comes here."

He could see by her confused expression that she did not understand.

"He's been here dozens of times," he said.

They received very few visitors at their home, at her husband's request. No faculty, no friends, and especially no students. Early on in their marriage, Irene wanted to host dinner parties for his colleagues, elegant catered affairs, thinking that it would help his career. He always refused. When she wanted to invite the neighbors over for a simple backyard barbecue, he always found a reason that they shouldn't.

She thought that it was because he was embarrassed at the condition of the house. It was old, one of the first built on the block. Admittedly, it could use a little TLC. She had often suggested having the house painted and the fence mended. She even offered to do it herself to save money. She was more than capable, having done a lot of miscellaneous work on her parents' house before they were married. He always said that there were better things on which to spend their time.

If it wasn't the exterior, Irene thought, it had to be the interior. She took pride in making it presentable. Each objet d'art and artifact was carefully dusted and then delicately moved to clean around it. With as many items as he had accumulated since joining the university, the process was never-ending. It seemed like every few months, he would come home with lavish decorations that he said he'd gotten at some antique shop on his lunch hour.

He insisted that any improvements be made *inside* the house. Over the years, the interior had been beautifully transformed. Still he refused guests.

Irene concluded that her husband simply preferred privacy. As a university professor, he was around people constantly; in classrooms, administration meetings, and whatnot. It was understandable that he would seek a more reclusive lifestyle at home. She loved him and knew that he loved her, so she had learned to accept his idiosyncrasy of solitude.

But this evening she was confused. He sounded convinced that the student, John Shaw, had visited before. 'Dozens of times,' he had emphasized. She knew this to be impossible. Not dozens—only once, today.

Granted, she wasn't in the house constantly. She belonged to a quilt club, volunteered at their church, took walks, went shopping, and occasionally went to lunch with some of the neighbors. Still, if someone had come to visit, she would have known.

"Dozens of times, Henri?" she asked, smirking. "I think I would have noticed."

"You always say that."

He lifted the glass and let the last few drops of whiskey drip onto his tongue. He wanted more. Maybe one more shot, just enough to fall asleep, but he didn't get up. He knew he wouldn't need to.

"Would you like me to pour you another?" Irene

asked.

He nodded, lifting up the glass. She went to the liquor cabinet and poured another ounce and a half.

Irene handed him the glass. "He said he was one of the students who went with you to Antigua."

"Yes, yes," he answered, sounding annoyed as if he had already addressed an uncomfortable subject satisfactorily. "Went with. Came back. And has been making a pest of himself ever since."

He raised the glass, gulped the shot, and set it down sharply on the end table.

Irene had learned over the years to avoid talking about his work when he was like this. But sometimes she found it too interesting to avoid. "Oh? How so?"

He bent forward. He rested his elbows on his knees and his face in his hands.

"Irene, *please*! Must you interrogate me about this boy night after night?"

Standing up quickly as if suddenly being stuck by a cattle prod, he shuffled toward the stairs. "I'm going to bed."

Once again, his actions surprised her. "Without dinner? I can fix you something."

"I'm not hungry," he said, his voice trailing away.

"It's just that I worry about you so."

He stopped at the bottom of the stairs, one hand on the bannister, his head turned downward. Then, as if experiencing an epiphany, turned around to face her. He smiled.

"My dear wife. I love you so. And I love how you worry about me. It is my only anchor. All these years, all these evenings. When everything around me is in entropy, the thing that has remained constant throughout it all is you." He put his hand to her warm and soft cheek. "I will certainly miss you when I leave."

Irene felt a chill and crossed her arms. "What do you mean when you leave? Are you planning on going somewhere?"

He removed his hand and nodded. "I've gone and returned many times. Many dozens of times."

Her head tilted. "I don't understand."

"I don't expect you to." His voice began to quake. "Just know that when John Shaw comes to visit tomorrow night, everything will change. I can't promise that it will be for the better, however."

Irene's eyes watered. She didn't know why. All she knew was that the man she loved, the man she'd spent the last twenty-eight years with, was talking nonsense. "You're scaring me now, Henri."

He realized he'd gone too far, said too much. He leaned forward and gently kissed her. "It's just the whiskey talking, my dear. Gibberish. That's all. Don't worry about anything. Everything is going to be all right."

They hugged for a long moment, and she smiled. This was the Henri with whom she'd fallen in love. The sensitive and caring husband. The protector. The romantic.

They released the hug, and he went up to their bedroom. He locked the door quietly behind him, went directly to the closet, opened the door, and knelt down. After pushing several pairs of shoes out of the way, he grabbed the corner of the carpet inside the closet and peeled it back, exposing the hardwood floor underneath.

Using a pocketknife, Rutherford pried up a floorboard, grabbed it with his fingertips, and set it aside. Then a second board. With the two sections removed, he reached into the hole and withdrew the gold puck he had found on Antigua.

With the talisman now removed from its hiding place, the light from the ceiling fixture reflected off its bumps. Points of light of various sizes filled the closet. Just like the very first time he ever held it, his fingers tingled. He felt the excitement rise in his throat. It was a giddy feeling, one of hope, anticipation, and surprise. How long had it been since he first felt that way on Antigua? Years? Decades? He'd lost count.

It had taken weeks, months, and years to figure out the power of the talisman. Not that he knew all its powers even now. It was a mystery as to where it came from, how old it was, what it was made of, and who owned it before him. But he knew *one* thing: it was a sophisticated instrument. This tool, unlike any other in the history of mankind, allowed the holder to go back in time.

Rutherford didn't pretend to understand the science of it. But through experimentation, when the halves were turned, or 'dialed' as he liked to say, he was able to relive the past few minutes, days, or weeks as if they had never happened. Remarkably, no one else knew they had relived the same experiences, traveled the same paths, made the same decisions, engaged in the same conversations, or formulated the same thoughts dozens of times prior.

The general populace also did not know that sometimes the outcome of those decisions and actions changed from the first time they had been experienced. As far as they knew, life was random, accidental, evolutionary, and entirely permanent. They had no reason to think otherwise.

Rutherford knew better. Unlike popular belief, there is no permanence to the past. The old adage that 'the past is past' was irrelevant and incorrect. The past was nothing more than an ever-evolving present, especially when the talisman provided infinite second chances.

While this was a frightening experience initially, like on Antigua when it had happened the first time, Rutherford became increasingly comfortable with turning back time and reliving the past.

He'd done it dozens of times. And he was about to do it again. In his wallowing and self-pity, he had inadvertently made Irene cry. He would have to go back and fix that. She was his love, his bedrock. In fact, the only stable element of his life. There was no way that he would let her feel an ounce of pain if he had the power to erase it. And he had—several times already.

This would be one of his last, if not *the* last, act of kindness that he would perform, he decided. He was tired of going back and fixing things and reliving those moments that he wished he'd handled differently.

The experience of time travel had been profitable, no question about it. It padded his wallet and savings account. It added countless valuable artifacts to his private collection. It adorned their home with beautiful decorations he could never have afforded otherwise. But it had also taken a tremendous physical toll on him.

The wrinkles across his forehead were now pronounced. The furrows between his eyebrows, which used to show up only when he was angry, were now permanent. His cheeks sagged and his hair was graying. Then there was the increased stiffness in his back, knees, and fingers.

The outward effects of repeatedly going back in time were evident. If there were any problems with his internal organs he wasn't aware of them. On the other hand, he wouldn't be surprised if an autopsy was performed after his death and the coroner discovered all sorts of weird anomalies. By then it wouldn't matter. He would have achieved all he wanted to achieve, obtained all he wanted to obtain, and wouldn't be around to be questioned. No more deceptions, no more lies, no more time-shifting. No more going back and reliving events which, he'd come to realize, should only be experienced once.

The trouble with time-shifting, the truly frustrating part as he had discovered, was that it was one-directional. Going *back* was easy. Forward, however, was impossible.

Going back provided an excellent opportunity to make different choices, fix those things that needed fixing, and, of course, take advantage of profitable opportunities whenever possible. In so doing, he was forced to continue on that timeline, living those same days over again all the way up to the present. His chronological age, however, never changed. As a result, he felt decades older than he really was.

Time-shifting had worn him out. It was frustrating. He generally always knew what the next day would bring, and it bored him.

Everyone else might be entitled to one 'yesterday' and one 'today.' He, on the other hand, was blessed— or cursed—with as many yesterdays as he desired. And he had desired quite a few.

Now he was ready to press on into the future like everyone else. He decided to leave the past right where it belonged—in the past.

Unfortunately, it wasn't that simple. He had discovered, multiple times, that the temptation to go back and 'fix' something that had already happened was insatiable. For a smoker, it could be likened to the draw of nicotine. For an alcoholic, liquor. For a drug user, crack cocaine. All it takes is a sniff, a taste, or a hit for those addictive personalities to fall back into a pattern of repetitive use.

So it was with him. Just knowing that the talisman was in his possession was enough to want to use it. And he did. Every time he had been late for an appointment, had an argument, or had been accused of some unscrupulous or unethical activity. He recognized that he was addicted to the power of the talisman. Unlike the smoker, the alcoholic, or the drug addict, however, he had nowhere to seek treatment. No hospital, psychologist, or rehab center would believe him. If he hadn't lived, and *relived*, these many time-shift experiences, he wouldn't have believed it either.

He had a way out. A way to end the merry-go-round of reliving his days over and over. The past several years have been spent planning his release from the power of the talisman, or his own lack of willpower. It all would end soon. The temptation. The manipulation of the past. The state of stalled time. His release, his freedom, and his peace rested squarely on John Shaw.

But now, with a loving wife downstairs who was visibly upset by his actions and his words, he had to make one more visit to the past.

After that, God help John Shaw.

14

RUTHERFORD SAT ON THE SIDE of the bed. He took a deep breath and exhaled slowly, as if mentally preparing for his last high before abstinence. Holding the talisman in his left hand, the edge facing him, bumps facing up, he squeezed with all his might and carefully turned the top half about a sixteenth of an inch counter-clockwise, the only direction it would go.

Then, it happened as it always did. Time changed. What was the present was now the past. There was no flash of light. No tumbling-through-space feeling. No spinning scenery like one might expect to see in an H.G. Wells-type movie. Just a momentary sense of complete darkness and a hint of vertigo.

The time-shift was imperceptible to everyone except him, for he was no longer sitting on the bed. Instead, he was now standing in the hallway of the lower level of Watkins, halfway between the archaeology lab and the stairs.

John Shaw stood in the doorway of the lab.

"I would like to examine the object too, professor," Shaw called from behind. "I think the university would agree that as co-discoverer, I have a right."

He had hoped to time-shift only about an hour to when he had first come home. He wanted to have the same conversation with Irene but with more love and less alcohol. Instead he'd turned the talisman too much. He'd gone too deeply into the past.

Dialing the talisman wasn't an exact science, and this had happened before. Sometimes he had only wanted to go back a day but had to relive the entire month over.

With an equal measure of frustration and capitulation, Rutherford answered, "Come by my house tomorrow night. We'll discuss it then."

John beamed. "Thank you, sir. I look forward to it."

Rutherford looked back. "No you won't. You will regret it. You will regret it until the day you die."

He climbed the stairs and hurried out of the building as quickly as he could. He didn't want to engage the boy any longer. There was a woman waiting for him less than a mile away who adored him and to whom he owed not an apology—for she wouldn't understand why—but a nice evening together. No snappy answers, no sarcasm, no alcohol, and definitely no talisman. She deserved that much, especially considering that there wouldn't be that many opportunities left.

15

JOHN COULDN'T SLEEP THAT NIGHT; the day kept replaying in his head. He couldn't imagine the day being any stranger. From Keith Fitzgerald claiming that Professor Rutherford had been fired, to the Registrar's office saying the same thing. It had to be some sort of practical joke, although they both sounded sincere, and more than a little bitter.

Then there were the odd comments the professor said in the lab. First, "Why are you doing this? You know it's fruitless. Nothing you say or do is going to make a difference." Was he harboring some resentment for the conversation that they had begun in his tent on Antigua? Had John violated some code of etiquette by wanting to discuss the thing that had sent them to the island in the first place—discovery of archaeological treasure? If he had done something wrong, he was at a loss to know what it was.

Then there was the professor's peculiar, "Not in this timeline" comment. Something about the odd comment felt familiar, but why?

Equally strange was the comment, "You've got to stop going there. I've told you for the last time!" The professor had sounded angry, threatening even. Since John had never been to his house before, the statement didn't make any sense. The professor must have confused him with someone else.

Lastly, and most disturbing, was the veiled threat, "You will regret it. You will regret it until the day you die." Was the professor warning him *not* to come to the house?

Ridiculous, he thought. This was Professor Rutherford. His teacher. Mentor. Why would someone whom he trusts be dangerous?

He wouldn't. As long as he was rational and thinking clearly. But what if he wasn't? What if the professor was suffering from some sort of dementia or paranoia or schizophrenia and didn't recognize John for who he really was? Or because of those ailments, didn't care. The mind can play tricks on people. Change them. Make them act irrationally.

Perhaps the professor had suffered some sort of stroke or mental breakdown and was having a hard time differentiating fact from fantasy. And because he was an intelligent man, a brilliant scholar, a respected researcher, no one questioned his sudden eccentricity.

Realizing that the professor may be the victim of some mental illness didn't change the facts. John still felt like he might be putting himself in grave danger by visiting the professor's home. The professor's use of the word "regret" resonated in his mind. He seemed so grave when he said it. It sounded as much like a warning as a threat.

John wondered whether the gold object had something to do with the professor's attitude and erratic behavior. The coincidence between finding the object and the professor's change of personality seemed closely knit.

It began to rain. A soft drizzle at first, then in large drops that pinged against the dorm room window. It reminded him of the noisy evenings on Antigua. Similar but different. Just like the professor's personality of late.

John didn't know what time it was, maybe eleven or eleven-thirty. With the drapes pulled tight, the darkness reminded him of the cave on Antigua. He could almost smell the damp undergrowth and feel the tingle in his fingers. His eyelids got heavy, and he finally drifted off to sleep.

16

THE NEXT DAY WAS FRIDAY. John sat in his Statistics and Business Theory class in the Charles M. Harper Center. It was a required class, and not one that he particularly enjoyed.

It was nearly impossible to concentrate. He was focused on the meeting he was to have at Professor Rutherford's house later that evening. There would be no shortage of questions that he wanted to ask about the gold object. Perhaps the more he learned of the thing, the better he would understand the professor's behavior.

He would have liked to talk to someone on campus about his feelings, suspicions, and observations but knew he couldn't. The only ones who might take an interest would be the research assistants who joined him on the expedition, but he wasn't close to them. Most were shallow and self-centered. In addition to that, Taylor Jennings was just plain mean-spirited. Hannah Miller was the exception. She was the one person he thought he could discuss this with but knew he wouldn't. She didn't possess any of the same negative traits as the others, but without trying, she intimidated him.

Hannah was in the same statistics class. She was attractive, intelligent, and quick-witted. He liked being around her, especially when they saw each other on the island. But, even then, he couldn't seem to get his courage up to converse with her on a personal level. All his life he'd been more of a scholar than a ladies' man, so engaging women in small talk was difficult. In that respect, and *only* that respect, he envied Taylor Jennings, who seemed suave when it came to members of the opposite sex.

Now, John wished that he had the sort of relationship with Hannah where he could discuss all that was going on in his life. He could imagine her being interested, sympathetic, and concerned. She'd want to know everything that he was thinking, everything he was worried about. They would talk, hold hands, talk some more, have dinner, and then … well, who knows.

There he went again. His mind had drifted from statistics to Hannah. A pleasant distraction certainly, but it was disadvantageous when trying to maintain a favorable grade point average. She sat two rows down from him in the large auditorium-style classroom. He had a clear view of the side of her face. Dammit for not having the courage to talk to her!

Without realizing it, he had daydreamed through the entire class. He would have to study all the harder so that he didn't fall behind.

The students rose from their seats and headed toward the rear of the auditorium. John timed it so that he and Hannah were exiting their rows at the same time. They met in the main aisle.

"I don't know which is worse," she said to him, initiating the conversation, "the sandblasted evenings of Antigua or this class."

John tried not to sound disappointed that she spoke first. He had spent the last ten minutes getting the courage up to say something to her. "They're both equally dry."

She smiled. "So true!"

They exited the building together. The sun was shining, the temperature cool. Colored leaves of all shapes fell from the trees and swirled on the ground as the wind pushed them from one side of the quad to the other. It reminded John of the ever-present influence of the sand on Antigua. They'd dig holes, and the wind and sand covered them. It was as if Mother Nature constantly tried to erase the memory of the intruders.

"Do you ever think about it?" John asked. "Antigua? The dig?"

They slowed, then stopped.

"Sometimes," she answered. "Quite a bit, actually."

He nodded. "Me too."

"I thought it was an interesting experience," she said, "but I'm glad to be back home. I'm not sure that I'm cut out for this type of work."

"What do you mean?" John asked.

She looked away for a moment, wanting to choose her words carefully. "I've always liked the idea of new adventures and discovering things. But, frankly, other than all of us getting to know each other better, the rest of the trip was pretty boring."

John nodded.

Hannah waited, hoping he would pick up the hint about getting to know each other.

"I think we could have done without Taylor, though," she continued. "Sheesh! What an egomaniac. I think you and I were the only normal ones."

Again, John nodded. His mouth opened slightly, but he seemed to be at a loss for words. She felt like blurting out, *"Stop being so shy! Don't you know that I'm interested in you?!"*

After the awkward silence, she said, "But I'll tell you something. I'm disappointed we couldn't stay a little longer. At least to complete the excavation and the analysis of the discovery."

John's eyes widened. "You know about that?"

Hannah's eyebrows rose. "I felt like confronting Rutherford about it."

"Me too!"

"It's a shame we had to leave it behind."

John paused, his voice trailed, disappointed. "You mean the skeleton."

Her head tilted slightly, and her eyes narrowed. "Of course the skeleton. What did you think?"

Flustered, feeling that she would somehow know that he was concealing something, he dropped the subject. "Well, I'd better get going. I've got to be at the Earlman building in … ," he checked his watch, "in less time than I have to get there."

She nodded. "I'm going over to the library. Opposite direction. So I guess I'll see you around."

No words came out, but inside his head he screamed at himself to say something. Ask her to dinner, or at least to go for coffee. The words remained frozen in his brain.

"Bye, John!" she called out as she turned and started down the cobblestone pathway.

As if he suddenly awoke from a semi-comatose state, he trotted toward her. She heard his footsteps and stopped, waiting for him to catch up. Her heart beat faster in anticipation.

"Hannah, I need to ask something."

She smiled, suspecting, or at least hoping, that she knew what he would ask. "Yes, what is it?"

His mouth went dry. He shifted his weight as he tried to choose the best words. "Does anything seem … different since coming back from the island?"

It wasn't the question that she expected. She was intrigued, nevertheless. "Different? How?"

He shook his head, trying to think of an analogy she would understand. "I don't know. Different. Strange. Unexpected."

The only thing that struck her as strange was the direction that the conversation had suddenly veered. There may be a time and place where they would break through their silos of being nothing more than classmates, fellow research assistants, and marginal friends, but apparently this wasn't it.

"I'm not sure I know what you mean," she answered, resolving herself to the fact that this was not a clumsy way of asking for a date. "Does something seem different to *you*?"

He wished that they shared a relationship where he could unfurl all the clues, concerns, and secrets that he harbored. She was so congenial, so approachable. They would make a good team. However, he had to talk with Professor Rutherford first. Details were needed, puzzle pieces were missing. When he had more data, he would share them with her, and maybe together they could come up with a logical picture. But not now.

"Yes," he finally admitted. "Some things seem different. Very different. And tonight I hope to find out why."

Now it was *his* turn to head off in the opposite direction.

Yes, she thought. Now that he mentioned it, at least one thing seemed different since they returned from Antigua. She watched as he ran down the sidewalk. She hoped it was for the better.

17

JOHN COULD THINK OF at least a few things that he would rather be doing than attending his Society and Social Trends of Colonial America class, another degree requirement. He would have much rather met Hannah for coffee at Starbucks in the student commons. At the very least, he would have liked to be over at Professor Rutherford's house, quizzing him about the gold object from the cave.

Between the two, he had plenty to daydream about during class. Remarkably, the two things had a lot in common. Hannah probably thought that he was a babbling fool for going on about things being "different." The professor probably just thought he was a pest for questioning something that was none of his business. After all, who was he to question a man held in such high regard? The professor didn't seem impressed or pleased that he was so persistent about discussing the object. No doubt he was in for a reprimand.

John knew he'd be putting his grades and research assistant position at risk, but it didn't matter. Education was now secondary to this investigation. The astonishing thing was he had no idea *why*. There seemed little reason that some dumb artifact found in a hole on a remote island would cause such infatuation. This probably wasn't the first time that a research assistant wasn't privy to every investigative step of a professor, and it probably wouldn't be the last.

Still, it felt as if he was being inexplicably drawn to the object, like some mysterious force was calling to him. But that was ridiculous, he realized. Inanimate objects were just that, inanimate.

John wondered whether he was really acting from a sense of selfishness and simply wanting to be part of the discovery. Was he so driven to succeed in archaeology that he would risk betraying a mentor to the Board of Trustees just so he could get partial credit for a discovery? He was on the verge of accusing the professor of impropriety. Demanding answers to things he probably shouldn't even be asking. His cheeks flushed with shame.

He knew what he should do. If it wasn't too late, if he hadn't offended the professor beyond all hope of forgiveness, he would go and offer up a confession. He would admit that something had come over him, although he wouldn't be able to explain what, and that he might be acting out of self-interest. He would apologize for his impudence and for any hurt feelings he may have caused.

Fortunately, he had been wise enough not to have mentioned the object to anyone. He had come close to spilling his guts with Hannah. Had she gone for coffee or dinner with him, he may have—probably would have—told her everything. What a fool he would have been. It's a good thing that they both had places to go, he thought, or he would have embarrassed himself even further.

He had to set things straight. Get his head back into his education. If the professor forgave him, he would work even harder at his studies. Work longer hours and not second-guess his mentor. He hoped that he hadn't ruined everything he'd worked for.

Only time would tell. He was due at the professor's house after class.

The clock above the whiteboard in the front of the room read four-thirty. Time had flown by. Class was over. Now he would find out whether he had a future in archaeology, or even at the school for that matter.

18

THE SMITH & WESSON snub-nosed .38 revolver was a powerful weapon. It was a more than adequate form of protection. Which was precisely the reason Henri Rutherford had purchased it in the first place. It was relatively light, accurate, and could be concealed easily.

In his business—not as an archaeology professor, for which he was best known at the University of Chicago, but as a black-market thief for which he was best known elsewhere—a handgun was a good thing to have. The nefarious characters with whom he had to deal were trustworthy only until they felt betrayed or cheated. The cost of a shady deal gone bad could easily be death. Fortunately, none of his many covert transactions went awry.

He only occasionally haggled on the price. It was far easier, and safer, to simply accept the going rate. He was, by nature, a greedy man, but he was no fool. The risk was always weighted in his direction. He was far more concerned about getting killed during a bad bargaining session in Tanzania, Cairo, or Italy than having the university find out his secret. He knew that his 'trading partner' was probably armed too, and even less hesitant to use it than he was.

Rutherford reminded himself on numerous occasions during negotiations that the item being fenced cost him nothing and that anything he received from its sale was pure profit. But it took great effort to think of the transaction that way. Greed is a mistress with no conscience. The more he stole, the more he earned. The more he earned, the more he wanted. The cycle didn't end. The revolver was as much a reminder to keep his greed in check as it was a form of protection.

Now, back in the safety of his own home, he sat in front of the desk in the den. He didn't have to worry about black market swindlers, corrupt government officials, or muggers lying in wait down dark alleyways. No, now he had a different villain in mind.

Rutherford checked his watch. John Shaw would be arriving within the hour. Maybe less. There wasn't much time.

He thumbed the release and swung out the empty cylinder. He removed six rounds from a small box of cartridges and slid them into each chamber. With the cylinder now full, he swung it back into the frame with a distinct click.

Sliding the top desk drawer open, he set the loaded revolver inside and then pushed it closed.

He knew that sending a projectile through the

air into another human's body was an act best left to mobsters, muggers, and soldiers, but desperation could empower anyone to do anything.

Some people seemed to be predisposed to kill. He wondered if he was one of them. After all, he took a shovel to the back of a young man's head on the island of Antigua and then left him for dead. Twice, as a matter of fact. Too bad the bastard didn't stay dead when he had the chance.

He smiled, thinking back on that evening so long ago. All the way home from Antigua, he had pondered the situation, mulled the possibilities. Fear gave way to common sense, and he realized that all the laws of the universe, however outlandish or bizarre, could ultimately be explained. This was no different. He hadn't dreamed the altercation with John Shaw, and he wasn't crazy. The explanation had to lie somewhere else. Now he knew. The talisman.

Rutherford slid open the desk drawer. He had to reassure himself that the Smith & Wesson was there. Seeing was believing. After living in a world that could change, revert really, with the turn of a dial on a puck, anything could happen.

Nothing seemed certain anymore. There was no permanence, as he had proven to himself over and over. He'd even come to believe that there was no future, only past and present. Then past and present again. If he didn't like what happened that day, that week, that month, he would simply twist the talisman and relive it and change it. It was a convenient crutch. One on which he relied far too many times.

He laid his hand on the cold steel of the revolver and sighed. He half expected the drawer to be empty. That he had once again gone back in time and relived his life to that point but had forgotten to put the gun in the drawer. Yet it was there, and very real. Knowing that it was in the drawer gave him a settling calm that he had been without for months.

The reassurance was fleeting, however. As he had discovered too often, what seemed to be permanent wasn't. Like when he repeatedly took a shovel to John Shaw's head only to see the boy walk and talk moments later. Or when he boarded the ship in Puerto Rico. He had retired to the guest quarters to examine and contemplate the talisman, only to find himself once again standing on the boardwalk ready to board the ship. That was when he concluded that the talisman was more than it seemed.

To prove it, he had boarded the ship, again. He went directly to his assigned cabin on the lower level without conversing with anyone and removed the talisman from his satchel. Sitting on the side of the bed, he held the puck sideways in front of him. Trembling, squeezing it tightly, he turned it ever so minutely.

Once again, he found himself on the boardwalk, several yards ahead of the research assistants. They were getting ready to pull the gangplank to the ship's deck. He stopped suddenly, realizing what had just happened. He tried to force himself to accept what seemed to be impossible. Several students came up behind him and asked what was wrong. He couldn't speak. Didn't want to. If he told them what he thought he was experiencing, they would have thought him insane. Instead, he checked his pocket for the talisman. After reassuring himself that it was still there, he hurried on board.

Once on the ship, he deliberately avoided the students. Especially John Shaw. They were all intelligent. The best of the class. They would almost certainly sense that something was wrong and grill him. On the contrary, nothing was 'wrong.' *Odd* maybe, but not wrong.

In his study, Rutherford slid open the desk drawer again. The gun was still there. He didn't touch it this time. There was no need. The present hadn't changed.

Seeing the revolver made him wish that he had it while aboard the *del Cadiz*, sailing from Puerto Rico. On the second evening while out to sea, he was in his cramped cabin examining the talisman, unaware that someone on the deck had been watching him through a porthole. The door of the cabin had burst open, and a stocky man stumbled in. His thick black hair was matted from sweat. His face was rugged and unshaven.

Rutherford quickly plopped his hat over the talisman, which was on the table in front of him, but it was too late. He was not fast enough to hide the dots on the walls reflecting off the bumpy surface of the thing.

"Ah, 'scuse me, señor," the man had mumbled.

Even from where he sat, Rutherford could smell the rum and cigarettes on the man's breath.

"What do you have there, señor?" the drunken sailor asked, smiling. His teeth were darkened by years of poor hygiene and smoking.

"Who are you?!" Rutherford asked, still reeling

from the surprise visit. "What do you want?!"

"I am Sanchez," the man slurred. "The captain has asked me to check on our esteemed guests." He closed the door behind him and drew the latch.

"I'm fine," Rutherford said, his throat dry, feeling uncomfortably vulnerable.

Sanchez was blocking the locked door, the only exit.

"Thank you for checking. Now, if you don't mind excusing me … ."

As if he hadn't heard the request, Sanchez inched forward. "The captain noticed that you haven't left your quarters. He wondered if you were ill. Perhaps the sea upsets you."

"Please tell the captain that I appreciate his concern," Rutherford answered, starting to perspire. It was then he noticed the sailor's hand in his pocket. "Please tell him that I'm fine. I just … prefer solitude."

Sanchez continued to inch forward a half step at a time, swaying as he tried to keep his balance, his ugly brown smile ever widening. When he was within six feet, the sailor brought out a pearl-handled switchblade, clearly not a tool of the mariner trade. Rutherford knew he was in trouble.

With a push of a button a four-inch blade sprung open and locked into place. Sanchez kept the knife at his side but there was no mistaking his intent. "I will ask you again, señor. What have you got there?"

Rutherford didn't take his eyes off his assailant. "A paperweight," he lied. "A souvenir."

"You are a very poor liar," Sanchez told him,

smiling. "I think it is much more. I am not a man of higher learning like you, but I know solid gold when I see it. And from the size of it I would say that it is probably worth a fortune."

Rutherford knew the drunkard was right, it *was* worth a fortune, either monetarily or in opportunity. He'd negotiated with similar entrepreneurs before and knew that despite their threats and posturing, they all wanted the same thing—to profit equally. If he could remain calm, he knew that he should be able to strike an accord.

"You flatter me, sir," Rutherford began, forcing himself to sound confident and sincere, "but this is just a trinket we came across in our travels. An open market vendor selling them portside in Antigua."

The sailor remained stationary, staring, listening. Tentatively, Rutherford reached under his hat to recover the talisman without taking his eyes off Sanchez, whose eyes widened at the sight of the round gold object.

"I'm sure that the vendor had no idea what it was," Rutherford said, "and frankly, neither do I. But like you, I can see that it has some gold content, although I seriously doubt that it is anything but gold-plated. I'm hoping to sell or trade it once we arrive in Cape Sable, as I have no interest in keeping such an extravagant paperweight."

Convinced that he had not only kept Sanchez at bay but also intrigued his would-be attacker, he decided to set the hook he'd cast.

"You would be doing me a huge favor if you would consider making me an offer on this monstrosity so that I don't have to deal with those U.S. Custom thieves in Florida."

Sanchez smiled. His foul rum-soaked breath filled the cabin, souring Rutherford's stomach. Then, as if he could contain it no longer, the sailor burst into laughter.

"You Americans! You all believe that you are the only ones who can make the rules. That we are all *estúpido*! No, señor, I have a different suggestion. You give me the gold object, and I let you live."

Rutherford began to tremble, and he couldn't catch his breath as he realized that the gambit had failed.

"Surely sir, we can come to some sort of agreement," Rutherford pleaded. He tried to sound like a confident negotiator but knew that more likely he just sounded pathetic.

Sanchez stopped smiling. His bushy eyebrows narrowed, and his eyes burned with hate or resentment or both. "I have a better suggestion. I cut out your heart and feed it to the fishes. Then I throw your fat disgusting body overboard when no one is looking. In the morning, we report you missing. We will, of course, suspect suicide."

A bead of sweat trickled past Rutherford's collar and down his back. He was in serious danger and quickly losing control of the situation.

"Suicide? That's ridiculous."

"Is it?" the man sneered. "You hide away in your quarters. What else are we to think? Who does that? A loner. A recluse. A despondent man who wants nothing more to do with humanity. So you go out for some night air. To stretch your legs. You go at night so you do not have to see other people. There is opportunity, so you take it. Climbing over the guard railing you drop into the dark water below. The current pulls you down and you are gone."

Rutherford knew that the tables had turned. He was now on the receiving end of manipulation with dire consequences to follow. It was true, he had lived a full, sometimes tumultuous life. He'd forged a career, made discoveries, fallen in love, traveled the world, and amassed a small fortune. In the end, if he were to be judged harshly, it would be because of the latter. And that judgment, he feared, was to happen sooner than he had expected. There, on board a transport ship halfway between Puerto Rico and Cape Sable, his life hung in the balance at the hand of some drunken sailor whose greed exceeded his own.

Sanchez stepped forward. With the knife in his left hand still at his side, he held out his right, palm up. "Now give me the gold."

Rutherford took his eyes off the sailor for the first time and looked down at the talisman in his hand. This small weighty object had been in his possession for three days and had caused him immeasurable stress and anxiety. It had also provided him with excitement and hope for huge financial gain. That was before Sanchez barged in. Now he was about to lose it all.

This peculiar discovery was nothing like he had ever seen before. Whether its powers were real or imagined was still to be determined. If real, it would be the discovery of the century. Nonetheless, it appeared to be solid gold and could certainly pad his wealth. It was worth protecting, no matter what.

"No," Rutherford answered. He set the talisman on the table, covering it with his palm. "No!" he repeated, more decidedly, looking up and shaking his head.

"You are a fool!" Sanchez sneered, lunging for the talisman.

Rutherford jumped to his feet, gripping the talisman tightly. With all his might, he swung his arm around toward the rushing Sanchez. The talisman crashed against Sanchez's right cheekbone with a loud whap, staggering him. It was a hard enough blow to level most men, but the alcohol in the sailor's bloodstream deadened the effect. If his cheekbone was broken, which was highly likely from the sound of it, he wouldn't know until morning. He turned his attention from the goal of obtaining the talisman to punishing the American.

Sanchez was nearly on top of him now. Pumped with adrenaline, Rutherford clenched his teeth. Holding his breath, he swung his arm around again. It was a wide arc, thrown wildly. The timing was perfect, however, for it struck Sanchez directly in the right temple.

Sanchez went down to a knee. His right hand shot up to the side of his head. Blood oozed from his ear. Rutherford leaned over prepared to deliver one final blow to the back of the head.

Suddenly, a sharp pain.

Sanchez had pushed the knife into Rutherford's side.

With a vengeful anger he had never felt before, Rutherford raised the talisman above his head with two hands and brought it down on the back of Sanchez's lower skull. The blow landed solidly. Sanchez collapsed to the floor, face down, unconscious.

With his attacker subdued, Rutherford assessed his situation. The knife was protruding from his side with only the hilt exposed. A circle of red stained his white shirt. The wound was bad, but he could barely feel it. Then, as if an angel of death was sending a preemptive telegram, he had the distinctive taste of blood in his mouth. He realized that he was bleeding internally. With the adrenaline of the duel wearing off, the pain in his side multiplied exponentially.

He was afraid to pull the knife out for fear that the bleeding would accelerate. But he was equally afraid to leave it in. Panic set in. He was immobilized. He needed help.

Now bleeding profusely, Rutherford stepped over the body of his attacker. He hoped that Sanchez was acting alone and not in conspiracy with other members of the crew. He was lightheaded. His legs were rubbery and the pain in his side was intense. Blood filled up his mouth and his vision blurred. He knew that while he might make it to the door, there was no way he would make it down the corridor and then up the stairs to the main deck to the bridge. He didn't want to alarm any of the research assistants, but it was clear, time was running out.

With one hand, he applied pressure on his side around the base of the blade's hilt. He stumbled to the door, turned the latch, and practically fell into the corridor. Leaning on the doorframe, he knew he didn't have long. If he could get to one of the student's rooms, perhaps they could summon the ship's physician, if there was one. Barring the absence of that, the ship's captain.

The ship felt like it was on choppy seas, being tossed side to side. But it was just his wobbly legs and distorted equilibrium. Rutherford shuffled down the corridor but could only move slowly. He wanted to stop, lean against the wall, and catch his breath. But he knew he probably didn't have much breath left. Every few feet he had to spit out a mouthful of blood. The end was near.

He banged on the first door he came to with his free hand, which still held the talisman. As he waited for the door to open, his legs gave way and he slumped to the floor, his back against the wall next to the door.

The door opened. Seeing no one, John Shaw stepped out into the hallway. "Professor!" he shouted, seeing Rutherford on the floor, bleeding, his head slumped forward. "What happened?!"

Rutherford heard the words and recognized the voice but could not answer. It was difficult to breathe with blood in his mouth and not enough air in his lungs. The wound in his side had gone numb, as had the lower half of his body. The murmur of pulsating diesel pistons from the engine room was fading. Although the lightbulbs all along the ceiling still shone brightly, it was getting darker. He was dying.

Then he remembered.

With what little strength he had left, Rutherford gripped the talisman with both hands. He didn't need his sight to know what to do. The only question was whether he had the strength and whether it would do any good.

He tried turning the halves, but his bloody and sweaty fingers couldn't get a grip. He squeezed harder, but once again his fingertips just slid around the edge. With every last ounce of strength he had left, he tried again. It turned. A little or a lot, he couldn't tell. In fact, in his near-death state he wasn't sure that it had turned at all.

The last thing that he heard was Shaw calling his name, muted, as if from a long distance.

For a split second, all went dark and then quickly became light. The pain was gone, he felt normal. The air smelled like briny water. A soft breeze passed through an open window, jostling his hair.

He was sitting on the passenger side of the pickup truck that they had used on Antigua. John Shaw was driving. They were approaching a white wood slat building with a red metal roof. Above the door was a sign: 'Saint William Equipment Rental & Supplies, est. 1928.' An abrupt stop jostled him and made him wonder if he had fallen asleep and imagined what had just happened.

Rutherford looked in all directions, getting his bearings. In the dream, he had been on a ship called the *del Cadiz* heading toward Puerto Rico when a drunken sailor named Sanchez attacked him. He'd been stabbed and was dying. There, in the the truck, he reached down to feel his side but there was no evidence of a stab wound.

After parking the trucks, the students returned the keys and gear to the old man behind the counter, and they boarded the ship to go to Puerto Rico. The ship was called *del Cadiz*.

It was no dream after all, Rutherford concluded. The talisman, that wonderful, miracle-making, tool from—somewhere, had given him life, or at least allowed him to relive it.

After boarding the *del Cadiz*, he found his cabin and promptly locked the door. He then wedged the top rail of a chair under the doorknob for extra protection. Then he threw a towel over the porthole window.

That evening, as expected, there was a noise at the door. The handle jiggled. But because it was now locked tight, the person went away after a few tries. That time, in *that* reality, *that* present, he managed to avoid a confrontation with the drunken Sanchez.

That second night, that terrible second night on the open seas on the way to Florida, he had almost died. *Would* have died if it hadn't been for the talisman.

~ ~ ~ ~ ~ ~

Now, in the present, Rutherford slid open the drawer in his desk and checked for the revolver. Still there.

John Shaw was due to arrive any minute.

19

JOHN SHAW HAD GONE to his Society and Social Trends of Colonial America class with two things occupying his thoughts: Hannah Miller and Professor Rutherford. By the time class let out, he was focused only on the latter.

With his backpack flung over one shoulder, John hurried out of class, down the hall, and out of the building. Dark clouds blanketed the sky, making it seem later than it was. The temperature had cooled by several degrees. A storm was brewing.

Past the main quadrangle, the campus buildings became fewer until the residential portion of Hyde Park sprung up and dominated. On 56th Street past University, Woodlawn, and Kimbark Avenues he went, walking quickly but short of running, until he got to Kenwood Avenue. There, nestled between two brick bungalow style homes, each meticulously maintained, sat the professor's humble home, which was badly in need of—everything.

Careful to swing open the picket fence gate for fear of it falling off its hinges, John closed it gently behind him. He tried to ignore the unkempt exterior of the house and focus on why he had gone there in the first place.

He climbed the steps and pressed the doorbell. Music rang through the house in a tune that sounded like a Chopin piano recital. Perhaps someone was playing the piano inside the house and the bell hadn't worked. He was tempted to push it again. Then the door opened and the music stopped as quickly as it had begun.

Mrs. Rutherford stood in the doorway, smiling. "Mr. Shaw, it is very nice to see you again," she said as sincerely as a favorite aunt expecting him for Sunday dinner.

"The professor invited me … ."

"Yes, yes," she said, stepping aside to let him pass. "He's waiting for you. Please come in. Henri is in his den."

John particularly noted her use of the word "his." No doubt his sanctuary, his personal study, of which she was probably invited into infrequently.

"Make yourself at home. I'll tell Henri that you are here."

Irene walked through the living room into the hall that led toward the rear of the house. Only after she was out of view did he permit himself to examine the room more closely.

A curved bay window faced the front yard. Thick

maroon drapes were pulled to each side, held back with gold ties and tassels. Sheer curtains underneath let in natural light without revealing too much of the outside world in the process. He doubted that they were ever fully opened. If they were, too much of the outside would be let into this private refuge that seemed to beg seclusion.

Luxurious furniture with embellishments and carvings was the primary décor of the living room. John remembered having seen photos of similar Rococo furniture that had been made for the Parisian monarchy. If genuine, it was possibly from the 18th century. He did not feel comfortable sitting on any of it. On one of the end tables were several links of a very heavy ship's chain with toned patina. On another table was a flat stone, intact enough to show a carved sphinx. Each appeared to be very old. Neither fit the period of the furniture.

Along one windowless wall were several tall glass-enclosed display cases. Each was filled with random curios and artifacts, most in good to excellent condition.

Not wanting to sit on the sofa or chairs that looked more like museum pieces than home furnishings, he stood at one of the display cases, admiring the variety of old coins there.

Beyond the living room, down the carpeted hall, he could see other objets d'art in a variety of shapes, sizes, and conditions mounted on the walls.

"Quite the art collector, you're thinking," Rutherford said, entering the room from John's blind side.

John spun around, embarrassed. He felt uncomfortable thinking he'd been caught snooping and not knowing how long he had been watched.

"It's all quite impressive," he said.

Rutherford nodded. "Yes, it is. Thank you."

"It must have taken … ."

" … a lifetime to get it all," Rutherford said, completing the sentence. "You say that every time."

John looked away for a moment, perplexed.

"Come, let's have a chat."

Rutherford led John down the hall to a set of white double doors, one of which was open. He waited until John entered, then followed, closing the door behind him.

The door closed with a distinctive click. John froze for a moment. The hairs on the back of his neck stood up, and he held his breath. His eyes darted around the room. He resisted the urge to spin around and face the professor. It felt like he had been lured into a trap, but he didn't want the professor to think that he thought so.

"Have a seat," Rutherford said, his expression blank.

John couldn't tell whether it was a request or an order.

An antique wooden office desk, solid and well-worn, was near the dual doors. Tall stacks of books, papers, and rolled-up maps covered the desk. Next to the window was a saddle brown leather couch cracked from age, facing the desk. Along the wall were two tall bookcases completely full of books and binders crammed in every which way.

Having seen the disarray of the exterior of the house, this was the way John would have expected each of the interior rooms to look. He sat on the couch. The professor sat behind the desk.

Storm clouds rolling in starved the remaining daylight. The natural light in the room, already dimmed by shuttered blinds, started to fade. Rutherford reached over and turned on the floor lamp next to the desk. The low wattage bulb filled the room with a soft yellow glow. Shadows filled the corners and accentuated the few remaining holes on the bookcases. The dull cast reminded John of the inside of the professor's tent on Antigua with the lantern above them.

"So here we are again," Rutherford said, smirking.

John didn't think anything of the comment. After all, they'd met yesterday in the lab, beginning the conversation that he hoped would conclude today. His mouth was dry. Unconsciously, his foot started tapping.

Leaning forward, John said, "Professor, there's something I want to say. Something I feel I *need* to say."

Rutherford sat back, his legs crossed and his fingertips touching. He was smiling, smug, obviously enjoying the bootlicking he was about to receive.

A low rumble of distant thunder distracted John for a moment as he glanced back toward the window. He drew a breath to steady his nerves preparing for his mea culpa. The wind had picked up significantly and began blowing leaves against the window of the office. A dog barked in the distance.

"Do you remember the first time that we had this discussion?" Rutherford asked.

John clenched his jaw, disappointed he wasn't being allowed to lead the conversation.

"The very first time. Do you remember?"

"Yes sir, I do. In your tent on Antigua. The evening we found the object."

"The talisman," Rutherford corrected.

"The … talisman," John repeated, to reinforce in his mind that the object now had a name.

"No. I mean the first time we had *this* discussion."

John diverted his eyes and tilted his head. He felt uncomfortable, slightly threatened, like in class when challenged with a question in which he thought he knew the answer, but the instructor had something entirely different in mind.

"At the hole!" John blurted. "When we found it in the hole."

Rutherford uncrossed his legs, dropped his hands to his lap and leaned forward. "You really *don't* remember, do you?"

John's face went blank and he shifted positions. It seemed that he had failed to answer the question correctly.

"Interesting," Rutherford murmured, stroking his bearded chin. His comment was barely audible above the patter of rain that had begun to fall. He stared past John toward the window, but the blinds were closed. "Intense curiosity, but no anger. No desire for retaliation. Repressed memory, perhaps."

Desperate to get back on track, John said, "Professor, I just wanted to … ."

Rutherford snapped out of his daydream. His

eyes narrowed and his voice deepened in a way that made his young protégé uncomfortable.

" '… apologize for my impudence,' " Rutherford said, completing John's sentence. " 'I didn't mean to question the intentions of a well-respected professor. I sincerely hope that this infraction hasn't hurt my standing in your class or my position as your research assistant.' "

John's jaw dropped. Over the past twenty-four hours he had carefully thought out his apology. Practiced the delivery in his head. He was now hearing the exact words told verbatim back to him.

Rutherford leaned forward. "Do you know the feeling of déjà vu, young Shaw?"

John was confused and feeling derailed. He shrugged, not knowing where the conversation was going or why he was being directed there.

"We've all felt that way," Rutherford began, leaning back in his chair, once again relaxed, and sounding the role of educator. "That short burst of sensation that we've experienced the same situation before in another time or place. The ancients used to believe that déjà vu was evidence that they were reliving the lives of spirits that walked the land before them. Thought that they couldn't remember any more than little snippets because they were not yet enlightened. Or that they were in some way inferior to their ancestors."

Lightning flashed and thunder rolled across the sky. The storm was approaching quickly. The rain splashed against the window in waves, but clearly the worst was yet to come.

"Professor … ."

"Of course, intellectuals of our day don't understand it any better. Most would tell you that what we are feeling is nothing more than rekindled memories. Similar experiences of a prior event, real or imagined. We both know better though, don't we?"

John's temples throbbed. He was baffled by the direction of this conversation.

"Professor, I just wanted you to know … ."

Rutherford interrupted. " ' … how much I enjoy being in your class and assisting in the lab.' "

John wondered whether the professor was psychic. That or such an astute judge of character that he knew what his students would say before they said it.

"Yes, yes, young Shaw," Rutherford acquiesced with a flip of his hand. He leaned back, then quickly leaned forward, "I forgive you! I accept your apology! You remain in good standing in my class. And you may certainly continue your position as my assistant. Happy?"

John could only nod. He forced himself to say, "If I've upset you … ."

Rutherford began wringing his hands together. His eyes squinched and he shook his head. "I just get so tired of saying the same thing over and over again. You come, apologize, and I forgive. You come, apologize, and I forgive. Damn, if it doesn't get redundant."

Another flash of lighting sent slivers of light through the edges of the blinds, dancing momentarily on the walls. A loud clap of thunder directly overhead made John jump. The rain, now a downpour, slammed against the window and thumped on the roof and awnings. The bulb in the lamp flickered.

Rutherford reached into his jacket pocket and removed the gold talisman. He cradled it with both hands, gently resting it on the desk.

"This is what you came to talk about," he said, with more than a hint of annoyance. "Let's get to it then."

John scratched his head. "Professor, I'm confused."

"Of course you are. You're *always* confused. And then I explain it to you, and you become even *more* confused." He laughed.

John suddenly wondered if the professor was mistaking him for someone else.

Rutherford looked down at the talisman, paused, and then shook his head. "It would be so much easier if you remembered that we had this conversation a dozen times already. Or if I would just forget. Or, even better, that it would turn out differently."

The professor wasn't making sense and John began to think that it was useless to have come. Worse, the professor was becoming more agitated and irritable by the minute. John wanted to leave; just stand up and leave.

"As you do not remember the conversation that we have had a dozen times over, I will explain *again*."

Cupping both hands over the talisman, he continued. "You have spent hours, days, pondering the talisman. And me *with* the talisman. You have wondered about selfishness. Questioned impropriety. The days have dragged on as you struggled to concentrate on things that you *should* be focused on. Like your studies. The evenings, lying in bed, have seemed even longer. Feeling that in order to get back to what you consider 'normal,' you must confront me, question my intention with the talisman. What am I doing with it? When will it be revealed, discussed? Why isn't it in the university display cases?"

John felt frozen. He wanted to answer, to say something, anything, but was enthralled with the professor's supposition. Even more amazing was the accuracy of the presumption.

Rutherford continued. "Something inside was urging you to action. Calling you out. Feeling pressured by your own conscience, you start to question your own desire to know. Your *right* to know. Your curiosity has become a source of embarrassment and you want to put it behind you. Clear the air. You resolve yourself to apologize. Feeling like I need to hear it."

He paused to stare at John, who was wide-eyed.

"And here we are."

"Yes ... ," John said, his voice trailing off, feeling numb, as if in a dream state. Real, but not believing. "But how could you know?"

Rutherford relaxed, smiled. "My dear boy, you've told me this over and over again this very night."

John's head was swimming. His temples throbbed. Nothing made sense. The professor's odd predictive comments sent a chill up his spine. Worse, he had the distinct feeling that something more ominous than a storm was building.

Rutherford held up the talisman with one hand.

"Ah, behold the explanation for your wonderment, young Shaw. A timepiece without the spring. A chronometer with reversing second hand. A veritable déjà vu-inducing device."

His voice rose, enjoying the telling.

"I hold before you Ponce de León's fountain of youth, without the water. H.G. Wells' time machine, without the seat."

John shook his head. "What do you mean?"

Rutherford lowered the weighty object back to the desktop. "I don't know how it works, mechanically speaking. But I know for a fact that it *does* work. I have conducted dozens of experiments with it over the years that I have had possession of it."

John finally found a flaw in the professor's logic and was quick to point it out. " 'Years,' Professor? We only just found it in August."

Rutherford nodded, realizing that he was getting ahead of himself. "Of course. That is what it must seem like to *you*." He laughed as if privy to an inside joke. "For *me*, however, many months have passed. Years, even. I have lived and relived these very days dozens of times over. You and I have had this discussion so often that I could predict your every movement and recite your every word."

John's headache intensified, as did the force of the storm outside. He usually didn't suffer from headaches except when under stress. This was one of those times. The professor, with his bizarre ranting, was starting to scare him.

"I know that you're wondering what I'm talking

about. How I got this way. And that you're concerned for your well-being."

John's cheeks flushed. "How … could you 'know' this?"

Rutherford rolled his eyes and sighed. He was frustrated with having to repeat what he'd already explained numerous times.

"Because you have told me the last time we discussed this. Or was it the time before? It's difficult to remember of late. They all start to smear together, one after another."

John shook his head as if to snap himself out of some sort of trance. "With all due respect, professor … ."

" ' … but I haven't the foggiest idea what you're talking about.' "

Once again, John was stunned. "How did you know I was going to use the word 'foggiest'?"

"Sometimes you say 'foggiest,' sometimes you say you don't have a clue. The future does change, but only slightly and never with any significance. What difference does it make? It all turns out the same."

John had heard enough. He stood up, ready to apologize again and excuse himself from this den of madness. The professor was obviously suffering from some sort of delusion or breakdown, and he didn't want to listen to any more insane babbling.

Rutherford calmly slid open the top drawer of this desk and removed the Smith & Wesson revolver. He looked at it for a moment and then pointed it at John's chest.

"You would think that after this many times you

would believe me. But you never do. So this is usually the point in the evening where I kill you."

John wondered if he had heard correctly. Had his revered professor actually threatened to *kill* him? He swallowed hard.

The bizarre nature of the situation caught John by such surprise that he didn't know what to do, what to say. But he felt like he should do or say *something*. A foolish man might make a run for the door. It was only feet from the man holding the weapon, so his chances of escape would be nil. The thought of groveling and begging for mercy crossed John's mind, but he immediately dismissed it as pathetic. He did not want to destroy his pride and spend his remaining moments of life that way. A fearless hero might lunge at his adversary, wrestle away the gun, and turn the tables on the attacker. This may work in the movies, but they were a long way from Hollywood.

Before John could think of an adequate response or course of action, Rutherford said, "I'm disappointed that you don't remember any of this. I really hoped you would this time."

John, not sure what reply would ensure his safety, simply shook his head.

With the gun still pointed straight ahead, Rutherford continued. "When do you remember being here last?"

John thought it best to just go along with the questioning. "Late yesterday afternoon. After school. I stopped by and your wife said you were at the lab."

"Sit down," the professor ordered.

John sat back on the couch, slowly, as if a jerky movement would accidentally cause the gun to discharge. His legs felt weak, and he was glad that he didn't need to count on them for support. He tried to swallow but couldn't muster enough saliva to make it worth the effort.

"The last time you were here in this room we discussed the talisman. How it had the ability to turn back time. I explained that the first time it happened was when we were on Antigua. One minute it was late in the evening and the next it was several hours earlier. Then, after living, or *reliving* really, those hours again, the same thing happened. It was instantly several hours earlier."

Rutherford deliberately omitted telling John about hitting him over the head repeatedly with the shovel and leaving him for dead—twice. There was nothing to gain trying to explain *that*.

"As you might imagine, I thought I was mistaken. Or dreaming. I even entertained the notion that I was slipping into madness."

A thought that John was beginning to entertain as well.

"But it was not my mind playing tricks on me. It was the talisman we found in the hole. Don't ask me how, because I don't have a rational explanation, but it has the ability to shift time. Turn back hours, days, and years. It is a device that permits the possessor to travel through time."

He leaned back in his chair, smiling, awaiting the response he knew would come.

"Time travel? That's … ."

" '… impossible.' No, my young Shaw. Not impossible. Not even unlikely. That poor fellow in the hole on Antigua must have died trying to protect the talisman. Or perhaps was killed because of it. I would have liked to explore the relationship of the skeleton to the thing. In many ways I feel I've been handed a sophisticated electronic device without the benefit of an owner's manual."

The professor sighed. He lowered the weapon, resting the grip on the desk, but continued pointing it in John's direction.

Perhaps there would be a chance for escape, John thought. If there was, he wanted to be ready.

"I could bore you with details of my adventures over the past fifteen or so years since returning from Antigua, but I won't."

He deliberately hesitated before continuing, knowing that John was trying to absorb the comment and do the math in his head.

They'd returned from Antigua at the end of August. It was now late October. Sixty days, tops. The reference to fifteen years must be nothing more than hyperbole.

The professor was smiling. A flash of light from a bolt of lightning snuck through the edges of the blinds and danced across the walls in horizontal lines. The flickering light and stark shadows accentuated the professor's odd expression, like something out of an old horror film.

"It's a bad storm," John said, in an awkward

attempt to defuse the tension.

Rutherford looked at his watch. "It will pass in precisely eleven minutes."

"Professor," John began, knowing full well that he was about to tread dangerous waters. "I don't know what's going on here. I don't know why you have a gun. And I don't know what you're talking about with shifting time and reliving the present. I don't mean any disrespect sir, but you've changed since coming back from the island. You don't seem yourself. Perhaps you need to … ." And then he stopped.

"Get help? Have a complete top-to-bottom physical? Have a long talk with a psychiatrist? Have myself committed to a hospital for the criminally insane? You never *could* complete that sentence."

"It's just that … this isn't normal."

Rutherford shook his head. "Of course you don't believe me. You never do. I've explained this over and over again, a dozen different ways."

His voice rose, frustration growing. "The talisman reverses time for a period, giving me the chance to live over the days and sometimes years that I just lived. I have lived fifteen years since returning from Antigua. Each day I relive, each year, is similar to the first time with minor exceptions. None significant enough to change history. I can't change things that seemed destined to happen, but I *have* been able to profit from it."

Rutherford's eyes lit up, and he smiled broadly. "And oh how I've profited! I've accumulated thousands of rare and priceless items. Made lucrative deals and even cheated more than my fair share of charlatans, deserving as they were. And here's the best part. I always escaped detection and prosecution by simply reliving that experience and changing a slight detail. Result? Complete exoneration!"

He waited for John to absorb what he said and grasp the concept. For John, this was once again a new and highly implausible concept.

"You don't believe me. I can see it in your eyes."

John's head was spinning. His temples throbbed. It was all too much to handle. He had gone on an archaeological dig over summer vacation, returned, started back in school a couple of weeks later, and was over at the professor's house to apologize. It all happened in a matter of months, not years. And now this wild tale of time travel, or 'shifting' as the professor called it.

In spite of the unlikeliness of the professor's tall tale, something about it made sense. He fought this thought. He didn't *want* to believe.

"If what you are saying is true, and in no way am I saying I believe it … ."

"Of course."

" … how have you retained the items you 'accumulated'? Wouldn't they disappear every time you … shifted. Because you hadn't yet accumulated them?"

Rutherford smiled. "Very astute, young Shaw!" He leaned forward. "I speculate that I retain the items because once I acquire them, I remove them from their *old* timeline and transfer them to *my* timeline. So, whenever and wherever I time-shift, they remain *my* possessions. Sounds strange, I know, but that's my best explanation. And because I am in possession of the talisman, I retain the memory of all the different timelines too."

"And if you *weren't* in possession of the 'talisman'?"

Rutherford stiffened, his expression somber. His grip on the revolver tightened. "Since I have never been without it, I couldn't say."

John had a cold chill. "Professor, why do you have a gun? Why are you threatening to kill me? What do I have to do with this?"

Rutherford laughed. "All good questions, young Shaw. I may finally be getting through to you."

He set the revolver on the desk. His hand rested on it, but his finger was now off the trigger.

John couldn't tell if the professor was letting his guard down or was subtly inviting an escape attempt. He decided to watch the signs and be ready to make a move if the opportunity presented itself.

"We have a history, you and I," the professor began, softly, sounding more like his old familiar self. "It has always been one-sided, until this moment, this pinpoint in time. Because I am the only one who remembers it! That is both a blessing and a curse. Certainly, from a point of view of being able to act covertly and pad my wealth, anonymity is a blessing. Living repetitive days over and over, is something different entirely. I hate it! Anticipating conversations and events with no element of surprise is agonizingly lonely, to say the least."

John leaned forward; his hands clasped together. His attention focused, as if trying to absorb an archeology lecture.

Rutherford continued. "I'm ashamed to admit that for quite some time, years in fact, I have considered you a threat. You knew of my—our—discovery of the talisman. You were bright enough to question standard operating procedure. And you had high enough morals to question what I may or may not be doing with it. By the time you pressured me into having the discussion we're currently having, I'd come to a difficult conclusion. That there was only one way to keep you from showing up at my house whenever I reached this point of the present. I killed you. Shot you dead, right here in this very spot."

He paused for a moment to let that sink in. "Foolishly, I thought that it would solve something. And it would have, I suppose, if I wasn't so damned greedy. When I time-shifted back to prevent an argument with my wife, or cover my tracks from selling an artifact from the university, or whatnot, you weren't dead any longer."

As if debating the accuracy of a science fiction novel that had loose ends of logic, John was now intrigued with the complexity of the professor's explanation.

"So you're saying that you … what? Brought me back to life after killing me?"

"No, no, no!" Rutherford said, sounding like he was arguing a commonly held hypothesis. "Not brought back to life. Because I had time-shifted to the past and was reliving those days as if they had never been experienced, you hadn't died yet. So every time I killed you … ."

"You killed me more than once?" John interrupted.

"Oh yes, many times! Twice on Antigua … ."

"On the island? You killed me on the island?!"

"Yes, but many more times right here in my house." He paused. "But it was so damned messy I stopped doing it."

John closed his eyes and shook his head. This was like a realistic dream with disconnected facts unsupported by science or common sense.

"As I say, you never stayed dead. Every time I shifted, the act of your murder hadn't yet happened, and I'd have to do it again. If I had just not time-shifted after that occurrence, if I had just exercised some self-control and let the present continue undisturbed, you would have remained dead. But lucky for you, I suppose, I can't stop going back in time and improving my situation."

"Lucky," John repeated. The word seemed hollow and ironic. Nothing that had happened or was being said, made him feel lucky.

"After a while, keeping in mind that months passed in between, I capitulated and decided to try and make you an ally. Perhaps if you understood and appreciated the power and possibilities of the talisman, you would be less relenting."

A low rumble of thunder rolled across the sky in the distance. The storm was moving out of the area. Rutherford looked at his watch. "Nine minutes. Hmm, earlier than last time."

John sensed that it was more than coincidence.

"You need proof," Rutherford said without prompting. "Just like before. So that's what I tried to do, provide proof."

He moved the revolver to the side. John pondered the possibility of rushing the professor while he was distracted but dismissed the idea. Even if he could overwhelm the larger man, which seemed unlikely, or push past him to get the gun, he wasn't sure he wanted to. There was more to the professor's story, and he wanted to hear it.

Rutherford laughed. "How naïve I was back then! I thought that if I explained the concept of time-shifting and then demonstrated it, you would be able to recall us having this conversation once we got to this point in the present. As it turns out, I couldn't prove it to you any more than I could kill you. Don't you see? When I time-shifted to the past, those days hadn't happened yet and you didn't know that we had even talked about this. I had to wait months to explain it all to you again. But just like now, and the time before that, and the time before that even, you don't recall our previous conversations or the demonstrations. Frankly, I've given up trying. No more demonstrations."

John wasn't sure if that meant that he was free to leave. "What now?"

Rutherford slipped the talisman into his coat pocket, stood up, and sauntered past the couch over to the window, leaving the pistol unguarded on the desk. John fought the urge to grab it and play hero. Even though it had been turned on him moments earlier, he no longer felt threatened.

Rutherford lifted a slat on one of the blinds and peered outside. The rain had diminished to nothing more than a light drizzle.

"Do you know what the single most desired quality of life is, my dear Shaw?"

John didn't need to think about it. He'd heard the professor lament about it since he first got there. He gave the answer he thought the professor expected.

"Power."

Rutherford, with his back to the room, smiled. "No. Nor is it wealth. For once those two are obtained the only thing remaining is immortality."

He turned to face John, but first looked to see if the pistol was still on the desk. His head dropped. John thought that it was a look of disappointment.

"The talisman certainly provides that opportunity. Want to live another day, another year, another decade? Take an opportunity, fix a wrong, gain an advantage? The talisman permits you to do that. Keep going back, keep living your days over again. Sounds wonderful, doesn't it?"

Rutherford began to slowly pace the room. "What's that old expression? Be careful what you wish for … ."

"You might just get it," John said.

Rutherford stopped. "Precisely." He glanced over to the desk. The gun was still there. "Do you know how old I am, Mr. Shaw? Take a guess."

John hated these types of games. No one was ever pleased with the answer. "Fifty-five? Fifty-six?"

Rutherford began to pace again. "I'm sixty-eight."

John tried hard to remain composed, but he felt his eyebrows rise, thus betraying his surprise at either the number or the claim.

"Well, you don't look a day over sixty," John said, hoping that his facetiousness would not be construed as offensive.

"So true. Of course, chronologically, I'm only fifty-three. But I have lived and relived fifteen additional years. They weren't *different* years, just repeated ones."

Feeling uncomfortable with the new direction of the conversation, John forced a compliment. "You look pretty good."

Sensing the strained attempt at flattery, Rutherford shrugged. "I look like hell. I feel like hell. I'm worn out both physically and mentally."

Rutherford stopped pacing. He stared at John for a moment and then glanced over at the Smith & Wesson. It was still lying there untouched. He sat down behind the desk and leaned back, exhausted.

"For me, the future doesn't roll in. Rather, it seeps in. I rarely see much of the future before I time-shift and relive the past and present over again. Subsequently, I am left feeling the draining effects of time's passage."

The whole concept of time-shifting and his own prior deaths was hard enough to grasp. John was even more confused by the direction that the conversation was going. Whatever the destination, he felt the journey was close to complete.

They locked eyes and John knew that his assumption was correct.

Rutherford slowly swiveled in his chair and reached for the revolver. His right hand rested on the gun. It remained there for a good ten seconds. His eyes darted from the pistol to John and then back again.

John felt his heart beat faster with adrenaline. He thought he ought to say something, but no words would come. He'd deceived himself thinking that he was out of danger. Now the professor was about to prove him wrong.

Rutherford lifted the revolver and stared at John. He was expressionless and trembling.

"I have a problem," he began, softly, as if in a confessional unloading his sins. "I know that. I can't continue this way, living yesterday and today over and over. But I can't stop. I can't. The talisman has become my opiate, my methamphetamine, my crack cocaine. Just having it is too much of a temptation to ... change things, to abuse the natural order of the universe."

After a long pause, he continued, his voice determined. "It's got to end, and it's got to end today."

Fear shot through John like one of the lightning bolts from earlier. In a nanosecond, he deduced that he was about to be shot. The realization froze him solid. He held his breath, his heart beating rapidly. Then, he had a thought.

"Prove it again!" he blurted. "One more time. Prove it again! Turn back time, shift, whatever. Show me. Make me understand. Just don't do *this*."

The professor's eyes began to glisten. His bottom lip rolled inward, and he exhaled. A single tear rolled over his round cheek, disappearing into his close-cropped gray beard. He fought to contain what little composure he had left. He shook his head, quickly dismissing the suggestion.

"It won't do any good."

"Maybe it will," John pleaded. "Show me. Shift time for me. Do it."

Suddenly, as if his entire body was shocked out of complacency, Rutherford leaned forward. His face reddened, and he raised his voice louder.

"Don't you see? You've asked this a dozen times before. And a dozen times I've obliged. 'Maybe *this* time. Maybe this one time.'" He slapped the desk with his free hand. "Every time I try to prove it to you, I have to live the days over again, but you never remember. Never! I'm not going through that again. I've had enough. Don't you understand?! I've lived more years than I care to. Endured more than I should have to."

He looked away, breathing deeply, desperate to retain his composure and at least a shred of dignity.

"There is only one thing left to do. And *you*, young Shaw, are going to help me do it."

The professor swung the revolver around and handed it, grip first, to John. "Take it," he said.

The realization hit John like a cold slap. The professor *did* intend murder. Or at least, a suicide masked as murder.

John leaned back, shaking his head. "No, I can't do this. Don't ask me."

"Take it!"

"I won't."

Rutherford looked down at the gun lying in the palm of his outstretched hand. Then, pleading, "You need to take it. Please. I need to give you something."

John began to think that this didn't sound like a man forcing a death wish. But, rather, a desperate man reaching out in need of help—who just happened to be holding a gun.

He decided that if one of them should have the gun it would be better if it wasn't in the hand of a man who obviously was wrestling with some psychological issues. He slowly reached out for the revolver. As soon as his fingers touched the cold steel the professor released the gun and pulled his hand away. If John hadn't gripped it quickly it would have fallen to the floor.

Sensing that time was of the essence, Rutherford reached into his coat pocket and removed the round gold talisman. The professor cradled it in his two hands like a newborn puppy, fragile crystal, or expensive artwork. He stared down at it, eyebrows raised, a tear in his eye. It was a look of adoration.

"We've come so very far, my friend. Grown so very close. I never thought I would ever say this, but I hope that we never meet again."

He glanced up at John and then quickly held out both hands still cradling the talisman. "Here, take this. Now!"

John didn't hesitate. Whether or not the talisman held some special power, he knew that it would be best if the professor divested himself of it. He reached out and snatched the puck.

Rutherford sat back and sighed, relieved. His eyes were closed peacefully, a slight smile on his lips. The tremble in his hands was gone. It was clear that a burden of some sort had been lifted from him.

"Professor," John began, knowing he was disturbing the first peaceful moment the professor seemed to enjoy since he'd arrived. "Why do I have a gun?"

Rutherford's eyes popped open. The moment of nirvana passed. It should have been obvious, after all he had told the boy, but he answered anyway, "To keep me from taking back the talisman, of course."

"I don't … ."

Rutherford held up his right hand, palm forward. "Don't! Don't say another word. I don't know what you are going to say, and I don't want to. This is an uncharted future for me. I don't want to spoil it."

He stood abruptly and walked the few steps to the den door.

"Go now. And don't come back."

John, stunned by everything that he'd seen and heard over the past hour, was even more shocked by the professor's stark rudeness. He stood up, cupping the gun in his right hand and clutching the talisman with his left. He slowly walked from the couch to the double doors where the professor was waiting for him.

Rutherford stared at the objects in John's hands, then met his eyes. "Heed my words, young Shaw. One of those two objects will save your life. The other will destroy you. Do you understand?"

John nodded but was not at all certain that he understood.

"I am trusting you to do the right thing. Do not inform the university that you have possession of the talisman. Do not donate it, sell it, or give it away. It is far too dangerous. Especially, and this is most important … ," he began as he reached out and squeezed John's forearm painfully, "above all do not be tempted to use it. Bury it or encase it in cement and drop it in the deepest depths of the ocean, just don't use it. Not once, not ever." He shook John's arm. "Promise me!"

John didn't know if he was dealing with a prominent professor in the throes of madness or a profound genius conquering the limits of time and space. Common sense told him that it was the former but gut emotion argued the latter.

"Promise me!"

John nodded.

"No! Say the words. Say that you promise."

The ferocity of the professor's words was frightening. Although he tried not to show his emotions, John was sure that his shocked facial expression betrayed him.

"Yes. Yes, of course!" he blurted. Then, softer, "Is there anything else I can do for you, professor? Anything?"

Rutherford released his grip on John's forearm and grinned. He liked the boy. This one was different from his other students. Smart, enthusiastic, persistent. Oh so persistent. He was also trustworthy and loyal. The talisman would be in good hands. Perhaps there was a reason they had found the talisman together and spent the past fifteen years centrally focused on it. He preferred that to thinking the sequence of life's events was nothing more than a random collection of happenstances, with no goal or purpose.

He was tired of pondering the origin of the talisman. Tired of protecting it. Tired of trying to control it. He was glad to finally be rid of it and, yet, felt torn at the same time. John was there when it was found and had as much right to it as anyone. Not only that, but he was full of youthful enthusiasm and strong moral fiber. If anyone could resist the temptation of the talisman, this one could. If not, heaven help him.

"And now," Rutherford said softly to his protégé, "there's only one thing left to do. Leave, and do not return."

Rutherford wanted to hug the boy. It's true that they'd had their share of disagreements over the years, all due to the talisman. But he now felt that John was his best hope for release from the chains that bound him. Instead of a hug, however, he put his hand on the boy's shoulder.

"There's nothing more you can do, other than hold to your promise." He took a last look at the items in John's hands and then quickly ushered him out of the den and down the hall to the front door.

Hearing footsteps in the hall, Irene stepped out from the kitchen. "Leaving already?" she asked from down the hall past the den. "Dinner is almost ready. You're welcome to join us if you'd like."

With his back to Irene to block her view, Rutherford whispered, "Put those in your pockets and let no one know you have them. *No* one."

John did as he was told. He untucked his shirt so that it covered the bulges.

"Mr. Shaw was just leaving."

Irene came up behind her husband and put her arm around his waist. She was smiling. "It was very nice of you to visit, Mr. Shaw, please come again."

The professor shook his head ever so slightly and

John knew that he was not welcome back—ever.

"Remember everything I told you. Everything."

John nodded. "Yes sir."

"It's time to go."

John didn't answer. Nor did he argue. He didn't fully understand, but he knew he had to respect the professor's wishes.

20

THE HEAVY FRONT DOOR CLOSED quickly behind him. John stood on the top step for several minutes, looking out at the damp and quiet neighborhood. He had to catch his breath, collect his thoughts. There was so much to absorb. So much conflicting information. He wondered what he was to do with the pistol, the gold ... 'talisman,' and the professor's outlandish claims.

The rain had stopped, but drips continued to fall from the house soffit and the leaves of the trees. He listened to the *plop-plop-plop* sound of rain on the sidewalk and street. The smell of wet asphalt permeated the air. He drank it in.

Ordinarily, it was a pleasant purging smell, giving the illusion that pollutants were being washed out of the air. Cleaning the streets and sidewalks, refreshing the earth. After all he had heard and promised this evening, it didn't smell refreshing or hopeful. It smelled like decay.

John was about to descend the steps when he heard a loud scream from inside the house.

He grabbed the door handle. It was unlocked. He cracked open the door and called in. "Hello! It's John. John Shaw. I heard a scream. Is everything all right?"

There was no answer.

He stepped in and called out again, a little louder, "Hello?! Is everything all right?!"

Muffled sobbing came from the other end of the house toward the kitchen. He hurried down the hallway, prepared to apologize for intruding.

He stopped at the den on the way to the kitchen and looked inside to see if the professor was still there. He wasn't. The kitchen was brightly lit and smelled of dinner cooking, but no one was there.

From the center of the kitchen the sobbing was louder, more intense, originating from the attached garage, through the open door across from the stove and refrigerator.

Still feeling like an intruder, John hurried to the open door. Light from the kitchen spilled into the garage only partially illuminating the space. He clearly heard a woman sobbing.

"Hello?" he called, not particularly loud for fear of startling the person. "It's me, John Shaw."

"Help!" Irene Rutherford called out, shrill and frantic. "Help me, please!"

He flipped on the light switch. Irene was standing in the center of the empty garage. Her arms were around the legs of the professor, dangling lifeless from a rafter. A white laundry line was wrapped tightly around his neck, his head cocked to one side, eyes closed. A wooden shop stool was on its side beneath him.

John rushed to her. She had been trying to support her husband's weight and save him from choking to death, but she wasn't strong enough to lift him. John knew that it didn't matter; his neck appeared to be broken.

Using a box cutter he found on a workbench along the wall, John stood on the stool, reached up, and quickly cut the rope. Together they lowered the professor's body to the concrete floor. Irene immediately threw herself on top of her husband's body and wailed. Her heart and world had quickly and unexpectedly been torn apart.

John ran back into the kitchen to phone for an ambulance. It was just a formality. They both knew that the professor was dead.

Part Two – The Transfer

21

JOHN RAN FULL GAIT BACK to the dormitory. He would have preferred to fly there, transport there, just *be* there.

This place, this seemingly normal middle-class neighborhood, was filled with terrors and horrors he had never imagined. Disturbing personality quirks. Weird time-travel scenarios. Multiple murders. Even suicide. It was all too much. If he could believe in time travel, or time-shifting as the professor called it, he would shift back to before he knew anything at all about the subject.

The streets and sidewalks glistened from the recent deluge. Water sluiced along the curb to storm drains. The wet slapping sound of his rubber-soled shoes hitting the pavement seemed to echo off the rows of bungalow homes. John panted as he ran, and his chest hurt from the thunderous beating of his heart.

He was alone, both physically and mentally. Not

a car or person was in sight. He wondered if the professor had somehow been right, if somehow time had come to a complete standstill, and he was locked in some godforsaken vacuum with no way out. No past or future.

He ran faster, increasing the echo off the homes. His thoughts fractured. Was anyone in those houses? Were they frozen in time? Did *they* have the ability to shift back to another time like the professor? Did *they* have their own version of the talisman? Is there a future at all if we can never get beyond our present?

Maybe there really is no tomorrow. Maybe the universe as we know it doesn't have the ability to have a future, to evolve beyond the present. Perhaps, this moment, this present, is all there is, all there will *ever* be. Which might explain why the professor never felt he had a future. There wasn't one. This day, this moment, could be the end of the world.

A car traveling down the cross street jarred him back to reality. He was not alone as he feared, just afraid and confused. When the car passed, the air went silent again.

He stopped at the corner and caught his breath. He was perspiring. A siren in the distance behind him cut the evening's dead air. It was getting louder by the second, headed no doubt, to the Rutherford home, now several blocks behind him. Suddenly, the siren stopped, no doubt reaching its destination. He didn't look back. He didn't dare.

His mouth was dry as dust, and his heart beat a drum solo on the inside of his chest. He was painfully aware of what they would find when they went in.

Poor Mrs. Rutherford, John thought, to find her husband that way. John had offered to stay with her until the ambulance arrived, for whatever good it might do her.

"There's nothing you can do," she had told him. "Nothing we could have done to stop it. He had his mind made up. You go now. And don't come back."

Don't come back.

It was what the professor had told him too.

With his hands on his hips, John threw his head back, caught his breath, and calmed himself. He began to hear noises he hadn't noticed before. Road hum from traffic on other streets. A garage door purring as it closed. Muffled conversation from a television through a slightly open window.

Maybe the neighborhood, the world, wasn't as eerily silent and foreboding as he thought seconds earlier.

It started to drizzle, just enough to urge him on to his destination. He began to run again, although without the same intensity. Now, it felt more like he was running *toward* something rather than away. A crack of thunder in the distance hinted that the storm might not yet be over. He knew he had to hurry.

22

THE NEXT MORNING, the news of the professor's death swept over the campus like a tsunami smothering a low-lying village. A dark aura hung in the air, matching the thick gray clouds that covered the sky. Rumors mixed with fact; speculation blended with reality.

The students weren't privy to many details other than Professor Rutherford was dead. Heart attack, stroke, accident, and even murder were all suspected causes. The school administration had yet to put out a formal announcement. That would happen later in the day.

Other than her parents, Hannah Miller was the first person on campus to learn about the professor's death. The news brought her to tears. While her father went to console Mrs. Rutherford and provide moral support, Hannah dressed quickly and went to the archaeology lab. She had a knot in her stomach, but it seemed the right place to reflect on the professor's life and mourn his passing. Plus, if the professor really did die by suicide as her father said, perhaps he left a clue as to why. Or better yet, a note. She had to know.

As a research assistant, Hannah had keys to both the building and the lab. It was a gray, overcast day. The little light that managed to seep into the foyer was soft and diffused, making the building feel abandoned.

Hannah's footsteps echoed through the empty halls as she descended the steps to the lower level. Very little of the light from the lobby pierced the darkness down there, and it felt like she was entering a tomb. She was neither paranoid nor the least bit superstitious, but for some reason it felt eerie.

Although she'd been to the lab a hundred times, this time felt different. She rubbed her arms and bit her lip.

There was nothing to be concerned about, she reminded herself. It was early on a weekend. The building had been locked. There was no one down there. The mere knowledge of the professor's death and the manner of that death, however, was sending her imagination into overdrive.

At the bottom of the stairs, a sliver of pale-yellow light coming from under the lab door made the hall seem less ominous. Someone may have left a light on from the night before. Or perhaps it was a bulb in one of the artifact display cases.

Just then, the light spilling into the hallway flickered. It could be a bad bulb, she thought, but more likely someone passing in front of the light, breaking the beam.

Knowing that her paranoia was not unfounded,

her fear gelled into curiosity and outrage. Someone was violating the sanctity of the professor's laboratory, and she was determined to find out who and why. Caution be damned.

Stealthily, Hannah made her way down the lower hallway. As she approached the door, it occurred to her that if it were, in fact, a burglar, it would have been better if she had a weapon. Even a flashlight could have been used as a club. She looked down the hallway in both directions, but there was nothing she could use to arm herself.

She briefly considered turning back and going for help but knew that by the time she notified campus security and they arrived, the burglar would be long gone. Professor Rutherford hadn't spent his career amassing an enviable collection of artifacts just to have someone steal or damage them. Plus, as the daughter of the president, she felt she had an obligation to protect university property. She was going in.

Hannah stood next to the lab door, her back against the wall. She positioned her set of keys in such a way that each key stuck out from between the fingers of her clenched fist. It wasn't much, but if she was able to get close enough she could swing her arm or jab her fist and cut up the intruder's face nicely. Presuming she could get close enough.

She listened, but it was silent inside the lab. If someone was in there, they weren't busting up the place.

Then she heard a scraping sound, like a steel file drawer sliding closed, and then a thump. It was muffled, like it came from across the room. Possibly inside the professor's office.

Wishing to retain the element of surprise, she crouched down and slowly turned the doorknob. When she was sure that it had disengaged from the striking plate, she gradually swung the door inward. It was a sturdy door and required every bit of strength she could muster to open from a crouched position. She managed to push it open about eighteen inches and was thankful that it did not squeak on the hinges.

Still hunched over, she took a deep breath and duck-walked into the lab, half expecting the intruder to be standing just inside the room, waiting for her. Once completely inside, she slowly closed the door over, careful not to let it latch and make a noise.

The blinds on the inside of the professor's office windows were cracked open just enough to see into the work area. A desk lamp was on, its shade angled down, illuminating the desktop. Due to its angle, she couldn't make out the identity of the figure in the shadows behind the desk.

A quick visual sweep of the room reassured her that no other accomplices were there and that the glass display cases were still intact and undisturbed.

Crawling on all fours to the outside wall of the office, Hannah was careful to stay under the windows. Once there, she realized that she didn't have a plan. With no weapon other than a set of keys, she was defenseless. She was not prepared to duke it out with some professional criminal or crazed hopped up druggie. Perhaps, if she could get a look at the person and provide their description to the campus security, they could apprehend the intruder. That is, if she could get a good enough look at them and still get out undetected.

Slowly, she rose up to peek in the window. A man had his back to her and was rifling through the second drawer of the file cabinet. He was thumbing through one hanging folder after another. Searching for test scores or future tests, she thought. Not unheard of on a college campus, but rare at the University of Chicago.

Within a minute, the man seemed to find something that interested him, and he froze. At first, Hannah thought that she had done something to draw his attention. Instead, he removed a folder, turned, and placed it on the desk under the lamp next to the windows. He adjusted the lampshade to better direct the light. It was then that Hannah recognized John Shaw.

She scowled and stood quickly, directly in front of John standing on the opposite side of the window.

Startled by Hannah's sudden appearance, John stumbled backward, his arms thrown back to catch himself. The back of his left hand caught the corner of the file cabinet. It stopped him from falling but tore open the skin from the wrist to a knuckle, and he began to bleed. Meanwhile, the desk chair rolled into the file cabinet with a loud *THANG*, adding to his surprise.

"Oh!" Hannah exclaimed.

She stood and ran to the door of the office, now more concerned with John's condition than his possible indiscretion. "Are you all right?!"

John regained his balance by the time Hannah entered the office and his face flushed. "You startled me!"

"Apparently."

"What are you *doing* here?"

"I can ask you the same thing," she said brusquely.

She lifted his hand and examined the bleeding wound. It was a deep scratch but not bad enough to warrant stitches. She took a clean shop towel from a folded stack on the top of the file cabinet and gently wrapped his hand with it. After tearing the ends, she tied them together to create a makeshift bandage.

He'd been watching her face the entire time that she was tending him. Even though they'd had several classes together and spent time together on Antigua, he'd not actually been this physically close to her before. He could smell the sweet floral scent of her hair and wanted to tell her that for quite some time he had admired her from afar. This, however, wasn't the best time. When she looked up, he looked away.

"Care to explain why you are going through the professor's files?"

"Thank you," he said, examining the homemade bandage.

Hannah crossed her arms and stared at him. "Answer me. Tell me what's going on."

"I'd rather not," he answered.

"You get straight A's," she said. "It's not likely you're trying to sneak a look at upcoming tests. Unless that *is* why you get straight A's."

John's voice rose. "Cheating? I would never do that!"

"I didn't think so. Then what? Trespassing

through a professor's belongings is subject to suspension. You may be his research assistant, but the professor wouldn't approve."

John looked down and flexed the fingers on his injured hand. He took a deep breath then looked up. "The professor is dead."

Hannah leaned against the edge of the desk, her energy spent from crawling and tending to John's injury. "I know. I heard this morning. Hanged himself."

John sat on the desk next to her. The grief-stricken and befuddled feelings of the previous evening once again washed over him. He nodded. "How did *you* find out?"

"His wife called my father. How about you?"

John knew he could lie and just say he'd heard it on the floor of his dorm. She'd believe that. But he didn't want to lie to her. Still, the truth was thorny and difficult to explain.

"I was there."

She turned her head and met his eyes. "You were *where*?"

"There. At his house. Last night."

She turned toward him, the pitch of her voice rising. "Did you know … ?"

John pushed himself to a standing position, bending his injured hand and sending a shooting pain up his arm in the process. He cradled the hand, now throbbing. "No! It happened after I left."

"What did you talk about when you were there? What was his mood? Did he give you any indication that he was suicidal?" She had many more questions but stopped to give him a chance to catch up.

John looked away, afraid that direct eye contact with her would cause him to spew out all that he knew about the professor and the situation. He had to remind himself that as much as he was attracted to her, she was still the daughter of the university president. Not knowing her depth of loyalty to her father or the university, John was nervous about divulging too much information.

He knew that a professor's suicide would certainly warrant an investigation and he would be questioned incessantly. Information would be discovered that revealed the professor to be not only a madman but also a thief and scoundrel. No, it would be best if Henri Rutherford were remembered as the outstanding professor and archaeologist that he was, not the demented eccentric he had become.

His pause did not go unnoticed. Hannah stood and moved to him. He was looking down, his brow furrowed, his lips tightly pressed. She felt sorry for him but didn't know why. She resisted the urge to put her arm around him. He would almost certainly think she was being too familiar.

"Can you talk about it?"

John looked up and turned to her. He badly wanted to share the burden of all that the professor had told him. To relieve himself of the responsibility of keeping it a secret. To debate what was truth and what was fantasy. If only she could keep a secret.

He slowly shook his head. "The professor must have had issues. It would be a shame to over-analyze them and come to the wrong conclusion."

She nodded, then smirked. "You're afraid I'll tell my father."

He wanted to laugh. She saw right through him. "The thought crossed my mind."

She slapped his right arm hard just below the shoulder with the back of her hand.

"That hurt!"

"Good," she said. "Maybe that will remind you that the professor was important to me too. If you want to share something in confidence then just say so. Just don't think of me as some sort of spy for the administration. Don't insult me like that."

John wanted to rub the sting out of his arm, but his left hand still throbbed. She was strong, self-confident, and wasn't hesitant to stand up for herself. He admired that.

She stood there with her hands on her hips, face scowling. Slowly, her anger dissipated and she dropped her arms.

"I'm sorry," he said. "It's just that I made a promise. But I don't know that I could keep it and I don't think I should share it."

"About the professor."

He nodded. "He was involved in a lot that we didn't know about. Some pretty questionable things."

"Such as?"

"Such as getting rich off the artifacts he was *supposed* to be bringing back to the university."

Hannah's jaw dropped. "He was … stealing?"

John started pacing inside the small narrow

office. It helped burn off nervous energy and bought him time to think.

"Stealing what's here and pocketing some things before they ever made it back."

Hannah put her hand to her mouth. "How could that be? Research assistants are with him at the time of the find, and everything is cataloged once it gets back here to the school."

"He's been doing it for years."

She shook her head. "That's hard to believe. Surely someone would have noticed things missing."

"That's why I came down here. For evidence."

John went back to the desk and leaned over the open file. He ran his index finger down the list of items that were hand-printed on the lined notebook paper. He remembered having seen several of those items in the professor's home: a flat sheet of marble, a foot square, with the carving of a sphinx; links from a ship's chain; and a Michoacán tripod tray with a serpent design around the edges. Dozens of other items were listed as well, but he didn't recall having seen them. He flipped over the paper. Five more sheets were underneath. The professor had been a busy man.

"Just as I thought. He kept a log of what was found, what they were worth, and what he did with them."

Hannah moved next to him and leaned over to get a better look.

"He either didn't think anyone would ever be on to him," John said, "or maybe he wanted someone to know in case something happened to him."

"How do you know what you're looking at?" Hannah asked. "Maybe this is just a list of things that interested him. Things to study."

"They interested him, all right. Look here." He pointed to the columns to the right of the item description. "He notes where he found the item and the date it was found. I saw some of them in his house. Other items have dollar amounts next to them. They must be the ones he sold."

Hannah straightened and shook her head. "This is not proof that he did anything wrong."

"Look at this," John said, pointing to one particular item. " 'Sloan Dalton spearhead, four inches, near perfect condition and symmetry. Found northern Arkansas, June 15, 2001. Extremely rare. UChicago cabinet 2B.' Then in different color ink … 'Flew to Rome, sold to JJ, $3,500.' It's dated September 8 of this year. Just two weeks after we returned from Antigua."

They looked up at each other, then back to the paper. She pointed to another item. "Look at this one," she said. " 'Openwork Faience Bracelet with Seated Deities, circa 305 BC. Found western Egypt, July 26, 1998. UofC cabinet 3A.' Then he wrote, 'Flew to Cairo, sold to FLN, September 7, $4,800.' "

"Here's one," John said. " 'Chalcidian Tinned Bronze Helmet, cracked rear guard, early 4th century. Found near Crete, July 1, 1978. UofC cabinet 1A. 'Flew to Rome, sold to JJ, September 8, $48,700.' "

She looked over at John. "They were all sold within a few days after we got back from Antigua."

He ran his finger down the list. "According to this, most of these had been in the university cabinets at one time."

Hannah was angry. "If he was selling university property on the black market, how come I don't remember seeing any of these things? If they were cataloged by cabinet and shelf, I *certainly* would have seen them!"

John had a suspicion, but it would have sounded crazy.

Then she pointed to several notations. "Cairo, Rome, Jerusalem, Crete … September 7, 8 … how did he fly to all these places and conduct those transactions in just two days?" She shook her head. "There's something wrong with this data. It's inconclusive. The only way he could have flown to each of these places was if he … ."

"Traveled back in time."

Hannah stared at him, then snickered. "I was going to say, 'beamed there,' but hey, time travel, sure, that works too."

John turned away, scratching the back of his head. Granted, the professor's story of time-shifting sounded less far-fetched after seeing a list of the items he had fenced, and when. He at least *believed* what he was saying. But John remembered how he felt when he first heard about the alleged power of the talisman. Hannah was sure to feel the same way.

Before he could decide what to say next, Hannah broke the stalemate. "There's something you're not telling me."

John didn't want to discuss what the professor had told him about time-shifting. Didn't want to remember his mentor dangling from the end of a handmade noose. Didn't want to be there, in that office, sifting through personal files, gathering evidence to support the admission from his revered professor that crimes had been committed. He choked down a dry swallow.

Hannah put her hand on his shoulder. "John, what is it?"

"There's more," he said finally. "A lot more."

"What is it? I can keep a confidence."

John hesitated, wanting to choose his words carefully. "There was another side of the professor. A darker side."

"*Besides* the thefts?"

He nodded. "He believed that he could … ," the words now seemed impossible to say, " … travel through time."

He stopped to see her reaction. There wasn't one. She waited.

"When we were on Antigua, we found something. A round gold object. It looked like a gold hockey puck with bumps on one side. He called it a talisman."

"The only thing we found on Antigua was the skeleton," Hannah said. "And we couldn't take that back with us. We came home disappointed, remember?"

John shook his head. "No. That's what he wanted you to think. Made me promise not to say anything. Said he wanted to study it without being disturbed. Now, knowing what I know about his black-market sideline, I think he intended to hock it."

She quickly flipped through the pages, then stopped. "Here is a mention of you and him finding a gold puck-like object. But that's all."

"He didn't sell it. Once he discovered what it was capable of, he decided to keep it. To use it."

"Use it?"

"Or so he said. He believed it would … ."

She waited but he didn't complete the sentence. "It would *what*?"

He watched for the reaction that he was sure would follow. "Allow him to travel through time."

As insane as it sounded, as ludicrous, he was glad to have spit it out.

"How did it work?"

John's eyebrows rose. It wasn't the response he expected. "I don't know. *He* didn't know. But it did. Or at least he was convinced that it did. According to him, he was able to go back in time and then relive all those days over again. Getting things. Selling things. Covering his tracks."

Hannah stared at him unblinkingly. John didn't know if that was a sign that she believed him, or something else.

"H.G. Wells-type stuff?" she asked. "Back and forth time travel?"

"Just back. Then he'd have to relive those days again. Said that he had lived about fifteen years since we got back from Antigua."

"We got back two months ago," she said.

"You and I got back two months ago. He had been going back in time months and years and reliving those months and years over again."

Hannah didn't flinch. Her expression focused.

"And we never knew?"

"No."

"So we have been living the same years over and over again with him but with no memory of it?"

It occurred to John that she was right. If the professor had been reliving the same days over again, as he claimed, then everyone else was living them over again too. How many times must they have had this same conversation?

Only once, John decided. Before he died, the professor said he was relieved to be experiencing the future for the first time. Since John was now in possession of the talisman and hadn't 'used' it, he couldn't have relived any days. If the professor was to be believed, these days, these moments, were all new.

"He couldn't handle it anymore … or didn't want to. So he gave it to me the night he died."

Hannah raised her hand to her chin and thought for a moment. "Hmm … Einstein, Hawking, van Stockum … they all pondered time travel. Not to mention writers of fiction, Wells, Finney, Vonnegut. So who knows?"

John's eyebrows rose. "You believe him?"

She shrugged as they locked eyes. "As students of archaeology, we see a lot of evidence without a lot of explanation. Who's to say what's possible and what isn't?"

He leaned toward her, attracted to her more than before, if that was even possible. "I have to say that you're taking this very well."

She inched closer, smiling, feeling a similar

attraction, hoping that a kiss was inevitable. "You have to admit that the possibility of reliving this moment over again sounds pretty exciting."

"Yes, if you even remember having lived it the first time … ."

She leaned in. Their lips met, and John kissed her back, warmly. It was a tender moment they both had hoped would happen eventually.

Suddenly, a noise from outside the office in the lab broke the moment. It was muted, distant, but in the empty lab, it was loud enough. It sounded like a click, as if the wind pushed a set of blinds against a window frame, but there were no external windows.

Just an old building settling, John decided, and didn't think any more about it. All this science fiction time travel talk had gotten him jumpy. He wondered if Hannah had heard it too. She hadn't. Or she didn't care. Her eyes were still closed.

The kiss resumed; the noise forgotten.

23

TIME TRAVEL. STEALING ARTIFACTS. Reliving days. It was beyond hard to believe; it was *ludicrous*. Still, Taylor Jennings was intrigued.

He had gone to the lab that morning to reflect, ponder, and pay homage to his professor. He hated funeral homes. There was no way he would visit that morbid building of death when they eventually put the corpse out on display. Watching people parade by a box with a stiff, wailing and carrying on, was depressing. Visiting the lab was his way of saying goodbye. Of paying respect. And perhaps pocket a loose artifact or two laying around.

As Taylor had approached the lab door early that Saturday morning, he heard voices but couldn't distinguish one from the other. Not that he cared if they were stealing or trashing, but he was fascinated by the mystery. He decided to investigate. His plan was to sneak up and scare the shit out of them. It was just what he needed after hearing about Rutherford's death. Sometimes all it takes is a good practical joke or prank to snap out of a funk.

He cracked open the door and peeked in. He couldn't see anyone, so he opened it another few inches. Still no one. Crouching down, he opened the door about two feet and snuck in, gently closing the door behind him. From just inside the lab he could see Hannah Miller and that country bumpkin John Shaw in Rutherford's office.

Crouching, Taylor moved closer to the office, slowly, quietly. He reevaluated his plan. Startling Shaw would be fun. Plowboy would probably wet himself. Hannah would no doubt be startled as well, but it wouldn't be nearly as much fun. She would almost certainly not see the humor in it and, worse, would resent him for the abrupt intrusion.

If he had any hope at all of bedding her, he couldn't have her mad at him. If there was one thing he wanted more than a degree from the prestigious University of Chicago, it was to bang the prettiest girl on campus. In fact, if Shaw hadn't been with her in the office, he might have tried to convince her to do it right there in Rutherford's office. Maybe right on his fucking desk! How hot would *that* be, he wondered. And if she resisted, maybe they would have done it anyway. It wouldn't have been the first time that he had forced his advances on a date.

Startling the pair was out, so was sex with Hannah, but maybe there was still something to gain from eavesdropping. And what he heard was astounding, not that he necessarily believed it. He kept waiting for Shaw to laugh or say that he was just joking, but he didn't. Shaw spoke of time travel with conviction and Hannah ate it up. Then they kissed. She was obviously a hopeless romantic, easily swayed by stories of fantasy and tall tales. He'd have to remember that.

Time travel—ridiculous. But there was one word they said that heightened his interest: gold. Gold that was discovered and never recorded in any of the university ledgers. If there was anything that interested him, it was *free money!*

The other thing that intrigued him, although extremely hard to believe, was living the years repeatedly. That was immortality. Immortality! If possible, that was *better* than gold. If he could get his hands on it, and it could actually do what Shaw said, then he could live forever. It was a win-win situation.

He had heard enough and crawled back the way he came in. The door may have closed behind him a little harder than he intended, so after he was in the hall he stood and ran up the stairs and out of the building. He didn't have much time and had to hurry.

Now standing in front of John Shaw's dorm room, Taylor looked both ways down the hall. It was still early on a Saturday; no one else was out and about yet. He removed his plastic student identification card and slipped it into the doorjamb and under the barrel latch. The lock popped, and the door swung inward.

Once in Shaw's room, Taylor closed the door gently, careful to turn the door handle and not permit the barrel latch to click into the striker plate. He didn't want a neighbor to think that Shaw was up, thereby drawing visitors, presuming he even had any friends. Taylor didn't know and didn't want to find out on the morning he was rummaging through the room.

Going right to work, he looked through the dresser and desk, checked under the bed, dug through the closet, and even sifted through a laundry basket of dirty clothes.

The entire process was infuriating. He half expected to turn up some weird farm boy shit like photos of Shaw and sheep, or a latex blow-up girlfriend. He found nothing, including this so-called 'talisman.' It could have just been bullshit. Lies to impress Hannah and get her into bed. It seemed to be working, the way that they locked lips. But his gut told him otherwise.

Shaw might be rural, full of idealistic country-folk old-fashioned values, but he didn't seem to be the lying kind. No, there was something to the story. But where *was* this thing?

Then it occurred to him. Of course! Shaw had it on him. But not for long, he thought. Not for long.

24

JOHN LOCKED THE DOOR OF THE LAB behind him. He had hoped to find conclusive evidence of the professor's time shifting claims, but all he found were conflicting and circumstantial notes. Hannah had left after they finished their kiss and had agreed to a dinner date at some yet-to-be-determined time.

What a difference sixteen hours made. Just the night before, he was engaged in a bizarre conversation with his professor, trying to sort out fact from delusion, and then trying to understand the logic of the suicide that followed. He wondered whether he would ever be able to erase the memory of *that* awful moment. But now, with the fresh memory of Hannah's kiss and embrace, all seemed right in the world.

John double-checked the lab door to make sure that it was locked. Just as he turned to head down the dimly lit hallway, all went black. Something had been flung over his head and shoulders. A thick blanket, he guessed from the size and weight of it.

Before he could react, he was shoved solidly against the cinderblock wall. The left side of his face hit hard. Except for a bit of luck, he would have been knocked unconscious. If he had not instinctively turned his head at the last moment, he surely would have broken his nose. As it was, it felt like he'd been hit with a brick. The searing pain spread through his skull, across his shoulders, and down his back. His chest had hit the wall at the same time as his face, hurting his ribcage, knocking the wind out of him. He gasped for breath as he was thrust to the floor.

Still covered and shrouded in complete darkness, he reached out to stop himself from falling, or at least defend himself. His arms swung wildly under the blanket, striking nothing. Just as he hit the floor, a large weight landed on his back, knocking out what little air he still had in his lungs. He gasped. The thick blanket pressed against his nose and mouth, making it especially difficult to breathe.

The attacker was kneeling on him. A bony knee jabbed into his spine, sending spears of pain up to his head and down his legs. He couldn't believe how quickly he had become immobile, compromised, and unable to defend himself.

A pair of hands started patting him down, front and back. It was a mugging, he realized. He wanted to tell the person that he was a student with very little money, maybe only a few dollars at best. They'd be welcome to it, if only they would get off his back and let him breathe! But he didn't have enough air to utter the necessary words.

He felt his wallet being drawn from his pocket. Then he heard it thrown to the floor. The attacker stood and the stabbing pain subsided. John started to catch his breath. Before he could push himself up from the floor he felt a hard slam to the head, most likely from the attacker's forearm or foot.

Lying face down on the tile hallway floor, in the darkness of the blanket shroud, he lost consciousness.

~ ~ ~ ~ ~ ~

When John woke, the blanket, or towel, or hood, or whatever it was, was gone. He had no idea how long he had been out. It felt like minutes but could have been hours. He checked his watch. Only twenty minutes had passed since he had locked up the lab. Interestingly enough, he still had his watch. For some reason, the mugger hadn't taken it.

He hurt all over. Chest, legs, back. But mostly the side of his head and his pride. He turned over and pushed himself up to a sitting position. The left side of his face throbbed, and he could taste blood in his mouth. Still sitting, but leaning against the wall, he took inventory of his condition. Sore back and ribs, but nothing broken—he hoped. He took a deep breath and exhaled. No noticeable internal injuries. John touched his face; one side was swollen and sore, but he could see.

His wallet was lying next to him. He grabbed it and checked the bill compartment. Twenty-eight dollars were still there. His mugger had a lot to learn about stealing.

He wished that he could have had the opportunity to confront his assailant face-to-face and get a few licks in. The fight wouldn't have been so one-sided, that's for sure.

Slowly, he got to his feet and stood there for a minute to see if he had the strength to hold up his own weight. His legs were a bit wobbly, but stable enough. He tried to walk. A few feet at first, then down the hallway. He felt like he had a bad hangover without the fun of the night before, but he'd live. The attacker apparently didn't intend to kill him, just make a point. Whatever that might be.

The thought suddenly occurred to him that the person might still be there waiting for him to regain consciousness. Maybe waiting with others to help finish the job. 'Don't start getting paranoid now, young Shaw,' he imagined the professor saying.

He looked back and forth down the hall, but it was too dark to see if anyone was lurking in the shadows. Deciding not to wait around to find out, he quickly shuffled through the dark hallway to the lit stairwell. At least in the light he stood a better chance of defending himself.

Climbing the stairs was awkward. John's back ached and his legs felt like there were lead weights attached to them. Every step was a struggle and just made his headache worse. He held onto the railing for support.

When he finally reached the landing at the top

of the stairs, he looked back, half expecting someone to be following him. The stairs were empty. He wiped his brow and took a deep breath. His chest still hurt, but he was now able to fill his lungs with air.

The walk across campus was challenging. The tightness in his legs had eased and the stabbing pain in his back subsided a bit, but his head still hurt like hell and his senses were on high alert. He expected another attack around every corner, out of every entrance, and next to every parked car. If he could have run, he would have.

Just seeing his dormitory building was enough to lift his spirits. He hurried the best he could into the safety of the building. Some students were milling around in the lobby, standing in groups, or slouching in lounge chairs. If they noticed him walk in, they didn't say anything, which was just as well. He didn't want to have to explain his bruised and bloodied face. As he walked through the lobby, he overheard just enough of their conversations to know that Professor Rutherford was the topic of the day.

After lumbering up the three stories to his room, John's legs, back, and head ached almost as much as when he was lying on the cold tile floor outside the archaeology lab in the Watkins building. Almost.

His room was midway down the hall. Music was playing from several of the rooms as residents were starting their day. One of them came out of the community restroom wearing a towel wrapped around his waist and carrying a black vinyl shaving kit. John recognized him as Freddie, a sociology student who lived at the opposite end of the hall.

"Hey, John," he said. Then, seeing the swelling and dried blood, "Holy shit, dude! What happened to you? Looks like you got hit by a train."

John kept walking. "Just a little accident, no big deal."

"I hope she was worth it, dude!" Freddie called from behind.

John, now in front of his door, fumbled with the key before inserting it into the lock. His left hand was still bandaged from the injury in the professor's office, while his right was stiff, bruised, and tender, making it hard to hold the key steady.

After several attempts, he managed to unlock the door and open it. His eyes widened with shock. The room had been ransacked. All the items that had been on the desk and dresser top were now on the floor. Drawers were open with clothes hanging half out. The bedspread, sheets, and mattress pad were all draped over the side of the bed. All the shirts and pants that had been hanging in the closet were now on a pile in the middle of the room.

John bit his lip as he took in the disarray. Who could have done this? And how did they get in?

Before he could even begin thinking of answers, a cold wave of fear enveloped him as he realized that they might still be in the room. Ignoring his aching body he knelt down and looked under the bed. Nothing. The only other place to hide in a dorm room that small was the closet. He didn't want to get into another altercation, but he didn't feel he had much choice.

Remembering the pistol that the professor had given him for protection, he hurried over to his dresser and dug through what few t-shirts and socks were left in the top drawer. The gun was gone. Instantly, the air in the room felt like it was sucked out. A wave of helplessness swept over him as he realized that not only was he defenseless, but the person responsible for this invasion of privacy was now armed.

With nothing else available to use in self-defense, he lifted the desk chair with his good—albeit sore—hand. He held it in front of him like a lion tamer getting ready to go into a hostile den.

With his injured left hand, he gripped the round handle of the accordion-style door. If someone was hiding there, he hoped to be able to spear them with one of the chair legs. It certainly would not inflict significant damage, but it might give him the element of surprise, and hence, the advantage. Hopefully, there wouldn't be a gun pointed at him.

With a quick hard pull of the handle, the door slid left. As the door was in motion he rushed forward with the chair legs extended in front of him. The chair legs banged loudly against the back wall of the closet.

No one was there. The jar of the sudden stop caused his chest to ram into the top of the backrest. His ribs, already sensitive from being slammed against the wall and floor in the lower level of Watkins, now felt like they were on fire.

He dropped the chair, relieved that another confrontation wouldn't ensue. Instead, he was left dealing with a feeling of dread and foreboding. He and his possessions, not that there were many, as well as his privacy, had all been violated. He felt dejected.

He sat on the edge of the bed while running his hand through his hair and looked around the room. If Freddie was right that he looked like a train had hit him, then that same train must have kept going and run smack-dab through his room.

A stark thought occurred to him. He only had two things of any value: the pistol and the talisman. Someone knew what he had, and they wanted them. The thief attacked him thinking that they were on his person before or after tearing up his room. But who?

Mrs. Rutherford may have known that her husband had a gun and a time-shifting device but couldn't find them after he died. She may have figured that he gave them to John and hired some goons to find them.

Perhaps that was the reason that President Miller had gone over to talk to Mrs. Rutherford this morning. Maybe he was in on it. A co-conspirator. Maybe this was all *his* idea. As president, he would have access to the security department and, hence, the keys to the class buildings and dorms. There was no evidence of forced entry to his room. The burglar must have had a key.

The worst possibility was that maybe Hannah couldn't be trusted as he had hoped. What did he really know of her anyway? She was the daughter of the university president. Where did he *think* her loyalties would be? He hated the thought that she might have lured him into her confidence by sounding sympathetic and even kissing him, and then went home and told her father all about the thefts. She may have even included the talisman among the lost articles, although not believing that it had any inherent powers. It was just something that belonged to the university, and *John* had it. President Miller could have then sent out some university security guards to find it.

With one hand pressing his ribcage, he went to the door and locked it. It was small consolation, however, if the burglar returned with a key.

He dug through the pile of strewn clothes in the closet and retrieved a duffel bag. Without wasting a minute, he shoved clothes into the bag. He had to get off campus, and he had to get out quickly before they came back, whoever *they* were. If they were after the talisman, they wouldn't give up looking for it. Next time, they might not be so generous as to let him walk away.

Other than his clothes and a few photographs, he didn't have any other possessions. He'd gone to the school without much, and he would be leaving similarly. Not even the portable stereo and shelf speakers belonged to him. They were on loan from one of the other residents on the floor. He was glad that they had not gotten stolen or damaged. Not only would he have felt bad if something happened to it while in his possession, but they held a secret.

He carefully removed the black foam grill from the front of one of the speakers and retrieved the talisman that he had hidden inside.

"What makes you so important, little fella?" he asked, softly, staring at the gold object in his hand. "I think the professor was right. Nobody better find out about you."

Suddenly, a knock on the door.

John snapped out of his moment of calm and

turned his head quickly toward the door. He half expected the person on the other side to either kick it in or bleed through like an apparition. Without a peephole, there was no way to tell whether the visitor was friend or foe. Given the circumstances, he had to presume the worst. Being a pessimist was not his nature, but his wounds hadn't healed yet and he wasn't looking forward to getting any new ones.

Another knock.

He had to get out of that room, but he was trapped like a caged animal. The room was on the third floor. A jump would either kill him or injure him badly enough to make him wish he *was* dead. There was only one way out.

He hatched a plan. With the stuffed duffel bag in front of him, he would crouch down next to the door and unlock it. The person on the other side would likely rush in at that point. They wouldn't notice him at first. He would spring up, shoving the bag forward, knocking them off balance and possibly to the floor. It wouldn't be much, but it might just buy him a moment to exit the room and escape. Once in the hallway, the attacker wouldn't dare make a scene and have the other residents come out to investigate.

Realistically, he didn't know if the plan would work, but he had to try.

He shoved the talisman into the front pocket of his jeans. The pocket was tight, he had to wriggle it in.

Without trying, it twisted ever so slightly.

Suddenly, the room went completely dark, and John was filled with a sense of vertigo. His mouth went dry, and his heart beat hard enough to hurt. He wondered if he was passing out. He fully expected to open his eyes and find himself on the floor as he had in Watkins. Only his eyes were not closed.

The feeling only lasted a second or two. Then, as if a dark veil had been lifted from him, he no longer felt light-headed and was able to see clearly again.

What he saw was not a disheveled dorm room but the lobby of the dormitory. He was now standing just inside the doors of the carpeted lobby. A number of students were milling around, standing in groups, or slumped in lounge chairs. He recognized them not only as being residents of the dorm, but from having seen them just twenty minutes earlier when he walked through there. The same ones, standing in the same places. If they noticed him they didn't say anything, which was just as well. He didn't want to have to explain his sudden appearance or his bruised and bloodied face. Was his face still bruised? He reached up to his cheek. Yes, still swollen and sensitive. *That* hadn't changed. His left hand was still bandaged. That hadn't changed either.

How did he wind up in the lobby when just a second earlier he was trying to plan an escape from his room?

As he walked through the lobby toward the stairwell, he overheard just enough of the student's conversations to know that they were discussing Professor Rutherford—just as they had before.

When he got to the top of the stairwell he walked down the hallway toward his room. Freddie came out of the restroom with a towel around his waist, carrying a black vinyl shaving kit.

"Hey, John," Freddie said. Then, "Holy shit, dude! What happened to you? Looks like you got hit by a train."

John didn't slow down. He knew what Freddie would say next.

"I hope she was worth it, dude!" Freddie called from behind.

Somehow, as unbelievable as it might have seemed, he was reliving the past twenty minutes over again, like some sort of déjà vu experience. This was what Professor Rutherford said happened to *him* with the talisman. Time-shifting, as he called it. What seemed ludicrous less than twenty-four hours ago now made perfect sense.

The talisman.

He reached down and felt it still in his right front pocket. It was no longer hidden in the speaker where he had left it when he went to the lab earlier that morning. When he 'shifted,' it had come with him.

John's hand was trembling. His heart was pounding. And for just a moment he held his breath, not realizing that he was even holding it.

What he had thought was impossible was now probable. This talisman, this gold *thing*, had permitted him to travel back in time and remember having done so. The professor *wasn't* a raving lunatic, a fool, or a liar. If the professor's time-shifting recollections were true, then everything else he said was probably true also. Now John missed Professor Rutherford more than ever. What else didn't he know about this strange artifact? What other mysterious powers did it possess?

He did know *one* thing, however. If he were reliving the same time over again, then his room would be trashed, and someone would soon be knocking at his door. He had to hurry.

Although the soreness and lack of dexterity of his fingers caused him to fumble with his keys again, he managed to get the door unlocked.

He wasted no time once he got into the room. It was trashed, just as he expected. No need to gawk or ponder. No need to check under the bed or in the closet this time either. No one was there, he was sure of it.

Knowing that there would soon be a knock on the door he quickly gathered his clothes and shoved them into the duffel bag. Then he put his ear against the door and listened. Just some muted music coming from down the hall. He knew, however, that someone could still be standing on the opposite side of the door.

Holding his breath and counting down from three, he whipped open the door and rushed out into the hall with the duffel bag in front of him as a shield. No one was there, but he didn't spend any time dwelling on it. He gently closed the door behind him.

With the bag now flung over his shoulder he trotted down to the stairwell at the opposite end of the hall from where he had come up. He opened the fire escape door and stepped into the stairwell, pulling the door closed behind him, careful not to let it shut completely.

With the stairwell door cracked open about an inch he was able to watch down the hall, at least as far as his room, which was as far as he needed to see. Two excruciatingly long minutes later, a figure approached his door, paused, and knocked.

Hannah Miller.

John's heart sank. She was the last person he wanted to see at his door. It took everything he had not to burst back onto the floor and demand an explanation just as she had done to him in the professor's office. It wouldn't have done any good. She would likely accuse him of being a thief and demand the thing he had no intention of giving up. She would also, no doubt, deny being involved with the beating and the vandalism.

John felt betrayed. Any hopes of dating her were now moot. So was any hope of graduating from the University of Chicago. He didn't feel safe there.

He'd been unwillingly thrust into an extraordinary and unique world of time travel. While he was sure that he didn't fully comprehend the magnitude of this anomaly, he was certain of his responsibility. If the professor, a well-respected member of the university and a genius by the standards of most, had gotten rich using its powers, then in the hands of a genuinely dishonest person, the spoils could be enormous.

Knowing the results of horse races at Churchill Downs, or a series of poker hands in Las Vegas, or just one mega-lottery could net the person millions. Tens of millions. More important than even the acquisition of wealth, the talisman also might be used to alter events and history. What would the country—the world—be like *then*?

John had reluctantly made a promise to protect

the talisman. At the time the promise was made, he was placating a respected—and armed—member of the faculty. Appeasement seemed like the safest, and only, course of action. But now! Knowing that the professor spoke the truth about the talisman and the potential for catastrophic danger, changed everything. Now, John knew that the promise made under duress needed to be kept in earnest. Even if it meant upending his college and career plans, it seemed clear that the integrity of humanity's timeline rested with him and him alone. He would not take that responsibility lightly. The trick was to make sure that he didn't get killed trying.

He let the stairwell door close the remaining inch, careful not to let it make a sound, and bounded down the stairs two at a time. Once out of the building, he headed directly off campus and never looked back. His college days were over. What was ahead was a mystery. He was sure that Professor Rutherford would have been envious.

25

AFTER LEAVING CAMPUS, John Shaw took a Greyhound bus southwest out of the city. The nearly six-hour ride brought him to within two miles of rural Ellis Grove, where he had grown up and where his family still resided. He walked the rest of the way.

Naturally, his parents wanted to know why he was home in the middle of the semester. Reluctantly, he told them that a unique device was found on Antigua. His professor had insisted that it needed to be hidden for safekeeping and entrusted John to be that protector.

John reassured them that the device wasn't dangerous or illegal, but that bad people might try to get it, and that was unacceptable. Unfortunately, that meant dropping out of school for a while and going away. So they shouldn't worry if they don't hear from him for an extended time, for he had a plan.

"Where will you go?"

"How long will you be gone?"

"When will we hear from you?"

"What is this 'device'?"

The questions continued, but he successfully avoided specifics in answering. They didn't need to know any details of his plans, and they didn't need to know about the death of the professor. And they certainly didn't need to know of the capability of the talisman.

His father was uneasy and paced the floor. His mother welled up, her hand covering her mouth. They wanted more answers, but any further knowledge might put them in danger from anyone still searching for the talisman—or him.

It was intended to be nothing more than a social visit. A quick infusion of home cooking, family camaraderie, and courage. As much as he wanted to, he knew he couldn't stay. He was a man entrusted with a fragile future, and that was a dangerous responsibility.

After a few days, his parents drove him as far as Granite City, about an hour north of their farm. John strongly encouraged them not to mention anything about their conversation or the device to anyone. His mother cried and his father hugged him. John choked back his own tears.

There, he took a bus to Moline, a small community west of Chicago on the border of Illinois and Iowa. It was the world headquarters for John Deere, manufacturer of agricultural equipment. His family was fiercely loyal to Deere. John had grown up operating their tractors on the family farm. In fact, he was driving and working on their tractors long before he ever learned how to drive a car. For that familiar reason alone, Moline seemed like as good a place to lay low as any.

Before leaving, he buried his cell phone under a bush in the back of their property next to the barn. He didn't want anyone tracking him down by using it as some sort of homing device.

Growing up in a rural community and assisting the family with repairing things on the property helped him find work as an entry-level maintenance man at George Washington Elementary School in Moline. He'd always taken great pleasure in taking things apart and fixing them. Working in a maintenance department seemed like a good fit and an easy transition.

He took a small studio apartment above the Hairport Beauty Shoppe three blocks from the school and settled into his new life.

26

THREE YEARS LATER

His primary responsibilities at George Washington were to sweep the school floors, wipe down cafeteria tables, empty trash receptacles, and anything else no one else would do. There wasn't much to it, but he made enough money for rent and food. It was a simple life. Lonely perhaps, but calm and secure. He liked it that way.

Occasionally, he would call his family from a pay phone to reassure them that he was healthy, safe, and doing fine. He never revealed his location, even when they asked. They appreciated the call, but continued to worry.

Out of fear that his small studio apartment would be broken into like his dorm room had been, he made sure that he was never without the talisman. His plan was to eventually build a house and set the talisman in between the studs under the drywall where no one would ever find it. Or maybe he'd bury the damned thing in the concrete foundation. Even better.

It was a nice thought, but he had no money with which to build a house or get a mortgage. Everything seemed to be in a holding pattern: his career, his love life, and his plans to permanently secure the talisman.

That is, until this morning.

~ ~ ~ ~ ~ ~

It started out as an ordinary day. After donning his gray overalls in the maintenance office, he pushed the dust mop down the main hallway as part of his daily ritual.

He'd only gotten about a third of the way down the hall when he heard a scream. It came from Miss Bloom's third grade room, directly across the hall from where he was standing. He quickly leaned the broom against the wall and rushed into the room.

The young teacher was in the alcove where the students hang their coats. A boy was hanging backwards from the four-inch wooden coat peg that projected up and out from the wall. His arms hung limp. His head drooped to one side. She was crying as she lifted him off the peg and laid him gently, but quickly, on the floor, supporting his head as she did so.

"Help!" she sobbed, realizing that someone had entered the room, not much caring who it was. "It's Bobby, he's … he needs help!"

John ran over. He could see that the back of the

boy's collar had gotten snagged on the peg and he became trapped. Most likely, the boy had tried to wiggle his way loose only to twist his shirt collar, choking him.

"I don't know what happened!" Miss Bloom said frantically. "We went out for recess, and I came back for a boy's jacket. That's when I found him!"

"He's not breathing," John said, kneeling down and putting his ear to the boy's chest.

"Oh my … !" she screeched, her hand to her mouth, tears rolling over her cheeks. "I'll go get help!"

She jumped up and ran out of the alcove and out of the classroom. John began mouth-to-mouth resuscitation on the boy. He tried several times, and several times more, but it was too late. The boy had choked to death hanging from a damned coat peg in a classroom. Such a young boy with a whole world ahead of him. Endless opportunities. An uncharted future. How could this happen, he wondered.

What a senseless, unpredictable world this is, John thought. One minute everything is calm, normal, and the next everything is upside down. Just like back at the university with Professor Rutherford. But that was the big city. You expect strange things there, almost anticipate them.

But this was Moline, a quiet, peaceful, non-eventful community. Not only had a life been extinguished, but the boy's parents will now spend their lives in mournful agony. A teacher will be traumatized, possibly to the point of having to change careers. Other parents will be paranoid about their own children's safety at the school. And this coatroom will forever be remembered as the place where

Bobby died. It was a heartbreaking thought.

Then, a thought occurred to him. There *was* something he could do, if he dared. Not once in all the time that he had been away from the university did he entertain using the talisman. Besides the danger and fear of the unknown, he had made a promise. *"Above all do not be tempted to use it,"* the professor had told him. *"Bury it or encase it in cement and drop it in the deepest depths of the ocean; just don't use it. Not once, not ever!"*

There were certainly a hundred reasons not to use the talisman but only one that mattered at that moment: a little boy named Bobby lying face up on the floor in front of him.

John had the chance to use the talisman for good. To perhaps save a boy's life. Surely the professor would have understood breaking a promise just this once for a noble cause.

John reached into his pocket and removed the gold puck. How did it work? Were there some specific words, some special incantation? It had worked before, back in the dorm, but he didn't know how—didn't *want* to know. At the time, he knew that if he understood how it worked, the temptation to use it would be great.

He turned it around in his hands, tapping it. Nothing. Then he rubbed it and made a wish that Bobby would sit up and resume his life again. Again, nothing. Then he shook it. Still nothing. Frustrated that he had a device that had the inexplicable power of time-shifting but couldn't use it, he put it between both palms and shook it violently. In so doing, he inadvertently twisted his palms in opposite directions, turning the parts ever so slightly.

The room blackened for a second and he felt disoriented, lightheaded. But it passed so quickly that he wondered if it had happened at all.

He was now alone in the maintenance room, standing in front of his locker, putting on his overalls. At that moment, he knew for certain that he had shifted. The talisman was still between his palms. He shoved it back in his pocket and quickly zipped up the overalls. He wasn't sure how far back in time he had gone or if it would be far enough, but he didn't want to take any chances, so he ran out of the locker room and down the empty hallway.

He ran past the gymnasium, the office, and the cafeteria. When he got to Miss Bloom's classroom it was empty. He looked in the coatroom. Empty too. He began to wonder just how far he had shifted back. Was it a day? A year? Had he just imagined traveling back in time at all?!

His heart pounded as he began to understand how the professor could become confused and paranoid. A disoriented fear rose up in him, lodging like a lump in his throat, and he froze in the middle of the empty classroom.

Then he heard voices. He hurried over to the opposite side of the room by the windows and crouched behind the teacher's desk. From there he was able to see into the coatroom without being spotted by three young boys coming into the classroom, one of whom he recognized as Bobby.

The students, about eight or nine years old each,

were giggling and playfully pushing each other. John watched as they went into the coatroom and stood next to that fateful peg.

"She'll flip out," the taller of them said, laughing.

"She'll freak!" said the blond-haired boy, equally excited.

"She'll puke!" said Bobby, who seemed to be in on whatever it was they were planning.

"Who's gonna do it?" Blond Boy asked.

"I wanna do it!" Tall Boy volunteered.

"You can't. You're too tall," Blond Boy explained. "Your feet'll touch the floor."

"Oh, yeah."

"I'll do it," Bobby said.

"Good," Blond Boy said. "Let's give him a boost."

They turned Bobby around and each grabbed an arm. With great strain they managed to lift up their friend about eight inches and hook the back of his collar on the protruding peg.

"Just remember to look dead when Miss Bloom finds you. I can't wait to see her face!"

"She'll scream!" Tall Boy said.

Bobby looked uncomfortable. His shirt was pulled tight against his chest, but he was smiling and in no significant pain or danger. "I hope she comes soon. It kinda hurts by my arms."

"I'll go tell her that I'm cold," Blond Boy said, "and that I want my jacket."

"Yeah!"

The two boys ran out of the classroom to go find their teacher on the playground.

So that was the plan, a practical joke. Amongst all the reasons to use the talisman to save Bobby, John could add saving two young boys from having serious psychological issues as a result of a harmless prank gone awry.

No sooner had the two boys left the classroom than the fabric gave way on Bobby's collar. John heard the tearing fibers and rushed into the coatroom knowing that gravity was about to pull Bobby down, tightening his shirt against his windpipe and cutting off his air supply. In a matter of minutes, he would be dead.

Bobby's eyes bulged. His mouth was wide open as if trying to scream, although no sound could escape. His arms flailed, his legs kicked the air. Panic had set in as he realized the true nature of his predicament. He was too scared to realize that help had arrived when John, "the maintenance guy," came running into the coatroom.

With one swift motion, John lifted Bobby off the peg and set him on the floor. The boy started crying and rubbing his throat.

John knelt next to him. "Are you all right?"

Bobby didn't answer. His cries just got harder.

Miss Bloom came into the classroom to retrieve the blond boy's coat and came running when she heard Bobby crying. She saw John next to the boy and wondered how the maintenance guy was involved.

"What happened here?!" she demanded, kneeling on the other side of her student. "What's wrong?"

"Do you want to tell her?" John asked.

Bobby, with his hands covering his face, just shook his head no.

"He was goofing around," John told her. "Got his shirt stuck on one of the pegs and couldn't get loose. I happened by and heard him."

"Is that what happened?" she asked Bobby.

He nodded, wiping away the tears. "I'm sorry."

"Lucky for him you happened by when you did," Miss Bloom said to John, hugging the boy.

John nodded. "Lucky."

The two other pranksters were standing just inside the classroom by the door, watching, wide-eyed. As he was walking out of the coatroom, John leaned over and whispered, "Something bad could have happened here, boys. Don't ever do anything like that again."

They both nodded, not understanding how the maintenance guy could know that *they* had been responsible or required scolding. It must be some sort of grown-up special power, they thought.

It was a wonderful day, a glorious day, John thought. By preventing Bobby from dying accidentally, he had broken out of his mindset of self-preservation and actually put someone else's well-being ahead of his own. It felt … invigorating.

So what if he had broken a promise? It was justified. A boy would live.

As good as he felt, he would have felt even better if the professor's words didn't linger in his memory, " *…just don't use it. Not once, not ever.* "

27

JOHN LEFT THE CLASSROOM for his next work assignment. He was exhilarated, nearly giddy, that he had done something significant, something meaningful. For the remainder of the day, could he do anything that would measure up to saving a life? Or the remainder of the year, or the rest of his life, for that matter? He didn't think so.

Suddenly, he was light-headed and his legs felt weak. He stopped, put a hand to the wall to steady himself, wondering whether these were lingering effects of having shifted. Some damage to his system at the molecular level. Perhaps this was the price one paid for messing with the universal law of continuous passage through time. He wondered whether this was what drove Professor Rutherford insane, ultimately to the point of suicide.

The students flooded back into the school from

the playground, passing him without saying a word. This, by itself, was not unusual. Only occasionally would one of them speak to him anyway, like when their locker was stuck, if someone threw up in the hall, or when they were looking for someone. Today, however, he wished that one of them would say something to him. Confirm that he was, in fact, still standing there and had not time-shifted to some parallel universe or turned invisible or … .

From behind, someone laid a hand on his shoulder. Startled, he spun around. Miss Bloom stood there smiling.

"I just wanted to thank you again. I can't imagine what might have happened if you hadn't come along when you did."

John sighed, relieved that she saw him and that he was right where he was supposed to be. He nodded and tried to smile. It was a feeble attempt and came across as a half smirk.

"Are you all right? You're perspiring."

He wiped his brow with his free hand. "I'm fine. Just a little warm."

"Really? I think it's quite chilly, actually. Maybe you have a fever."

John took a deep breath and exhaled. The pressure in his chest was gone as well as the lightheadedness and dry mouth. He was back to normal. Whatever it was had passed.

"I'm fine. Really."

She nodded. "Okay, if you say so. Bobby's mother is going to come pick him up. He's gone through enough for one day."

"I'm glad I could help."

Miss Bloom waved and returned to her classroom.

There was no explanation for the odd feeling that had come over him. If he hadn't been in possession of one of the oddest artifacts ever discovered, he would have dismissed the feeling as unimportant. But he knew that the feeling had to be related in some way to the talisman, or the time-shifting that he had just done, and it scared the hell out of him.

Having used the talisman to help the boy, John could see how it could be abused. A dishonest man could steal and manipulate the future for his selfish interest. On the other hand, an honest, well-intentioned person could time-shift for the betterment of society. Go back and relive days, months, years, and right things that got skewed. Fix society, save lives, prevent crimes.

John wondered whether the professor wrestled with the same good-use versus bad-use scenarios. Was it the moral implications or the physical exhaustion that drove the professor to desperation, believing that suicide was his only recourse? John vowed that it wouldn't happen to him. He realized that he had to follow the professor's final advice to get rid of it in some secure fashion.

In the cafeteria, John started unfolding the eight-foot tables that had been stacked on their sides on rolling carts. Wayne Wilkinson, the maintenance supervisor of the school and John's boss, came to assist as he did every day.

While most of the students thought that the old white-haired guy was a sourpuss and an unapproachable loner, John saw him differently. He respected Wayne. His supervisor kept to himself for the most part, it's true, but that was because he was focused on the jobs that needed to be done, and nothing more. He was certainly knowledgeable about everything maintenance.

There is no question that Wayne took a chance on hiring a young man with limited experience, and for that alone, John was grateful.

With more than four hundred students at the school, three hallways, six school buses, and a furnace that was always in need of repair, Wayne had desperately needed an assistant to get it all done. He could see that John was a bright, enthusiastic young man willing to learn. He may have wondered why John dropped out of the University of Chicago, but he never asked. John had learned a lot from Wayne over the past three years and knew that he could learn a lot more.

As John pulled tables, he formulated a plan to be rid of the talisman permanently. It had to be put it in a safe spot where no one would ever find it. Tossing it into the Mississippi River or Lake Michigan or even an ocean, for that matter, wasn't as secure as it might seem. If the tide brought it to shore or a commercial fishing boat netted it, it would be in the hands of the next poor fool. Burying it sounded secure, but construction was ongoing, and it wouldn't take much to uncover it during land site development.

All along he liked his plan of building it into the home in which he lived, stuck between the walls behind thick drywall where it would be inaccessible, but he would still know exactly where it was. There was no chance that someone would come across it accidentally. Even if they broke into his house, they would never find it.

No matter what, he would always feel responsible for it. He owed Professor Rutherford that much at least.

The question now was not *what* to do with the talisman to protect it, but *how* to do it. He earned slightly more than minimum wage working for the school district. He didn't dare try to find a job in his chosen field of archaeology. Doing so would only increase the chance that someone would track him and find the talisman. He hadn't forgotten that someone had roughed him up in the Watkins hallway and broken into his dorm room. There was no reason to think that they would give up, and the first place they would look would be in the field in which he had an education.

He was putting a little money away every paycheck to save for his house, but it would be years, perhaps decades, before he amassed enough savings to put a down payment on a place of his own. By that time, they might find him and the talisman. Whoever 'they' were.

He needed money, and lots of it. There were many ways to get it, if he was willing to bide his time. Unfortunately, time was just another thing that he didn't have.

Actually, the more he thought about it, time was the only thing that he *did* have. It came in the shape of a gold puck with bumps on the top of it. He tapped his pocket to reassure himself that the talisman was still there. It was. His hope of building a house could be realized, but it meant using the device to help achieve his goal of never using the device. Convoluted logic, certainly, but it was the only way.

Knowing the week's winning lottery numbers and choosing those numbers in advance would do it. He could get the winning numbers that evening when they posted them on television. A quick time shift and he could go to the grocery store right down the street and buy a ticket with those winning numbers. Within a matter of days he would not only have enough money to build a house, but probably enough to retire!

It was a foolproof plan. Not only doable, but fast and convenient. No one would ever be the wiser that he had seen the future and was using it to his advantage. Easy money!

For a long moment he pondered how to best spend the money he was about to 'win.' Then, he began to tremble as he remembered something his father once told him: "Nothing worth having comes easy."

John shook his head. *"That would be tantamount to stealing,"* he said to himself. *"Is that who I am? Is that what I've become?!"*

His heart sank. He was back where he started.

Then, he realized there was a viable alternative. The only *legal* and *ethical* way to acquire the amount of money needed was to get more experience. More experience equates to knowledge which translates into promotions and higher salary.

He waited until all the tables were set up, not that it really mattered anyway. If the talisman worked as it should, he would be reliving this moment again eventually, except he would be making more money and be that much closer to his goal.

When he finished, John went directly to the maintenance office. Wayne would be returning to the office after surveying the symmetry of the tables, so he had to hurry.

He closed and locked the door behind him. Sitting behind Wayne's desk, he retrieved the talisman from his pocket. He ran his fingertips over the various sized bumps and wondered what meaning they held. They obviously meant something to whoever made it. The edge was smooth, solid. What had he done to make it work when he was in the coatroom of Miss Bloom's class? Or when he was sitting on the floor of his disheveled dorm room when there was a knock at the door?

It felt like he was trying to figure out a stranger's combination lock. Or line up the rows and columns on a Rubik's cube. Or discover the secret of how to build a sailboat inside a glass bottle. All seemingly impossible, but all were easy once you knew the secret. He just needed to discover the secret combination to *this* thing.

He turned on the desk lamp and held the talisman under the lampshade. The light reflected off the bumps, spraying various-sized dots onto the walls and ceiling like a non-rotating disco ball.

Then he noticed the ultra-thin line that ran the circumference of the disk. "What's this?"

Holding both halves with his fingertips, he strained to unscrew the top from the bottom. The halves moved ever so slightly in opposite directions. He felt a slight sense of vertigo and the room went pitch black for a split second, even though his eyes were still wide open. He knew what was happening. He was time-shifting. He'd discovered the combination, or at least how to pop the lock.

When the light in the room returned to normal a second later, he was standing outside his apartment door wearing blue jeans and a sweatshirt. It was early morning, the sun was shining, the birds were chirping. But what day was it? He looked at the date feature on his wristwatch. It was the same day, just earlier.

Instead of walking to work as he usually did, he ran. He wanted to start quizzing Wayne on how to do some of the things he hadn't been allowed to do because he had no experience, like repairing the furnace or the air conditioning compressor.

After gleaning enough knowledge about those, he would use the talisman and rewind time to learn about repairing school bus engines. And then again to learn plumbing. And then again to learn electrical. And then the budgeting process of the maintenance department. There was always more to learn, and he would go back as many times as necessary to gain skills and be more valuable to the school. Each time, he would be smarter and more experienced than the last.

Wayne and the rest of the school board would not know that he had turned back time and relived those days already. As far as they were concerned, he had been hired with that much knowledge. A renaissance maintenance man, they might call him. They would see how experienced and essential he was and pay him accordingly. Then he would build his house and rid himself of the talisman forever.

Before he reached the school, three blocks from the apartment, he felt the same lightheaded feeling that he experienced after using the talisman to help the boy in the coatroom. Only now it was a bit more intense than before. He was dizzy with a touch of nausea. It was similar to the feeling of time-shifting, but without the blackening effect or the resultant shift. He slowed to a walk for fear that he would lose his balance and fall over. The feeling passed almost as quickly as it came but left him wondering what it meant.

He told himself it was nothing, but he wasn't convinced.

28

WAYNE WILKINSON COULDN'T BELIEVE his luck. He had been begging for an assistant for the better part of six years. To have them now hire someone with the skill set of John Shaw was remarkable. What was even more remarkable was that the boy came from an exclusive school studying geology, pathology, or one of those other '–olgies'. Dropped out for some reason. Maybe he just preferred fixing things. Who could blame him, since the boy knew how to fix damned near everything.

At twenty-four, the boy knew just about everything they required, Wayne thought. Must have had prior experience somewhere, since they don't teach diesel technology, plumbing, or electrical at the University of Chicago. Or heating and air-conditioning, for that matter. At least he didn't think so. It made things so much easier than training some rookie. All he had to do was tell John that one of the buses was sputtering, and the boy would jump on it. By lunchtime, he had that engine tuned and purring. Amazing!

Another thing that was equally amazing was how John had developed techniques and shortcuts so similar to those of his own. It was as if he had personally trained the boy on all aspects of the job. In only three weeks John Shaw's skills matched those of his own.

Such a level of experience and skill came at a hefty price. While he had requested an entry-level assistant, they hired someone of Shaw's caliber. Not that he complained, it's just that once they saw the boy's skill set in action, the school district increased his salary to double what Wayne had budgeted. The boy was worth it though; he was sharp.

Still, Wayne couldn't help wondering whether the school board had deliberately hired someone with that much experience specifically to replace him. He'd been in the business world long enough to know that companies, even school districts, would rather have a younger employee than an older one. Age discrimination was illegal, of course, but it still happened all the time. Why invest in an old guy who will be retiring soon when a young guy can be molded into whatever they want and will likely stick around longer?

Wayne's only complaint—concern, really—was that the boy seemed to have some sort of health issue. On several occasions he looked ready to pass out. He had to sit down or hold onto something to keep from falling over. When asked about it, John said that he was all right and explained that it was probably just the heat getting to him, or lack of breakfast.

Wayne wasn't buying it. To him, the symptoms, which started almost immediately after John was hired, looked to be those of someone suffering from a bad hangover. Or maybe anorexia. Maybe even drug dependency. He hoped not. The boy's work skills and attitude were exemplary.

The other thing that concerned him may or may not have had anything to do with John Shaw at all.

Shortly after the boy started working for the school, a man wearing a dark suit and sunglasses was seen hanging around the property. The first time Wayne saw him, he was standing next to a fancy sports car across the street from the playground, just watching.

After the man showed up a second time a few days later sitting inside the car, Wayne reported it to the principal. The school was very sensitive about people other than parents lingering around the school. There were too many instances of abductions and shootings in the news to take any chances. The principal shared the same concern, but since the man was off school property, there was little they could do. Still, she promised to alert the Moline Police and mention it to the teaching staff.

For some reason, John always seemed agitated whenever the man was spotted nearby. Perhaps he, too, was concerned for the safety of the children. Maybe the guy was a drug dealer and John's connection. On the other hand, he could be with the Drug Enforcement Agency, and they had John under surveillance for selling. It was also possible that the man was a job recruiter wanting to steal John away.

Of the three scenarios, Wayne hoped that the man

was a recruiter. He didn't want to lose his prized assistant, but if the boy was on drugs he'd lose him eventually to incarceration or death anyway.

29

JOHN COULDN'T HAVE BEEN more pleased. His plan was working like a charm. He figured out that by turning the two parts of the talisman counter-clockwise, he was able to time-shift backward. Turning it any more than an eighth or quarter inch sent him back weeks or months. It was not an exact science. There was no way to turn the halves with any sort of accuracy. He applied pressure, they turned, he shifted.

Common sense told him that if he turned the parts *clock*wise, he would travel in the other direction, to the future. It would have made things so much easier for him. As much as he tried—and he tried often—he couldn't move them any other way than counterclockwise, which was something that the professor must have realized early on and accepted.

It was always a surprise where—and when—he would return. Usually, he went back about two weeks, but sometimes further. It meant reliving those days, just like Professor Rutherford claimed. Unlike the professor, who used the days for personal greed and thievery, John spent his time increasing his training and knowledge.

Whenever Wayne would mention that he was going to go work on something with which John was unfamiliar, John would shadow him. He would ask the typical who-what-why-when-how questions. Wayne liked teaching John the tricks of the trade, especially little-known facts and shortcuts.

"Trade secrets," Wayne would boast, "are worth their weight in gold."

Shortly thereafter, John would shift and go back to before that incident, but now with complete knowledge of those trade secrets. He did that repeatedly until he felt he knew just about as much as his mentor.

In a way, John felt a little guilty, as if he were using his boss for personal gain, and if he was honest about it, he probably was. Any covert manipulation was done not out of spite, maliciousness, or profit, however. His goal was a loftier one. It was born out of a greater good to earn enough money to hide and protect the talisman.

The plan was seamless. He had gleaned a career's worth of valuable knowledge and hands-on experience, conveniently taught by the person he most needed to impress. There was only one last time-shift to make. Back to the day that he first applied for work at George Washington Elementary School.

Both the principal and the school district superintendent were astounded that someone so young knew so much about so many things. He was "a natural at facility maintenance," they said. It was no wonder that he had stopped taking boring archaeology classes. Clearly, his calling was to have a set of maintenance tools strapped around his waist, and it was a stroke of luck to land him. With Wayne Wilkinson guiding him as a mentor, he was sure to be a key employee. Possibly even supervising all the facilities in the district eventually.

John was hired on the spot and given a hefty salary, far more than he had hoped. It was an amount that he would have had to wait years to earn the conventional way. Now, he was earning it on day one.

John's meteoric leap from maintenance assistant to facilities superstar did not come without an ample supply of difficulties.

First, there was the redundancy of living the same days over and over again. He deliberately attempted to do exactly what he had done in the previous timeline. Wearing the same clothes, eating the same food, watching the same television programs. At times, the routine was boring to the point of excruciating. He persevered nevertheless. He didn't want to chance disrupting the natural timeline any more than necessary.

If those science fiction writers were correct, that any little change in the timeline could have huge repercussions, he wanted to be extremely careful. Also, he wanted to retain a sense of continuity to his own life even if he was repeating it. It was a somewhat comforting thought that he was traveling down the same path of life as everyone else. Even if he wasn't.

Unfortunately, the plan was not as easy to execute

as it was to conceptualize. Just as a path in the forest may appear stable and unchanged, it is, regardless, in a constant state of flux. There are elements at work that are not obvious. The wind, the sun, and the rain, all leave their own indelible, albeit sometimes miniscule, changes. Every falling branch, scampering squirrel, sprouting growth, and hiking person leaves a mark, makes a change.

John knew that no matter how hard he tried, there would be changes that were beyond his control. Small and inconsequential, meaningless and trivial, but changes nevertheless. He resolved himself to that realization, which made it easier when he had to step off the path.

The first time that he deliberately departed from the set timeline was when he intervened to save Bobby from accidentally choking to death on a coat hook in Miss Bloom's class. Actually, in his current timeline, that event hadn't even occurred yet and wouldn't for another two and a half years. It happened before he began his trek backward to begin his education on facilities management.

Invariably, every shift presented opportunities to positively intervene in events, although none were as dramatic or as significant as the incident with Bobby. Regardless of the possible ramifications, he couldn't turn his back on helping others whenever he was aware there was a need.

For instance, there was Mrs. Muldoon, the kindly old widow who lived next door to his apartment. She walked to the Dairy Mart down the block nearly every morning for her coffee, newspaper, and bag of groceries.

One morning, after John had shifted and was heading to work to learn how to tear down a diesel bus engine, he saw Mrs. Muldoon coming out of the Dairy Mart. She was cradling a bag of groceries and holding a cup of coffee. She didn't notice that some children had carelessly left their bicycles lying just outside the door. Her foot caught the handlebar on one bike and she fell face down on the ground. The bag of groceries split open, and the contents spilled out across the sidewalk and into the street. The hot coffee burst and splashed against her face, chest, and arm. Worse, she twisted her ankle, split her lip, and bruised the right side of her face. An ambulance was called, and the paramedics tended to her.

The next time that John shifted, he walked past the Dairy Mart at that precise moment and moved the bicycles away from the store entrance. She never knew that he had saved her a lot of pain and a trip to the hospital.

On another occasion, he was at the laundromat. He noticed a young mother with her two children. The kids raced back and forth the length of the room past the washers, dryers, and folding tables. Between trying to get them to settle down and sort her laundry, the mother hadn't noticed that she had mixed a new red t-shirt in with her whites.

When the load was ready to go into the dryer she discovered she was transferring a load of pink items. She covered her mouth and began to cry. Meanwhile, her rambunctious children tried to see if they could get to one of the candy bars in the vending machine by sticking their arms up and under the return chute flap. The girl, about five years old, got her arm wedged under the flap.

Not only couldn't she reach the candy, but she couldn't extract her arm. She began to screech, more from panic than pain.

The boy, a year or two older than his sister, ran to his mother for help, but she was distracted and upset by her laundry faux pas.

He kept calling, "Mama! Mama! It's Jamie! It's Jamie!"

Thinking that it was just another case of tattletale, she ignored him. When he started pulling on her shirt and wouldn't relent, she bent over and nearly screamed, "What is it?!"

Terrified that he was in trouble, he just pointed to his sister who was across the room, hysterical and desperately trying to retract her arm from the vending machine.

The mother ran to her daughter, her son close behind. She lifted the chute flap just enough so that the girl could extract her arm. It all happened so quickly that by the time John realized what was going on it was nearly over. There was nothing he could do—that time.

The next time he shifted, however, it was a different story. After putting his clothes in the washer he waited for the kids to start fiddling with the return chute of the vending machine and went over to them.

"Excuse me," he said pleasantly.

They stepped aside. He put some change into the machine. "Hmm, I can't decide. What's the best candy to have?"

"M&M's," Jamie said.

"Butterfinger," her brother answered.

"I guess I'll have to get both."

John pushed the corresponding number, and the bag of M&M's fell into the chute. He put in more change and pushed the corresponding number for the Butterfinger.

"You must be hungry, mister," the boy said.

"Not as hungry as I thought," John answered as he pushed open the chute and removed the candy. "In fact, I've changed my mind. Here, you both can have them," he said, handing them the candy.

"Thanks mister!" the boy said, running to his mother to ask permission to eat the candy.

"Yeah, thanks!" Jamie said, following her brother.

It felt good to be able to save the girl the pain and panic of getting stuck, John thought. And to remove that much more from their mother's stress level was a bonus. No one else knew what could have happened.

After that, every time that he shifted, he made a point to bring enough change to the laundromat to buy a couple of candy bars.

John realized that these incidents most likely altered the natural course of the timeline, but so minutely, so inconsequentially, that he couldn't see the logic of *not* doing them. He decided to help wherever he could. It was the right thing to do.

Every time that John found someone to help, he wrote down what it was that he had done. He didn't want to forget the action he had taken for fear that those original events would happen unaltered without him. Knowing that Mrs. Muldoon would fall, Jamie would get her arm stuck in the vending chute, and Bobby would strangle, he wanted to be there to prevent those things from happening.

He found that if he carried the list on his person, it went with him to the next shift. Every morning before leaving for work, he reviewed his notes to see where he had to be and at what time. It was a bit of a burden thinking that he might forget to intervene, but it was a welcome distraction from repeating the same day with no deviation.

The only trouble with intervening in other people's events was not the philosophical nature of it or even the scheduling of it, but rather the physical drain of the time-shift. After gleaning as much teaching as Wayne would impart on a particular subject, John would twist the talisman and shift back a few days or weeks and do it all again. Immediately after shifting, he would feel a brief sense of lightheadedness and vertigo. It was a destabilizing feeling, and he sometimes had to hold onto whatever was nearby to keep his balance.

The first time that he felt the odd, disorienting feeling was shortly after shifting to help Bobby in the coatroom. The feeling intensified each time after that. Whereas it started as a little lightheadedness, it progressed to nearly blacking out by the time he had shifted nine or ten times. Perhaps the talisman, besides having the power to transport him back in time, was also capable of giving him brain cancer, clogged arteries, or some weird disease. He couldn't very well go to a doctor and request treatment because of how it would sound:

"What brings you in to see us today?"

"Well, doctor, every time I travel back in time I get dizzy. Sometimes to the point of

passing out."
"Hmm, sounds like a classic case of time travel delirium. Take two aspirins and call me in the morning."
Or…

"Sometimes I feel disoriented."
"Are you eating okay? Drinking lots of water? Been time traveling a lot lately?"
"Well, as a matter of fact … ."

No, there was no rational way to explain his symptoms without sounding like a total nutcase.

It bothered him that these time-shifting feelings of vertigo sometimes happened in front of Wayne. After having been given the "grand tour" on each first day of work, he had to stop and lean against the wall. His vision had become tunneled, and the room started spinning. He felt flushed, and anything Wayne was saying at the time sounded garbled and distant. Then, almost as soon as it started, it disappeared. Wayne, standing in front of him, would ask if anything was wrong. His new boss, already skeptical about the authenticity of the skills cited on his resume, always looked at him suspiciously.

John successfully bluffed his way through those particular episodes, but each time that he shifted and relived the day again, the feeling returned more intensely. If his maintenance skills weren't growing exponentially with each shift, he doubted that Wayne would be as tolerant as he was.

Fortunately, after shifting multiple times, John had learned everything he felt he needed to make a good living. Despite the unsettling feeling of vertigo every time he shifted, he was satisfied with how well the plan was unfolding. He was well-educated, well-paid, and well on his way to hiding the talisman where no one would ever find it.

Everything would be copacetic, if it weren't for that stranger. That weird guy with the sunglasses who always seemed to be hanging around the school, near the property. Standing. Watching.

The first time that John noticed the guy was after the second time shift. He was standing across the street from the school after John had learned how to fix an air conditioner compressor unit. The man hadn't been there in other timelines, he was sure of it.

It was more than a bit strange that every time John shifted from then on, the man showed up. When he did, it was always a little different than the time before. Sometimes he would be sitting in his car, walking along the sidewalk, or leaning against a streetlight. The only consistencies with his appearances were that he wore a dark suit and wrap-around sunglasses. That, and he was always staring in John's direction.

He was common, unrecognizable, but he also seemed eerily familiar.

John couldn't be sure that the guy was there watching *him*, but it felt that way. Just coincidence, he thought. Probably wasn't even there watching him at all. He was probably just some freaky pedophile checking out the little kids. That was the worst thought of all.

He tried to ignore Mystery Man and keep his mind on his work and training, but it was difficult. Was he a robber? A university goon? Some sort of time cop, aware of the shifts John had been making and there to arrest him and throw him in some intergalactic penitentiary?

He had come so far, learned so much. It was difficult not to wonder whether his plan could be in jeopardy this close to completion. He dismissed the thought as simply paranoia.

Denial didn't help. He knew he had damned well better complete his plan and rid himself of the talisman, the sooner the better. Mystery Man was real and had an agenda. John just hoped that he wasn't on it.

30

JOHN MADE WHAT HE EXPECTED was his last time-shift and landed the day before having gotten his job at George Washington Elementary.

The first time that he was hired he was a naïve and inexperienced twenty-one year old college dropout. He was just looking to lay low and make enough money to get by while figuring out what to do with both his life and the talisman, which he had reluctantly inherited.

That was almost four years ago. Now, with the help of the talisman, the very thing he wished to disassociate himself from, he was twenty-one again. Fully trained with more experience than someone twice his age.

This was to be the last trip through the timeline, as he was prepared to work at the school for at least as long as it took to get a mortgage and build a house. Perhaps even retire from there. The job wasn't so bad, and Moline was a nice community. Quiet, unassuming. A good place in which to grow old. He hoped that he would get that chance.

It was Sunday, and John brought his duffel bag full of dirty clothes to the laundromat. As the washing machine was going through its cycle, he took some change and went to the vending machine as he usually did.

Little Jamie and her brother were just finishing their marathon race past the rows of washers, dryers, and folding tables. They ran to the vending machine and John didn't need to ask. He knew exactly what they wanted. They had done this many times before.

He inserted his money, punched the buttons, and extracted a bag of M&Ms and a Butterfinger. After handing the candy to them he walked past their mother who was hurriedly stuffing her own machine.

Jamie and her brother ran to her side.

"It's candy, Mommy. Can we have it?"

Jamie held up the bag of M&Ms. Her brother held up the Butterfinger.

"Where did you get candy?"

They both pointed to John who was standing nearby, smiling. "That man," Jamie said, anxious to enjoy her treat.

The mother's head tilted, and her eyes narrowed as she stared at John as if he were a social outcast, a predator, a deviant. After yanking the candy out of the children's hands, she tossed them on the folding table next to John.

"I don't know what you're thinking, but my

children are taught not to take candy from strangers."

She grabbed each child by the forearm and pulled them to the opposite side of her. She then returned to loading her Maytag.

Confused at the unexpected turn of events, John apologized. "I completely understand. I'm sorry."

But he *didn't* understand. In all the other timelines, the confrontation with the mother hadn't happened. He saved Jamie the pain of getting her arm stuck and bought them candy. That's it. The mother read nothing into the gesture, felt no threat, and went home with two happy children and a load of pink clothes.

Now, as John returned to his own machine, he looked back to see her setting the red shirt aside. There would be no load of pink clothes in *this* timeline. For some reason, those experiences turned out differently than before. Not a huge earth-shaking metamorphosis, but just enough that the normal timeline changed. Almost imperceptibly. But it *did* change. The timeline which had always been predictable was now vulnerable, or at least unexpected.

Then he remembered.

Mystery Man.

Perhaps the word was out in the community that some stranger was milling around the elementary school, and the mother suspected John of being that person. They were roughly the same height, and with sunglasses on, nobody knew *who* Mystery Man was.

Not possible, he concluded. According to something that Wayne said in a different timeline, the stranger only started showing up *after* John was working at the school. In *this* timeline, John hadn't even started working there yet.

No, this was just a coincidence. Millions of such changes must happen every day with no one noticing. There was no reason to think that things weren't exactly as they were supposed to be. Only *he* knew that they weren't as they had *originally* been.

This last change—buying candy for the kids in the laundromat—produced different results than the last several shifts. The experience shook him.

He'd gotten complacent. The order of the universe, even when he aligned it himself, was obviously not as predictable as he had begun to think. The disturbing part was wondering what larger effects might be ahead.

This uncertainty left him anxious. He stayed close to his apartment through the remainder of the weekend, not wanting to disrupt the current timeline. He was too close to achieving his goal to have some weird twist in the timeline mess up everything. While it was boring just watching television programs he had already seen many times over, and rereading books that he had already read, it was safe. He didn't know why he should feel *unsafe*, but he did. He paced, felt jumpy, like having had way too much caffeine. It was likely only anticipation for starting his new job.

There really was no reason to feel so apprehensive, he reminded himself. He knew the school, he knew his boss, and he knew the job inside and out. Other new hires would never feel so self-assured. Darn that woman in the laundromat. If she had just reacted the same way she had in the last several timelines, he would be filled with enthusiasm and excitement for his new, and hopefully last, trek through this present. Instead, he fretted about what would go wrong.

Rationally, there wasn't much that *could* go wrong. It was a fine plan, and it was unfolding as expected. Still, he couldn't help but wonder whether he was suffering from some residual effects of all the time-shifting he had been doing. Perhaps this was what Professor Rutherford was going through right before he ended his life. An autopsy might have shown some chemical imbalance in the professor's brain which caused him to deteriorate mentally. If so, the talisman could have been the cause.

John didn't know anything about identifying mental illness but he imagined it was much like what he was currently going through. He questioned the logic of reality and was becoming fearful of it. He wondered what would be next. Would he devolve to full-blown paranoia?

This could have been the very thing the professor had been thinking right before the end. That the redundancy of the present was monotonous. That it was disturbingly volatile. Or perhaps he felt like he was running on a treadmill with no hope of venturing into the future, the great unknown. Maybe something else, something John hadn't thought of or experienced yet. Could there be something else looming, waiting, ready to morph from normal into grotesque?

John rolled his eyes and smiled. What an imagination, he thought. Other than the occasional unexpected detour, like the events at the laundromat, it wasn't likely that there would be any huge departures from what was going to happen anyway.

By evening, he had relaxed and put those thoughts behind him. He'd been too permissive with his imagination; it was time to shut it down for the day. At least when he was asleep, he wouldn't have to worry about the future. Or the ever-repeating present, the time-shifting delirium, the onset of mental illness, the fear of a potential suicide, or the mysterious boogeymen.

Tomorrow, although not a *new* day, was at least a fresh start. The chance at an optimistic future. Once he worked another three years at George Washington he will catch up with the present. A present that he had already lived. Then, at last, it will be the beginning of the future.

Time travel was peculiar.

31

THE NEXT MORNING JOHN woke before the alarm. He felt rested and refreshed.

He stared at himself in the bathroom mirror and noted that he looked older than his twenty-one years. There were fine furrows on his forehead. His cheeks had minor wrinkles, politely called laugh lines.

Time-shifting was starting to take its toll. Much like it had taken a toll on the professor. The face looking back at him was supposed to be a college student. Or a research lab technician. Or a junior archaeologist. Instead, it was the face of someone who had lived more years than their chronological age would indicate. Someone who had also experienced more career opportunities than any student fresh out of school.

Someone who had taken a sharp turn off their timeline and gone in a completely different direction.

"Hey, what did you do with John Shaw the

archaeologist?" he asked the face in the mirror. "Left him in the past," the face replied.

Great. Now he was talking to himself. Time to go to work, he thought, before he went completely batty.

He finished dressing, choosing a pair of jeans and a long-sleeve button down shirt. He probably could have gotten away with a t-shirt if he wanted, since he'd be wearing coveralls once he got there, but it just didn't feel right to be so casual on his first day. Plus, he didn't want to rub Wayne's nose in the fact that some young guy dressed like a college kid on summer break was coming on board with as much knowledge as him and making about the same amount of money.

No use drawing undue attention to himself or creating any ill will with his mentor. Just keep to the plan.

It was a luxury to be able to walk to work from his apartment. No need to have a car and all the expenses and headaches that go along with one. Of course, once he started accumulating some money, he'd *have* to own a car, since he pictured his house to be somewhere on the outskirts of town. Most of the rest of Moline was already built up with residential or commercial construction. There was some land available at the north end of the county near the river. It would be an ideal location, he thought.

Now that he was about to make some serious money, he could actually start to entertain the thought in earnest.

As he approached the Dairy Mart on the way to the school, the familiar bicycles were lying near the door as expected. He wondered whether he should remove them again or leave them for Mrs. Muldoon to fall over as she had the very first time before he ever interfered. Even if he removed the bikes, there was no guarantee that the old woman would be safe or that something else wouldn't happen instead. The incident at the laundromat proved that. On the other hand, he didn't have the heart to leave them there and watch as she fell down and injured herself, presuming that she didn't see them again.

There was no way of telling what would, or would not, happen.

He hurried over to the front entrance just as Mrs. Muldoon was coming out of the Dairy Mart cradling a bag of groceries and holding a large cup of hot coffee. John pulled the bikes aside and the old woman walked out of the store uninjured. Unlike the other times he had removed the bikes, she noticed what he had done and stopped.

"Why thank you, young man. I didn't even see them there."

John smiled. "My pleasure."

"Have a wonderful day," she said, shuffling on her way.

John stood there for a minute to see what might happen. Would the kids who owned the bikes come out to yell at him for touching their rides? Would a lightning bolt come out of the sky to strike him dead for being a nice guy or for interfering?

No one came out of the store, and the sky remained friendly.

He hurried down the sidewalk to George Washington Elementary School, his steps a little lighter.

He smiled. A new job awaited, along with a new timeline, a new present, and then, if all went well, a future.

Part Three – The Return

32

THERE WEREN'T MANY THINGS that Taylor Jennings detested more than time travel. For one thing, it was confusing. It was always a gamble how far back you would go. Sometimes a day, sometimes a week or a year. Maybe it wouldn't be so bad if you could be precise about how far you wanted to go, or where.

As advanced as science was to permit time travel in the first place, no one thought to put a steering mechanism on the damned thing? Or a GPS system? No, let's invent a fucking time travel device and not tell the traveler how to get where they are going! Brilliant.

Whenever he arrived back in the past, *his* past, he was disoriented. There was no welcoming committee greeting him when he arrived, telling him what day it was or how far back he had gone.

Everyone was living their lives as if it was the very first time that they had ever experienced it. Ignorant fools. They had no idea that he could make them relive their days as many times as he wanted. Over and over again. He was the great puppeteer. Geppetto with superpowers.

Not that he could enjoy the performance. In order to view their choreographed dance, he had to be there too. Stepping through the same crappy days as them. It wouldn't be so bad if he could shoot back to the past, do what he went there to do, then return to the present. *His* present. But no. The inventors failed to include a 'forward' option in their time travel device. Thanks. Thanks a lot.

Another thing that annoyed him about time travel was the pathetic nature of the people who were in his past, experiencing their *present*. It was like rewatching a movie, or staring at an old postcard, or rereading a letter. Familiar, predictable, boring. For him, these people were just shadows and memories come to life. They'd already lived those days. It's not like their lives were all that interesting to begin with and worthy of a repeat performance.

Worse than just observing the mundane and pathetic lives of Moline, Illinois residents was to actually live it with them. Because it was impossible to travel forward to his own present, he would have to live out his miserable days there with them until he caught up with his own timeline.

Just like his first stint in Moline, he was adamant about keeping a low profile. There was no way that he wanted to make friends or socialize. He was there on a mission and wasn't going to be happy until he returned home. The present should be just that—the present, period. It should not be the past-present for those who are reliving it or the present-present for those who were living it for the first time.

Time travel sucked. Or, more specifically, *one-way* time travel sucked.

Taylor had just finished dressing after spending the night at the twenty-unit Blue Whore motel. Actually, it was called the Blue Horizon, but the blue neon on the 'i-z-o-n' letters was burned out and at night it looked like Blue Hor. It amused him, so he continued calling it by its derogatory nickname.

There was nothing fancy about the Blue Whore, unless you consider a rack of flyers promoting pseudo-tourist attractions next to the registration desk and a Pepsi machine on the sidewalk next to the front entrance as 'fancy.'

Moline had other motels, but the Blue Whore was closest to the George Washington Elementary School, so he was willing to sacrifice comfort and amenities for convenience.

The old couple who ran the joint were sappy-nice the times that he checked in. They usually enjoyed a whopping twenty-percent occupancy rate, so when Taylor said that he wanted to have an extended stay the first time he was there, they were ecstatic.

They had extended stay patrons in the past, especially when the Risk board game regional championship was held at the Holiday Inn over the Thanksgiving weekend and the chain was fully booked. The Blue Whore benefited from booking the overflow from most of the other, nicer, motels in the area. If they had a niche, that was it.

When he said he wanted to stay a month or more the old folks were beside themselves. They fumbled through their drawers looking for the proper extended stay paperwork that permitted them to offer a lower rate. It was amusing to watch them searching, digging, and talking to themselves.

The old geezers didn't have a clue that he had checked in before. On their timeline it was the first and only time he had been there. With his suit, tie, and sunglasses they guessed that he was just another exec- utive-type passing through. Attending a meeting at the John Deere corporate headquarters, perhaps.

He let them think that. He couldn't very well say, *"No, I'm not with Deere. I'm from the future, traveling back to your time on a special mission of the United States government. Got change for the Pepsi machine?"*

Who knows, maybe these rubes would buy it. It was small town types like these that always seemed to be the ones who see Sasquatch, flying saucers, or weird ghost-like apparitions in the stairwell. They were always the ones taken aboard alien spacecraft and spit back out to regale us about the out-of-town visitors with big heads, big eyes, and big ambitions.

He was tempted to tell them the truth but decided against it. Not that he wouldn't have enjoyed toying with them and seeing their wide-eyed expressions of disbelief, but frankly, he didn't want anything more from them than a key.

Taylor hoped that this mission would conclude

soon. If he had to listen to the old dame talk about her "famous corn muffins" just one more time, he was likely to punch her right in her wrinkled old puss. That in itself might make traveling back to Moline worth it, but he restrained himself.

After finishing tying his thin black tie, he slipped on his black suit jacket. He liked dressing in black. It made him feel like an outlaw. It had become his signature. Everyone back at the agency noticed it, but they didn't have the guts to say something. He was too respected, too revered, too *feared* to mess with.

If all went well with this mission, he would run the agency. Already he was the highest-ranking member of his division. A phenom. A wunderkind. The fucking Bill Gates of physics. He'd heard it all before. And how right they were.

After brushing some specks of lint off his shoulders, he picked up the Smith & Wesson and put it in his jacket pocket. Then, opening up a zippered shaving kit, he removed a syringe with a red protective cap. It was filled with a yellowish liquid. He carefully put it into the other pocket.

Would this be the day that he would finally get to use them and get on with his mission? For the love of everything holy, he hoped so.

He didn't know how many more days he could stand to be in Moline, or listen to that old bat talking about her corn muffins or chronic lumbago. If someone had to die today, he half wished that it would be her. Maybe he would kill her and her frumpy old husband just for kicks. *After* the mission, of course. *After* he took care of business.

He wasn't an assassin by nature, but the mission—the one that he himself suggested—forced him to take on that role. He had killed once; he could do it again.

The mere fact that he was still standing in his room at the Blue Whore instead of back home with his beautiful wife was testament that he would have to kill again.

"Let's hope that this is the day," he thought. "The *last* day."

33

IN THE FEW BLOCKS that John had to walk to the school, the sky had quickly darkened to an ashen gray. A light mist began to fall. The odor of wet asphalt reminded him of when he left the professor's house that fateful night. It was the smell of starting over. He trotted the last block.

He didn't remember it raining the other times he had lived through this timeline. He was pretty sure it hadn't. The woman's reaction at the laundromat and now the rain. Slight changes, minor and insignificant to the whole perhaps, but changes nevertheless.

He was reasonably certain that none of these little timeline ripples would produce the catastrophic disasters predicted by science fiction writers. Still, he was left with an eerie feeling of unpredictability. Much like the average person feels as they travel through their present headed into their unknown future. Much like he felt before he acquired the talisman.

John had taken the future for granted. For the past several years, he'd relived the present so many times that he knew to the minute how long it would take to get to work, what Wayne would say when he got there, and a hundred other miscellaneous details. Today, there seemed to be uncertainty. It was exhilarating.

The falling mist turned into a light drizzle. He was getting wetter by the step. His feet slapped the wet pavement as he ran. Fortunately, he was only about fifty yards from the front entrance of the school. He knew that being damp under his coveralls might be uncomfortable, but he would be so focused on the final stages of his grand plan that he wouldn't care. Soon he would be venturing into the future, and he could finally be rid of the talisman. Then, at last, his present, and that of everyone else, would be in sync.

As he approached the rows of parked cars along the curb in front of the school, he noticed someone standing between two cars.

Mystery Man.

John stopped running. Something felt wrong. This time Mystery Man was standing directly on school property. Yet another difference from other timelines. Before, he had kept to the safety of the area across the street or in his car at a distance where the school would have no cause to call the authorities.

Mystery Man might have been a parent, dropping his child off for school if the school year had officially started. It hadn't. It would be another two weeks before the students returned.

This was no parent. He was looking in John's direction, but John couldn't be sure that he was actually looking at him since he was wearing dark sunglasses.

John would have to pass Mystery Man in order to get to the courtyard at the front entrance of the school. Should he say hello? Ignore him? He didn't want to overreact, but he didn't want to be a fool either.

With all the preparations for changing the present and planning for the future, he'd failed to consider the danger that he had left behind at the University of Chicago. Mystery Man felt like a threat.

The rain had stopped but the sky was still dark and overcast. Mystery Man was standing between a new black Corvette and a light blue minivan.

John kept walking. He couldn't tell if the man was armed, but he sensed danger. The back of his neck tingled.

Had there been another entrance to the school close by, John would have gone there to avoid Mystery Man, but he was nearest to the main double doors. Even if he could have avoided the man, John knew that it would only be a temporary reprieve. A confrontation was coming. A showdown. There didn't seem to be a way to avoid it.

"John Shaw," the man called out, stepping onto the sidewalk. It was a statement, not a question. He knew to whom he was speaking.

John's mouth went dry. Denial would be fruitless. He wondered for a split second whether this was a police officer. A detective perhaps. Had he broken some law? Not unless someone believed that he had stolen the talisman from the university.

Hannah Miller.

Of course. She likely told her father, and they called the cops. Or hired a private investigator. And now, they had finally found him.

In the few yards it took to reach Mystery Man, John weighed his options. He could run. The man was a little older, by maybe ten or fifteen years, but looked to be in good shape. John was in good shape too, but he was no athlete, so it could be a footrace and a close one at that. Besides, making a mad dash for the school entrance seemed like a sure way to destroy a good impression on his first day.

Another alternative would be to sucker punch the guy and take his chances. Bad idea. If this guy was, in fact, a detective or private investigator, then he probably knew all sorts of fighting techniques. Worse, he probably had a gun.

He could always time-shift backward and remove himself from that present entirely. That meant reliving the previous days again and they would likely meet eventually anyway.

No, his options were few.

Slowing, but not stopping, John answered curtly, "Good morning." He deliberately did not confirm nor deny his identity.

Mystery Man took a step forward, away from the cars. John stopped, preparing for a defensive maneuver if necessary.

"Been a long time, plowboy."

'Plowboy'? The last—and only—time that he

had been called that was back on Antigua by... .

"Taylor? Taylor Jennings?"

Using both hands, the man removed his sunglasses and slipped them into the breast pocket of his suit jacket. He grinned. "Surprise!"

Without his sunglasses, the man *did* resemble Taylor; dark hair, brown eyes, square chin, smirky smile. But he was noticeably older than the Taylor he remembered. He had more wrinkles across the forehead. Puffiness under his eyes. A few gray hairs. If this was in fact Taylor Jennings as he claimed, he looked to be in his mid to late thirties. More likely, it was an older brother, or cousin, or just someone with remarkably similar features.

Seeing that John was skeptical, Taylor asked, "Don't you recognize me, old friend?"

"I recognize who you want me to *think* you are."

Taylor threw his head back and laughed. "Always the archaeologist, eh? Always looking for more evidence before making a conclusive decision. Yeah, me too."

His voice sounded like Taylor's, but John was still not convinced.

Taylor pivoted and looked around at the school and the middle-income homes across the street.

"For the life of me, I don't understand what you are doing in this piss-hole. And working as a garbage man at a kiddie school? This is the best you could do?"

John scowled. "I happen to like Moline. It's a nice, quiet community. And I'm a maintenance engineer. Not a garbage man."

"Hmm ... a 'maintenance engineer.' Well, I guess that's a step up from being a country bumpkin."

Despite the obvious age difference between them, John was starting to believe that somehow this *was* the Taylor Jennings he knew from the University of Chicago.

"But actually," Taylor sneered, "you're not a 'maintenance engineer' *yet*, are you? Unless I am mistaken, this will be your first day."

John's cheeks flushed. He wanted to step away from this conversation, hurry into the school, and begin his new career. To carry on with his plan. But he knew that Mystery Man—now revealed as Taylor—wasn't done with him yet.

"You're right. And I'd like to get on with it. So, if you don't mind … ."

He took a step toward the school.

Taylor countered the step and they both stopped, still maintaining equal distance from each other. "Oh, but I *do* mind. We haven't had a chance to catch up yet. It's been a long time."

John thought for a moment. It was mid-August. The new school year hadn't started. He dropped out of UChicago only a few months ago. Of course, it seemed much longer than that to him, since he had worked for nearly three years at the school before using the talisman to shift backward and relive those days over again.

"I don't know what you mean. I saw you on campus … what, two, three months ago?"

Taylor nodded. "In the *current* timeline, of course."

John's stomach flipped. He knew that he was being toyed with. "What do you mean?"

Taylor's eyebrows rose, as did the volume of his voice. "You don't know what I mean? Really?!" He rubbed his chin. "Hmm, let me see if I can refresh your memory. You dropped out and moved to this hick town so no one would find you. Then you got a job pushing a broom at this school. So far so good?"

John didn't answer.

"Then, in an effort to obtain immortality you used the talisman to travel back in time so you wouldn't get any older."

He got the reason wrong, but he knew about the talisman! And he knew the *capability* of the talisman! But how, John wondered. And what else did he know? John grew more concerned by the second for his safety and for that of the talisman.

Taylor smiled. "Ah! So I got a base hit! You know what I am talking about now. Your eyes betray you, my friend."

"I don't recall us ever being 'friends,' Taylor."

"We're making progress. You finally accept that I am who I say I am."

John nodded slowly. "You're Taylor all right. But you look like crap."

"Do I? I guess time hasn't been kind to me. You see, it may have been only three months since you've seen *me*, but it's been ten years since I've seen *you*."

A light rain began to fall.

Looking up, Taylor said, "We should step into my car before we get soaked."

"I really should go," John answered. "They're expecting me. I don't want to be late on my first day."

Taylor laughed. Then a sinister smile spread across his face. "You really *are* slow, aren't you, plowboy?

You're not going to make your first day. Not this time. Or should I say, not this *timeline*."

John stiffened. "You're not getting the talisman," he said, reaching for the puck in his pocket. His plan was to shift and remove himself from the situation. He would worry about how to avoid Taylor the next time he got to that point in the present. Next time, he wouldn't be caught by surprise, and he'd be better prepared. He tapped his pants pockets. First the front then the rear. Then the front again.

The talisman was gone.

Taylor waited a moment to say anything, a smug little smile on his face. He seemed to enjoy watching John search for his last good hope.

"You're wasting your time."

"What do you mean?" John asked, shoving his hands into each pocket again just to be sure that it really wasn't there. He distinctly remembered putting it into his pocket along with his wallet and keys. Or was that yesterday? It was such a natural routine, could he have forgotten it just this once? Not likely.

Taylor smiled and then shook his head, tired of this game. "You're not going to find it," he said. "I've had it for years."

Suddenly, John knew that it was true, although he couldn't begin to explain *how* he knew.

Taylor pointed to the Corvette. "Now get in. Let's talk. We've got business to discuss."

34

IT STARTED RAINING HARDER. Drops plinked down on car hoods and trunks. Water sluiced alongside the curb like a rushing river current, pushing floating leaves downstream to some unknown destination.

If it was true that Taylor had the talisman as he claimed, running away would be futile. He could just shift time and they'd be doing this all again in a few days or weeks. If he was bluffing, John knew he'd find out soon enough.

John opened the door. "Nice car."

"Like it? It's a rental. I was going to get a more practical one. Energy efficient and all that. But I figured, what the hell. They discontinued making the Corvette years ago, so I thought I'd treat myself."

John wondered what he meant. This was a brand-new Corvette, and he hadn't heard anything about them discontinuing the model. When he got in the car and closed the door he noticed the new car smell. Distinctive and pleasant. Sweet, like new plastic and leather.

Taylor got behind the wheel and slammed the door. He shifted his weight in the leather seats and ran his hands over the steering wheel. "They don't make cars like this anymore. Everything is 'green' and 'energy efficient' nowadays. We've forgotten the little luxuries in life."

"What's this about, Taylor?"

Taylor pushed the ignition button on the dashboard, and the powerful engine roared to life. "Damn! Did you know that I could go from zero to sixty in five-point-one seconds? Burns too much fossil fuel, the environmentalists said. Made 'em discontinue the model." He turned to look at John. "I'd love to show you, but I don't want to draw attention. Maybe some other timeline."

He backed the sports car out of the parking spot, and wheeled onto Polk Street in front of the school.

The rain was steady now. The sky grew gray and moody.

"I don't remember it raining the last time we did this, do you?"

John looked at Taylor. It was true, he hadn't remembered it raining in this timeline, but what did Taylor know of it, and what did he mean about the 'last time'?

Taylor glanced over and smiled. "You are so transparent, plowboy. I can read every emotion, every question on your face. You want to know what I meant.

You want to know where we're going. You want to know why you no longer have the talisman."

Right on all counts, John thought. It was as if Taylor *could* read his thoughts … just like Professor Rutherford had. Only the professor couldn't really read thoughts. He knew what John was going to say because they had done the same thing and had the same conversation in a previous timeline. Still, John had the distinct feeling of déjà vu. Like some fragmented pieces of a memory were being stored somewhere in the dark recesses of his mind, poking through like bone fragments embedded in the sand.

Taylor drove to the end of the block, turned left onto Valley Road, and headed west, toward the edge of town. He kept to the speed limit, careful not to attract attention.

"What I don't get, and what you've never been able to explain to me, is why *here*? Why Moline, of all places?"

John watched as they passed the last row of red brick storefront buildings. Raindrops ran nearly horizontal across the passenger-side window, like flowing tears.

"They build John Deere tractors here," John finally answered. "On the farm my father had a Deere. Just reminded me of home, I guess."

Taylor nodded. "Sure. That makes sense. Thanks for sharing. I don't know why you never told me before."

"What are you talking about?"

Taylor smiled, enjoying the cat-and-mouse game. "The last time we did this. The last time we took a ride together."

"We've *never* taken a ride together," John said, although even as the words were leaving his lips, he wasn't sure that he actually believed it. "We've barely spoken to each other."

"Au contraire, mon ami! We've had numerous conversations. You have limited memories of other timelines because you *once* had the talisman. But you don't remember *everything* because you are no longer in possession of it. If you still had it, your memory would be as clear as mine."

The engine hummed as they cruised out of town. Quaint antique stores, clothing boutiques, the coffee shop, the realtor's office, and the hardware store were replaced by open farm fields. Soon they would be in the dense woods on the outskirts of the county. Then the Mississippi River.

The rain was heavy and visibility poor, but it didn't matter, Taylor knew exactly where he was going.

"For you, this is all happening for the first time. For me, it all happened a long time ago."

"The talisman," John repeated softly to himself.

"Precisely."

It was like having seen a movie already but forgetting the plot, John thought. "So we went for a ride sometime in your past, my future, and you stole the talisman … ."

Taylor looked over sharply, his voice rose. "Stole? No, not 'stole.' You gave it to me. Willingly." Shaking his head, he muttered, "I hate time travel. It's so fucking redundant." Then, to John, "At least there are some differences, right? Like the rain. And you telling me about Deere. That was different. I like that. Breaks up the monotony."

Taylor had something up his sleeve, and if he truly had the talisman, John knew he was in grave danger.

John shook his head. "I wouldn't have given it to you willingly."

"Ah, but you did! You saw the logic in it."

"You would have had to kill me."

Taylor grinned. "Oh, but I *did* kill you. Much later, after you stopped cooperating. That's why I'm so optimistic this time. Things are different this time. Like the rain. Maybe *this* time you get to live! Wouldn't that be nice?!"

They were a mile past the open farm fields now. Trees grew densely, tall pines, oak, maple. Thick green foliage. It would be another month or two before the leaves changed colors. Autumn was always a beautiful time of the year, John thought. Sprays of red, yellow, orange, and magenta. He hoped he lived long enough to see it.

Taylor turned right at a stop sign and headed down a paved side road with gravel shoulders.

A red wooden sign with faded white letters staked on the side of the road identified the area as the William B. Simmons Forest Preserve.

The narrow asphalt road wound through the trees toward the river. John had never explored that part of the county, so none of it looked familiar. Taylor apparently knew it quite well. The Corvette picked up speed as it hugged the switchback turns.

"I love this cruise! No one comes through here,

so I open it up a bit."

John could see on the speedometer that they were taking the turns at forty-five miles per hour and going nearly ninety on the straightaway. He hoped that Taylor was wrong and that someone was around to see a crazy driver and report him to the authorities. He also hoped that the Corvette stayed on the road.

Suddenly, Taylor hit the brakes. The Corvette skidded in a straight line. Now going about thirty miles per hour, he quickly turned left down an unmarked gravel access road with minimal fishtailing.

"Wow! I love that part!"

The gravel access road ended in less than a mile on a rocky bluff overlooking the Mississippi. The U.S. Army Corps of Engineers used the road to inspect the river bank every eighteen months for erosion. It was not intended for general public use. As such, there were no protective barriers or guardrails keeping an errant vehicle from careening off the path and into the river some fifty feet below.

Taylor stomped hard on the brakes, the tires locked, and the car slid in a straight line directly toward the edge of the embankment. Mud and gravel sprayed up into the wheel wells, and John would have been thrown forward if the seat belt hadn't held firm.

The Corvette came to stop with the nose less than a yard from the edge.

John released the breath he hadn't realized he'd been holding. "And the purpose of that?!"

Taylor ran his fingertips over the steering wheel again, as if he were deciding to purchase the vehicle.

"Just living life on the edge," he said, laughing. "That's another reason I hate time travel. Things are so *predictable*. Even speeding down that road wasn't as big a rush as it was the first time. Will there be a turn? A deer? A felled tree? You wonder, you anticipate, but you just don't know. It's the unpredictability that makes things interesting."

The rain was letting up. What little was still falling couldn't get through the dense layers of tree branches high above.

Through the clearing ahead, John could see the surface of the river still being pelted with raindrops. Out the side window past the narrow gravel drive was thick brush that no doubt made great groundcover for deer, wild turkey, and a host of other animals. He couldn't help but think that their location was a good make-out spot for promiscuous teenagers. He wondered if anyone other than the Army Corps of Engineers even knew it was there.

John's heartbeat sped up, even faster than it had been. His senses were on full alert. He knew it was a precarious situation. Taylor wasn't to be trusted. If something happened to him, who knows how long it would be until they found his remains. When was the last time the Engineers were at that spot? In hindsight, he realized he probably shouldn't have gone for a ride in the first place. It might have been safer to take his chances and make a run for it.

Not that it would have made much of a difference, he reminded himself. If Taylor had the talisman, he'd just shift and do it again anyway.

"Explain something to me, Taylor."

"Of course," Taylor answered pleasantly, looking over while unbuckling his seatbelt. "Ask away. I've got my own questions as well."

John unbuckled, hoping for a chance to escape. "You don't look the same," he said.

"You don't either."

"You look older," John said.

"So do you."

"*Much* older."

"Ten years to be exact," Taylor explained.

"But we're the same age."

Taylor shook his head. "Used to be, but not anymore."

"You're not making sense."

"I'll explain—again. You left Chicago and came here. After a few years you bounced backward a handful of times and relived those years. All said and told, you've lived about twenty-six years—give or take—even though your birth certificate would indicate that you're only twenty-one. I, on the other hand, have lived ten additional years since the last time we met."

John diverted his gaze. The concept of continuous timelines and chronological ages was difficult enough to understand, but this didn't make any sense at all. He turned back toward Taylor.

"That's illogical. Regardless of what we did or where we did it, we'd still be the same chronological age."

Taylor stuck his index finger up. "Ah! Unless we both didn't live ten years past the last time we met."

"You mean … ."

"You died."

John recalled what Taylor said earlier: *'Oh, but I did kill you.'* True or not, the mere mention of it was startling. He flushed and started to perspire. It was bad enough feeling vulnerable, but he was more concerned for the fate of the talisman.

If Taylor had a reason for bringing him to the middle of the woods, or for killing him—if that was destined to happen—then there had to be a good reason.

"Maybe now is a good time to tell me what's going on."

Taylor threw his head back and smiled. He'd been waiting for this moment. "Okay. I know all about the talisman," he said, proudly. "It's a huge part of my life, actually. And I have *you* to thank."

"You're welcome."

Taylor stared at John. He hadn't remembered the sarcasm before. Interesting.

"Don't mention it. You see, I was there in the lab when you talked to Hannah about the talisman and Rutherford. I snuck in thinking I would catch someone in the act. The act of *what* I didn't know, but then I heard you explaining the whole concept of time-shifting. Naturally, I thought you a wacko, but you made a convincing case. Hannah seemed to buy into the story, so maybe there was something to it. I had to know for myself. I searched your dorm room, but it wasn't there."

John turned quickly. "*You* jumped me in the hall."

Taylor nodded. "So where was it?"

John shrugged, seeing little reason to lie. "Hidden

in one of the speakers."

Taylor closed his eyes for a second, picturing the room and the one location he had failed to check.

Then, smiling, "Sure. Good thinking! Anyway, I figured that you were either lying to impress a girl or were genuinely onto something and willing to protect this thing at all cost. I didn't figure you to be either a liar or a lady's man, so I gambled you were in earnest. Hannah came to class on Monday all concerned that you weren't there. Said she was worried. She'd gone to your dorm room a couple days earlier, but there was no answer when she knocked. Thought we should go look for you. I wanted to know where you were too, but for an entirely different reason. She dragged me to the dorm, and we got the resident assistant to open your room. It was trashed, of course, but then again I knew that it would be, right? Now she's *really* worried. Very touching. I took her to lunch to calm her down … and then dinner."

John felt terrible. He had mistakenly thought that Hannah—sweet, caring Hannah—was involved with the burglary. As bad as he felt about having suspected her, he forced his attention back to the sinister man in the car next to him.

"Did you do anything to her?"

"She needed someone to talk to. Someone to confide in. She talked about *you* a lot. She was quite taken with you, apparently. Must have been attracted to some cow pie kicking quality. We spent a lot of time together. A *lot* of time."

John's voice rose. "What did you do?!"

"She never talked about the talisman or what you

told her in the professor's office that day. I'll give her that much. She can keep a secret all right. I never told her that I had heard it all anyway. I kept waiting for her to slip up and tell me where she thought you went or what you were doing. She didn't, but I kept hoping. After a while I stopped thinking that she would lead me to you, so I shifted directions."

John scowled. "Tell me! What did you do?!"

Taylor smiled. His fish was nibbling, but he wasn't ready to set the hook. "Knowing how she felt about you I considered it a personal challenge to put an end to that."

John fought the urge to lean over the center console and attack Taylor, even at the risk of his own safety. "If you hurt her, so help me I'll … I'll … ."

Taylor didn't flinch. "You'll *what*, plowboy?" He paused, savoring the moment. "I *did* do something to her actually—I married her."

John's heart sank. "You … what?"

Taylor laughed. "That's great! I love the part where you find out that I wound up with the girl you were attracted to. Funny how things work out, huh? Yeah, it took a while. But with you missing, I turned on the charm, dazzled her with some bullshit, and eventually earned her trust. Convinced her I wasn't the asshole she thought I was. Bingo! I bagged a trophy wife!"

"When?" John asked weakly. His strength depleted like air leaked from a balloon.

"Right after graduation. About a month ago in this timeline," Taylor answered. Then, after a pause, he continued, knowing what John would ask next. "No, we never had kids."

For a brief moment it was like having a breath of fresh air. He couldn't picture another generation of Taylor Jennings running around. Especially when the mother would be a woman whom he admired and respected.

"So now both of you are archaeologists, I suppose," John pressed.

"Looks like the rain's stopping," Taylor noted, staring out the front window. "For the moment at least." Then, turning toward John, "No, actually we're not. Hannah lost interest in archaeology after you disappeared, and I changed majors."

Taylor waited for the question he knew would come.

John felt that they were on the precipice of something important. "To what?"

"Funny you should ask," Taylor answered, slyly. "I dropped archaeology and took on physics."

He had John's full attention.

"If the talisman did have powers as you claimed, then I wanted to understand them. It took all I had to finish a new major over the remaining two years. Lots of evening and weekend classes. Cramming. I was motivated. I was either going to see you go to jail or I was going to solve the mystery of the talisman. A win-win, as far as I could see."

John shook his head. "You really should get a hobby."

"I *have* a hobby. You!"

"I don't know why. You said it yourself, I'm a wacko."

Taylor nodded. "Yeah, that's what they said at the agency. Took me a while to convince them otherwise. I know the truth, though. You're crazy all right. Crazy like a fucking fox."

"You give me too much credit."

"Probably." He lowered the driver's side window.

John kept one eye on the key fob sitting on the center console as Taylor turned off the engine, desperate for any opportunity to grab the fob and run.

Taylor smiled as he carefully tucked the fob into his pocket. "Not this time, plowboy," he said.

The rain had stopped, and birds began to chirp. Water continued to drip from the tree branches.

"I got a job with Homeland Security. In their I.S. department. I.S., that's … ."

"Information Systems, I know."

"Right. With my educational background in physics, it didn't take them long to see that I was over-qualified. They submitted my name for a position at the Department of Defense. They were developing a new division. A top-secret group of brainiacs brought in to ponder anything and everything … lasers, microbiological weapons, hypnosis, impenetrable armor … whatever they wanted to think about."

Taylor grinned, hardly able to keep it all from spewing out faster than he wanted to tell it.

"I interviewed with a panel of big brass. Generals, admirals, scientists, even the secretary of defense himself. At first, they didn't even want to talk to me. They were looking for middle-aged scientists acclaimed in their respective fields, not some young punk who was an archaeological student one minute and a physics scholar the next. You should have seen their faces. You'd have thought I took a crap on their nice mahogany boardroom table! They had to be thinking, 'The nerve of this kid. What idiot at Homeland Security can we nail for this?' Naturally, they were skeptical. At the time, I didn't know what I was being interviewed for. But I knew that unless I could convince them to give me a chance I was going to be out the door faster than a sheep with you standing behind it." He chortled.

John was not amused. He listened but was looking for an opportunity to either escape or overtake this loudmouthed braggart. Taylor was streetwise and undoubtedly dangerous. He had proven it by the altercation in the Watkins hallway. But that had been an ambush. In a fair fight, John felt he could hold his own. He just needed the right opportunity.

"I could tell from the look in their eyes that they weren't even going to invite me to sit down for the interview, so I tossed my two hundred sixty-eight page thesis on time-shifting onto the table in front of them. 'What's this?' they ask. 'The future,' I told them. 'And the past.' They don't know what to make of it, of course, but they take a cursory look through it anyway. Interesting, they admitted, but lacking any quantitative evidence.

"They were right. I couldn't prove any of it. I didn't possess the *one* thing that would substantiate what I was saying. But *you* did. I walked out of that room embarrassed, humiliated. Naturally, I blamed you for that too."

"Naturally."

"There was only one thing to do. I had to track you down. I found out where your family lived and went to visit them."

John waited for more. He froze, biting his lip. This man was capable of anything.

"Not surprisingly, they didn't give you up. Hadn't heard from you. Didn't have a clue as to your whereabouts. Or so they said."

"You didn't … ."

Taylor shook his head slowly. "You disappoint me, John. I'm no monster. I have nothing against your family. I'm just trying to preserve the peace and stability of the future."

"You mean *control* the future."

Taylor shrugged. "Same thing."

John slumped. His situation seemed more dire by the second.

"Using Hannah's money, I hired a private investigator to find you. She thought it was a great idea. Very excited. I didn't tell her that my goal and hers were not the same. It only took a couple of months for the private investigator to find out that you were laying low in bumpkinville. Of course, I told Hannah that he came up empty."

"Of course."

"Never been to Moline before. Nice place, if you like stagnation. Ever had the Blue Whore's corn muffins? Yummy."

John didn't know what Taylor was talking about, nor did he care, but the sarcasm was evident. He was still plotting to get out of this mess alive. Somehow.

"I started following you. Watching you at the school. Trying to find the best time to 'convince' you to let me have the talisman for the good of the country. One day I waited for you to leave for work and broke into your apartment. Just like in your dorm room, I couldn't find what I was looking for. By the way, I appreciate the nifty Smith & Wesson I found in your dorm room. Thanks."

"Sure."

"Drove over to the school and met you in the lot, much like this morning. Ring a bell?"

John shook his head.

"Hmm … probably because I now have the talisman. You would remember more if *you* still had it. Maybe I should give it back to you and we can see if you remember then. What do you think?"

John didn't bother to answer. It was rhetorical.

Taylor grinned. "Anyway, I didn't waste any time. We took a ride, and I shot you in this very spot. And that's when I became the proud owner of the talisman."

"You said I gave it to you willingly."

Taylor nodded. "You did. And then you jumped me. I shot you in self-defense."

John's chest hurt from the anger seething within. "So I suppose you're going to kill me again."

Taylor shifted in his semi-reclined leather seat, trying to get comfortable. "I don't have to. You see, I already have the talisman from the last time. After I got the piece, I went back home to Evanston. As much as I wanted to, I knew that I couldn't prance back into the

Department of Defense with the talisman and declare that I now had proof. So I experimented with the thing. Took a while to figure it out since you died before telling me how it worked."

Taylor waited for a response that never came.

"Interesting experience traveling back in time," he continued. "It was weird having to relive all those days again. I made the most of it, though. I kept reliving the last two years of college over and over again. It felt like déjà vu except that I retained my knowledge from the previous timeline. I was able to take advanced physics classes, do internships, and build on the knowledge I already had. It was like getting a bachelors, masters, and doctorate in physics in two years. The professors thought I was brilliant. A natural born physicist. The brightest they'd ever seen. It was only because I was able to keep building on the previous year's education."

John knew the feeling well. He was doing the same thing, but with a completely different motive.

"Once again, I took the job with Homeland Security only so that I would have security clearance and credibility with the Department of Defense. Of course, when I applied for their open position, they looked at me with the same degree of skepticism as before. This time, however, not only did I have a time travel dissertation to share, but I also had a sample of the actual device. They didn't take my word on the capability of the talisman at face value. I had to prove it to them. So I did."

Taylor squirmed in his seat, trying to sit up, but was only partially successful. His excitement and pride were evident, and he smiled in the telling.

"I had each one of them write something on a piece of paper, date it, and sign it. I didn't care what they wrote, just something that they alone would recognize when I presented it to them again when I returned to that timeline. Then we put the notes and business cards in a large envelope. One of the generals put in one of his medals. They sealed the envelope, and the secretary of defense signed his name across the flap. We even used my camera to film them doing it.

"Honestly, I wasn't sure that it would work. If it didn't, I was screwed. With the envelope under my arm and the camera in my pocket, I used the talisman to shift out of that boardroom and back to the university. I had to finish the last two months of school, but this time I had the envelope and camera with me.

"Eventually, I showed up in the boardroom of the Department of Defense. When I told them the preposterous story of owning a time travel device, this time I had proof. I handed the sealed envelope to the secretary of defense. Although he had no memory of meeting me before, he recognized his signature across the flap. Running a pen under the flap, he opened it and spilled the contents on the table in front of them. They were intrigued, but unconvinced. Then I showed them the video. You should have seen their eyes!

"The part that ultimately convinced them that I must be telling the truth, was when the general recognized the medal that fell out onto the table. He immediately checked his chest, and that exact medal was missing from the others. After a lengthy discussion and a quick review of my dissertation, they practically carried me out of that boardroom on their shoulders. I was hailed a hero. A wunderkind. Another fucking Stephen Hawking! Five and a half hours later I was a member of the most elite and secretive division of the Department of Defense.

"Of course I couldn't explain how it worked because I didn't know. We put the country's top scientists on the project. We studied it for years but couldn't figure out what made it work. After quite a bit of experimentation there was one thing they were certain about. The talisman was only one-directional. They knew that it would be decades before they could figure out the inner workings of the thing. But there were other huge questions. Where did it come from? If we couldn't recreate it, could we get others? How do we go *forward* in time?"

With the key fob out of reach, John had to formulate a different plan. He could open the door and make a run for it, but without overtaking Taylor or recovering the talisman, it would be wasted effort. He had to keep Taylor distracted.

"So you're a bigwig on some secret committee. That explains the suit."

Taylor grinned. "I love the sarcasm. It's so refreshing not to have you roll over and die like last time." He continued. "The concept of time travel was intriguing for everyone on the committee for a lot of different reasons. Homeland security. Weather predictability. Planning and budgeting. Not to mention the obvious military uses. As a nation we would be omnipotent. Can you imagine? If we got hit with a devastating hurricane or tornado we could shift and take extra precautions. If we were ever attacked, we could shift and prevent the attack. Protect ourselves or strike first."

John added, "If a politician was elected who you didn't support, you could shift and make sure that it didn't happen."

Taylor nodded, oblivious to the mockery. "The possibilities are endless. We'd be the most powerful nation on earth."

"I thought we *were* the most powerful nation on earth."

Taylor rolled his eyes. He had explained this in a different timeline and was finding it wearisome.

"Someone once said, 'He who controls the weather controls the planet.' Imagine what you could do if you controlled *time*."

John knew that Taylor was dangerous, but now he suspected him to be a psychopath as well. What was even more frightening was that there was a whole committee of people just like him, with the power of the United States government behind them.

"Studying a device that would permit us to travel back in time to change what needed changing was a career opportunity of a lifetime. Of course, no one outside our small top-secret division knew we had such a device. And I led it. *My* theories, *my* goals, *my* device."

Taylor's face lit up with a twisted and frightening expression that could only be derived from holding the power of the universe.

"Our goals were simple. Figure out how the

damned thing worked and then determine whether our enemies were capable of peeling back time too."

It was a concept that John hadn't spent much time pondering. It was a disconcerting thought that there might be other devices like the talisman out there.

"We didn't have the technology to understand how a time-shifting device worked, but I knew that we should be able to develop something that had the ability to detect *when* the timeline changed. I requested a subcommittee to develop a time signature detection device. Something that could tell when the normal timeline was disrupted."

John wanted to ask but didn't need to. Taylor knew what the question would be.

"Oh, it wasn't as difficult as you might think. We had unlimited funds and an enviable bank of brilliant minds."

John started to hatch a plan. Overtake Taylor while he rambled on, and recover the talisman, which he no doubt had on him. Then either time-shift or slide down the embankment to the river and escape downstream. He could try going through the woods, but Taylor had probably already scoped out that area and would have the advantage. Worse, he knew that Taylor was armed. John would clearly be prey, and easy prey at that.

"Naturally, I was asked to head up that subcommittee. It took a few years, but eventually we had developed the technology we were looking for. You're familiar with the Very Large Array outside Socorro, New Mexico? Measures radio waves coming from outer space. It's similar to that. We called it the Time Displacement

Array or TDA. It measures a host of factors that parallel one another. Sudden and erratic molecular peculiarities, atmospheric density fluctuations, harmonic disruptions … that sort of thing. It then identifies where the anomaly occurred. Every time that you went backward, the talisman sent out a vibe, a signature. You were sending us a signal in the future! Just like we know how far away a star is by measuring how long it takes light to travel to us, we were able to trace molecular disruption to Moline. It was harder, however, to tell just *when* the disruptions occurred."

John found the concept of eavesdropping from the future disturbing, but not surprising. The talisman had mixed up his understanding of the world to the point that he hardly recognized it anymore. What is 'now,' what is 'then,' when is *any* of it?

"The TDA worked quite well. We learned that if there were any other time-shifting devices in the world, they weren't being used."

John was confused. "You said you were from ten years in the future."

Taylor smiled. "You were listening."

"What are you doing here *now*?"

"Going backward is beneficial, but going forward is critical. After studying the talisman for more than ten years, we concluded that the talisman did not have the capability to go forward. Something was missing. A command, a technique, or another piece. We decided to go back to the source. Back to the person who had it first."

"Me."

"You."

They stared at each other for a good thirty seconds that felt uncomfortably longer.

"Well?" Taylor asked.

"Well, what?"

Taylor raised his voice. "You piece of shit. Why must we do this *every* time?"

With his left hand, he reached into his jacket pocket and pulled out the revolver.

"Last time I had to threaten you to get you to hand over the talisman. Now I've got to threaten you to hand over information." He paused, drew a breath, held it, then exhaled slowly. "John, you died last time. This is your chance to live. You can go back and sweep floors at your school, shovel shit at the farm, run naked with small furry farm animals, whatever. It doesn't have to end the same way."

John had, until that moment, felt that he had a chance of escape. Now, the scale had tipped, and he felt powerless. Was this what had happened the first time?

Taylor smirked. "You see that I hold all the cards. Answer my questions and you live. You don't, you die. Again. This time, forever."

John froze and held his breath.

"And don't even think about jumping out of the car. You'll be dead before you step on the gravel."

John's head dropped and his voice lowered. He rubbed his forehead "What do you want to know?"

"Ah! That's what I was hoping to hear. Okay, first, where did you get the talisman? Be specific."

John didn't hesitate, there was no point. "On

Antigua. At the last place I was excavating. I don't recall the plot marker."

Taylor nodded. He knew that to be true, since he heard John tell Hannah something similar. "Very good. How do you go forward? Time-shift to the future?"

"I don't know," he answered, "I've only been able to go backward. Professor Rutherford told me the same thing."

Again, Taylor seemed pleased. "Excellent. That's what our group concluded too. You're doing fine. Now the question we've all been waiting for … what else was with it? Some instructions? Other artifacts? Another talisman?"

John shook his head. "Nothing, other than a skeleton."

"There must have been *something*. Whoever invented this thing wouldn't have just permitted one-way travel. Doesn't make sense. There has to be a way to go forward. It's only logical."

"Logic has nothing to do with it."

Without warning, Taylor swung his arm to the right and hit John square in the face with the side of the revolver. John's eyes watered from the sudden strike and blood began to flow from his nose. He reached up with both hands and cupped his face, which burned. His nose was broken, his palms wet with blood.

"You bastard!" John yelled through his fingers.

Taylor was calm but brusque. "I'm afraid you've only seen the beginning of what I can do if you don't change your story."

"I wouldn't help you now if my life depended on it."

Taylor grinned. "Oh, but your life *does* depend on it."

He pointed the pistol downward and shot John in the left calf. The discharge was deafening. John's ears rang, his whole skull hurt. But that discomfort was miniscule compared to the sharp, stabbing pain in his leg that rushed up his spine to his head. He let out a guttural scream and bent over to grab his leaking leg with both hands.

"You're banged up a little," Taylor told him calmly, "but you can still hobble out of this in one piece. You can make it back to town and get patched up."

Fueled by adrenaline and rage, John took a swing at Taylor, who anticipated the move and blocked the punch easily. It would be impossible to fight his way out of the situation. John had waited too long. He was losing strength by the second.

"What else was with the talisman when you found it?"

Grimacing from the hot pain in his leg that wouldn't dissipate, John said through clenched teeth, "Just a skeleton. Nothing else."

"Wrong answer." Taylor lowered the gun once more and fired into John's other leg, hitting him just above the ankle.

Above the booming crack of the gun discharging, John heard his tibia shatter. His eyes squeezed shut and he wailed.

"Now you have to rely on me to carry you out. I'd still be happy to do it. I really would. But you've got to give me something. Everything has a price. And the price of your life is useful information. So far, you've given me shit."

John was bleeding profusely from both legs. He knew that without proper medical attention—and soon—he would go into shock and pass out. The pain was excruciating. Even if it were possible to battle Taylor and win—unlikely now with his injuries—he couldn't drive himself out of the woods without great difficulty. Still, he knew he couldn't just sit there and wait to die in the car.

With trembling fingers wet with blood, he fumbled with the handle and opened the door. Almost immediately, he fell face-forward on the ground. It would have been a painful landing if he had felt it. His face and legs were numb.

With little more than sheer determination, John used his upper body strength to pull at the ground and extricate himself completely from the car. It took longer than he would have liked, but finally his limp legs flopped out. He wondered why Taylor didn't finish the job when he had the chance.

A moment later, he had his answer. The driver's door opened. Then, still trying to crawl away from the vehicle using only his arms, he heard the crunching sound of footsteps slowly approaching.

"Some things never change," Taylor said, now towering above him.

"I told you … the truth," John struggled to say, rolling onto his back, expecting the kill shot to come with every breath.

"Just like you told me the truth the first time

about not having the talisman? No, I'm afraid that I just can't trust you."

Calmly and methodically, Taylor stuck the pistol in his waistband and extracted the hypodermic needle from his jacket.

After removing the protective cap from the needle, he knelt down. "You don't look so good, friend."

"You're not my friend," John said, coughing out the blood dripping down the back of his throat.

"Arrogant to the end. Well, I'm going to help you anyway."

With one swift motion, he stuck the needle into John's left thigh and discharged the contents. "There. That will help the pain."

It did. The yellow liquid coursed quickly through John's body, alleviating all discomfort. He may have been bleeding from any of several sources, but he couldn't tell. He was calm, relaxed, and at peace, much like he might feel prior to surgery after being adequately anesthetized. He'd been injected with some sort of pain reliever, morphine perhaps. He felt like he'd just laid down to sleep but wasn't tired. He could still clearly hear the birds chirping and the river water lapping and gurgling as it flowed downstream, but the sounds were in slow motion. He blinked, but it seemed to take several seconds for his lids to make the journey.

"Can you hear me, friend?"

It was Taylor's voice. Muffled, labored. Sounding far away. Like a clouded dream.

"Hear … you."

He knew he'd been given a powerful drug. He

didn't care. If this was the end, he was thankful he wasn't going to be in pain when it happened.

"I've given you a sedative with a hit of sodium pentothal. Do you know what that is?"

John watched as drops of rain fell in slow motion from treetops. A few landed on his face.

"Truth … serum."

Taylor nodded. "Some people call it that."

John wanted to roll over, crawl away, put distance between him and Taylor, but his body wouldn't cooperate. All his muscles, although pain-free, were now lethargic.

"You know I'm trying to help you, right?"

John didn't want to answer. He just wanted to close his eyes and drift off to sleep or death, if that was what it had come to. Instead, he heard words leaving his numb lips. "Help … me."

"That's right. I'm trying to help you. I'll be honest, you're hurt pretty bad, John. But I can help you some more. Do you want me to help you?"

"Help … me."

"I will. Just answer one key, very important question. Can you hear me?"

"Hear … you."

"Good! Now John, was there anything else with the talisman when you found it?"

John could move his eyes, but little else. It was like being in a dream. Nothing seemed real. Even the injury to his legs and face seemed to have been part of an earlier dream. He no longer felt anger and hate. Not because he was all that forgiving of what Taylor had done. Rather, the drug fooled him into complacency.

There was one emotion he still felt, however, and he hung onto it for dear life. His feelings toward Hannah Miller. What a fool, he thought, to have let her slip through his fingers and out of his life. At a time when he needed her most, he turned his back on her. Things might have been much different if he had not been so hasty to sneak out of the dorm that last day. They would have faced Taylor and the challenge of what to do with the talisman together. Wasted days, he thought.

"John? Are you listening to me? Can you hear me?"

"Hear … you. Yes."

"Good. I'll ask you again. Was there anything else with the talisman? I need to know how to go *forward* into the future."

"Forward … future."

His patience was spent, but Taylor maintained his composure. It would help with the serum. They may have called it a truth serum, but it wasn't foolproof. The patient had to trust the person asking the questions. If they felt threatened, there could be resistance.

"Yes, forward. What do you know? Answer me, John. I want to get you help."

His life hadn't worked out the way that he thought it would, John realized. He didn't succeed on the family farm, much to his parents' disappointment. Didn't succeed at the University of Chicago. Didn't succeed as an archaeologist. Didn't succeed at George Washington Elementary School. Didn't succeed with Hannah Miller. And certainly didn't succeed at keeping the talisman out of the hands of someone who intends to use it for evil. Not that he expected everything to go his way in life, but to fail at *everything*?

The smell of damp leaves and soil filled the air. Raindrops fell gently from branches above him. Water rushed downstream in hushed tones. He closed his eyes. There was no reason to think that this wasn't his last few minutes on earth. If it was any consolation, he knew that he had always *tried* to do the right thing. If he was to be judged fairly in the afterlife, that should count for something.

A crow cawed in the distance. Another answered. He was reminded of a cartoon he'd seen once where an eagle was in an attack position, talons flared, ready to pounce upon a tiny mouse. The mouse, realizing that the end was inevitable, chose not to roll over and accept its end. Instead, it stood its ground and flipped its middle finger to the eagle. John smiled, or at least he thought he did, feeling very much like the mouse. With every ounce of physical and mental energy that he could muster, he fought the drug to leave this world like that mouse. If he couldn't live, he could at least inconvenience his killer.

"Talisman … bumps," he forced himself to lie. The words came out slurred and garbled. Blood and tears trickled over his dirt smeared cheeks.

Taylor leaned forward directly over John's face, his excitement building. "That's it, John. What about the talisman's bumps?"

"Talisman … bumps. Fit on … other half."

"Other half? What other half?"

John wanted to just close his eyes and go to sleep but fought the urge with what little energy he had left. "Other … half. With … holes."

Taylor was giddy. "Another half? The half that goes to the future."

"To … future. Fits … on top … of bumps."

"I knew it! I knew there had to be another piece! Where is it? Where is the second half?"

"Second … half."

Taylor bit his lip, growing impatient. He knew that John didn't have long before unconsciousness.

"Yes, yes, where is it?!"

John heard the words, but their meaning didn't register. Second half? Second half of *what*? His thoughts were fuzzy. Breathing was difficult. Pain was returning to his legs. Then he remembered. Taylor was grilling him for information about the talisman. There was no second half. He knew that for certain. It was all he could do not to spew out the truth. Instead, he drew from a reserve of strength he didn't even know he had to carry the charade through.

"Inside … cave. Other … half."

"You left it! Why in the world would you leave it?!"

John wanted to laugh but neither his cheeks nor vocal cords would have cooperated if he even had the strength to try.

"Professor … in hurry. Left."

Taylor sat back on his haunches. "I do remember that he pushed us to leave quickly. But why didn't you grab them both at the same time? It doesn't make sense."

John was exhausted. Between the sedative nature of the drug and the loss of blood, he had very little strength. He was starting to think about his grandparents, who had died when he was just a boy. Nana and Grandpaps. They were so loving, caring, gracious, and supportive. Rural people. The close-knit family type. There might be a chance to see them again. Also, the family dog. A border collie named Dutch who died when John was twelve. They would be there to greet him. All of them. He was sure of it. Wherever *there* was. And he would wait for his parents. Look after them while they are still living, if permitted. Hug them when they arrive.

"Why didn't you take it?" Taylor asked, forcefully.

"No … time. Professor … anxious."

"So it might still be there," Taylor muttered to himself.

"Still … there. Still … there."

Taylor stood up and looked down at John who was bleeding profusely. The gravel and fallen leaves glistened with crimson around him.

"That's exactly what I wanted to know. You've been a tremendous help to your country."

John knew what was next. He didn't have any hopes of emergency first aid, or a hurried ride to the nearest hospital. It was difficult to keep his eyes open, and he couldn't move. His arms were useless. Looking straight up through the treetops, he could see the clouds breaking up and blue sky peeking through. It was going to be a lovely day. He smelled the fresh scent of pine wafting on a gentle breeze. Birds were chirping in the trees. And, best of all, he thought he heard Dutch barking in the distance.

John watched as Taylor moved closer, directly above him, blocking his view of the opening sky and covering him in shadow. Three feet above his head was the Smith & Wesson revolver that Professor Rutherford had given him for protection.

He never heard the final shot.

35

TAYLOR HAD NO INTENTION of returning the Corvette. The first time that he had returned to this timeline, he had rented a nondescript sedan and killed John inside the car. Shot him in the head. Blood everywhere. A messy scene. The fact that John crawled out this time was an interesting twist, but it didn't matter. The end result was the same.

Eventually, the Army Corps of Engineers would come out to survey the erosion of the shore. Only then would they discover the abandoned Corvette and John Shaw's body, or what was left of it after the critters of the woods were done with it. Since he had used a phony ID to rent the car, there would be nothing to tie Taylor Jennings to the vehicle or the crime. It would just be one of those unresolved crimes that every small town seemed to have in the books. Perfect.

Standing next to the bluff overlooking the

Mississippi River, Taylor removed the talisman from his pants pocket. He didn't want to waste any more time. He'd spent more time in Moline than he wanted and was anxious to get on with it. His plan was simple: time-shift back to Antigua, get to the cave, snatch the other half of the talisman from the partially excavated hole, assemble the two pieces, and time-shift forward to his own timeline and resume his life as a physics god.

The cocktail of sodium pentothal and morphine had worked like a charm. Taylor was glad that one of the scientists back at the agency had thought of it. Foolishly, he had killed Shaw the first time before bothering to ask how the talisman worked or whether it had any limitations.

After the Department of Defense concluded that the talisman was flawed, or else had an integral part missing, they became convinced that Shaw was the key to the mystery. Someone had to go back, and Taylor knew that it had to be him alone. He trusted no one when it came to handling the talisman.

Shaw had been very helpful. Not only did he give up the talisman, but this time he gave up the truth. There *was* another component to this time travel device. But Shaw was too stupid to grab it when he had the chance. Just following orders. When has anything productive been gained by following orders? It figures that a country bumpkin would be more concerned with impressing a professor than with doing what needed to be done. He *deserved* to die for his misguided loyalty.

Enough waiting around, Taylor thought. There was an artifact to gather and then get on with life. The Department of Defense trusted him to use the talisman to go back in time, secure any other components, and return as quickly as possible. Along with this level of trust came a high degree of respect. He fantasized about how they would treat him when he returned. The secretary of defense would certainly shower him with accolades and financial rewards. The president would want to meet him, possibly offering up a cabinet position. Promotions, responsibilities, and authority would all be bestowed upon him. He would be one of the most influential men in government. A member of the inner circle.

Suddenly it occurred to him. One of the most influential men in government? One of the inner circle? What was he thinking?! With only half of the talisman he was already a powerful man in charge of a top-secret defense committee. With a totally functional time travel device, he could easily be *the* most influential man in government and *in control* of the inner circle.

Of course! He'd been setting his sights too low. Willing to accept too little. Knowledge of time-shifting gained him access to the most important people in government. Ownership of the talisman gained him power and authority. Possession of the enhanced forward and reverse talisman would make him god-like. He wouldn't need to head some committee or department. He wouldn't need to abide by any rules, laws, or authoritative body. With an all-powerful time travel device *he* could make the rules, the laws, and direct the authoritative bodies.

It took a while, but he finally got it. He who controls time, controls the world. And with a fully functional time travel device, there was absolutely no reason why *he* shouldn't be that person!

It was time to go.

He wiped his fingerprints off the Smith & Wesson and dropped it next to Shaw's body. It had proven its worth, but he wouldn't need it where he was going.

Removing the talisman from his pocket, he held it in front of him. He didn't need to fumble with it or figure out how to make it work. He'd used it before.

Holding it sideways with both hands, he carefully twisted the halves. The movement was measured in minuscule increments, so twisting too much would send him further back than he needed, and twisting too little wouldn't send him back far enough. Another idiot design feature, he thought. The designer should have put little marks on the disk to indicate how far you wanted to travel. Oh well, it was what it was.

The river and trees before him faded to black, and he felt a slight sensation of lightheadedness. The rushing water, birds, and crickets all fell silent.

As quickly as the world had gone dark, it suddenly became visible again.

He was standing in the middle of the grassy commons area of the University of Chicago. The sun was shining, and he was wearing a burgundy-colored graduation gown. In one hand he held a black leather-bound diploma with the UChicago insignia stamped in gold, and in the other he held the talisman. Hannah Miller was standing next to him, wearing a white graduation gown and holding her own diploma. Two hundred graduating seniors and their parents were milling around the area, talking, laughing, and congratulating each other.

"Quite the occasion," Hannah said, looking over

the crowd.

Taylor nodded, still getting his bearings after having just shifted from the deep woods outside Moline, several months in the future.

Noticing that he was quiet after delivering an eloquent valedictory speech at the commencement, she asked, "You all right? You don't look so good."

He nodded again. "Fine."

"Too bad that John Shaw couldn't be here."

"Yeah, too bad."

"I wonder what ever happened to him."

Taylor smiled. He knew exactly what happened to Shaw. He was lying dead in the forest at this very moment, a bullet in his head. Well, actually, he *will* be once the current timeline catches up.

"Well, you know what's next, don't you?" she asked.

He hoped he knew the answer, but of course he didn't dare say.

"What?"

"Our future, silly."

"Our future," he repeated. "Of course."

"Now that we're out of school, we'll have to start planning … ."

"Hold that thought, okay?" He looked around. Students, parents, and faculty were milling everywhere. He hadn't gone back far enough and had to find an opportunity to shift again.

"After the graduation party at my parents' house we should talk about setting the date … ."

Taylor looked at her sternly. "Can you wait a

minute? Please!"

On top of trying to straighten out the timeline and take a controlling interest in it, he had Hannah bugging him about their future together. If all went well, they wouldn't have one. In the original timeline, he had smooth-talked her, hoping she would give up information about Shaw or the talisman, neither of which she did.

Nevertheless, she was a catch. Drop-dead gorgeous, smart, and her family had money. A trifecta. He could have done worse, so he stayed with her. But he had no sincere feelings for her. Now, with the opportunity to course his way through the future any way he wanted, he wasn't so sure he wanted to be tied to any one person. He would be the most powerful person on the planet. A deity. In the next timeline, she would only slow him down.

Anxious to shift further back, he didn't wait until he was alone. He tossed the diploma on the ground and grasped the talisman with both hands.

"What are you doing?" Hannah asked. Then, noticing the object in his hand, "What's that?"

Taylor didn't bother answering. There was no need. He expected to be long gone before the words ever left his lips.

Although she had never seen it before, it looked like the object that John had described in Professor Rutherford's office a couple of years earlier. Her smile disappeared as she stared at it. "That looks like the … ."

Before she could finish her sentence, everything faded to black. Everyone milling around the area disappeared. All sounds were swallowed up in the silence.

Taylor felt lightheaded and slightly nauseous but wasn't concerned. He knew he was shifting.

Then, as if opening his eyes, a new set of images came into view. He was sitting in the university auditorium, three rows from the front, with Hannah sitting next to him. He looked around the room. They were in their history class, but the instructor wasn't there. Class hadn't yet begun.

" … the weirdest thing," Hannah was saying, "but he wasn't there when I went to check on him. Today he's not in class. I'm worried. Come with me after class and let's go look for him."

He realized that she was referring to John having gone missing after the professor's death. She and Shaw had met in the lab, discussed the talisman, and now he was nowhere to be found. In the original timeline, Taylor had jumped at the chance to spend time with her. It was to be the beginning of their relationship. In *this* timeline, however, he didn't have the time or the desire to start something up with her. He was on a quest for something bigger and more important than a bedroom romp or a romantic commitment.

He looked over, seeing the look of concern and love on her face. But her expression was not a reflection of her feelings for *him*. Even though she would marry him eventually, he wondered if he had ever truly possessed her heart. He dismissed the self-pity as irrelevant. In a nanosecond, she was going to be history.

"Are you okay?" she asked. "You look … different. Older."

"Didn't get much sleep last night," he lied. She

bought it.

"Me either. I'm worried about him," she repeated.

"I heard you the first time," he said sharply, keeping his voice low.

She leaned toward him. "So, are we going to go look for him?"

"Not this time."

Hannah tilted her head slightly. She was confused.

He lifted the talisman, not caring that he might be seen. Careful not to twist too much, he turned the halves ever so slightly. He didn't want to go back further than absolutely necessary.

The room went completely black and deeply silent. He felt the familiar feeling of vertigo, which he recognized immediately.

The next moment he felt hot sun on the back of his neck. He was kneeling on the ground inside a stringed-off area of gravel and sand. He was wearing the same clothes that he wore while on Antigua in the original timeline. Looking around, he saw his archaeological research colleagues, Harrison to the left and Louis to the right. They were kneeling in their own stringed-off areas.

He was back.

36

THE SUN WAS SETTING. Orange lit up the horizon, flickering on the ocean waves. It was late in the day.

He didn't know exactly *when* Shaw and the professor found the talisman, but the group hadn't yet left the island, so there was still time to retrieve it.

The temperature was in the nineties, the humidity thick. Taylor's clothes stuck to him and smelled. His skin felt gritty. He stood up and wiped his face and neck with a handkerchief. It felt like sandpaper.

He shot a glance down at his free hand for reassurance that he still had the talisman. He sighed with relief knowing that it had not somehow gotten lost in the shift.

Professor Rutherford was off talking to Shaw and pointing to an area at the far end of their assigned dig area. It was at the base of a sloping ascent that was covered in rocks and plant growth.

"Try here," he faintly heard the professor say.

Good, they hadn't found it yet.

Suddenly, Taylor had a terrible thought. If Shaw and Rutherford uncover the talisman, what happens to the one that he currently held in his hand? Would there be two of the same talisman disks? Unlikely, since there was only ever one. More likely, from his understanding of physics, the one that he currently had would disappear because now it only existed in *this* particular timeline. He wasn't sure *what* would happen, but he didn't want to chance being without it.

The solution, he realized, was to go back further. *Before* Shaw and Rutherford found the talisman. That way, if the one he currently held disappeared, he'd still find the original one in the cave.

Quickly, he dialed the talisman. As expected, the world went dark and silent.

When visibility returned, Taylor was surprised to see that he was not back at the university before their trip, but still on Antigua. The students were gone, and the stringed off areas were flat and untouched. To the east, where the tents had been staked, was just flat ground.

All along, every time that he had shifted, he followed his own timeline backward. From the Department of Defense laboratories to Moline. From the University of Chicago graduation ceremonies to inside a classroom. Then, to the archaeological dig on Antigua. In each case, he was always retracing his own timeline. This latest step backward should have landed him sometime earlier in his life; at the university, or maybe still in high school.

It hadn't. Something wasn't right.

His heart raced. Perhaps it was just some weird anomaly. Nothing to worry about. He twisted the talisman again hoping to land back on his previously lived timeline.

Darkness. Silence.

After a moment, the familiar feeling of light-headedness dissipated, but the complete darkness did not. Wind was blowing through the trees, crickets chirped, and waves lapped on a rocky shore. Because of the noises, he knew that he was done shifting, but where he was and why he wasn't able to see anything was a mystery.

After a few seconds of disorientation, Taylor realized that it must be the dead of night. He crouched down and ran his fingers along the ground. Loose gravel and sand. Slowly, his eyes became accustomed to the blackness. Up ahead, about a hundred and fifty yards, there was a glowing pinpoint of flickering yellowish light.

The waning crescent moon provided very little light. Barely able to see more than a couple of yards ahead, he made his way toward the flickering light. It was emanating from a kerosene lantern that hung from a pole attached to the back end of a wooden wagon, reminiscent of those used at the turn of the century. Several horses tied up next to each other sensed his approach and began to whinny. Further along were two wagons loaded with crates, pickaxes, shovels, brooms, and other rudimentary mining equipment sticking out of them.

Suddenly, he heard the clicking bolt action of a rifle somewhere in the darkness near the wagons.

"Who's there?" a husky voice called. "Identify yourself or be sayin' your prayers!"

Two more flickering lights appeared, closer to ground level and dimmer than the one by the wagon, likely from lanterns inside two canvas tents that he hadn't noticed in the dark. The occupants of the tent scurried outside to see what the commotion was about.

The man with the rifle fired, but with it being dark, Taylor was a difficult target. The shooter may have thought that it was just an animal that happened upon their area, but he didn't care. Animal or robber, they were both a threat.

Taylor wasn't going to take a chance that the man would draw a bead on him, so he took off running in the direction from which he just came. Nearly blind in the darkness and unsure of his footing, he tripped on the uneven surface, likely the beginning of an excavated area, and fell face down. His forehead hit something hard, a rock or shovel head. He got to his knees as a stream of wetness cascaded over the bridge of his nose and past his cheek. He was bleeding, but that wasn't the worst of it. He had dropped the talisman.

Desperate, panting, and starting to panic, Taylor swept the gravel with both hands. The need to hold the gold disk again was so intense that it might be compared to a drug user trying to find a syringe on the first day of detox. Feeling around, he confirmed that he had, in fact, fallen into a shallow excavation site. He even felt the string that had tripped him up.

"Damn archaeologists," he muttered, wishing that he hadn't deliberately dropped Shaw's pistol at the scene of the crime back in Moline.

Another shot rang out behind him. The people in the tents were now out and moving quickly toward him with their lanterns.

Just when he was about to call out to the men to try and explain his presence—hard as that might be— or more likely, beg for mercy, the fingertips of his hand brushed against something larger and smoother than the fistful of gravel he'd been pawing at. His hand wrapped around the talisman disk and he pulled it to his chest like a long-lost family heirloom.

Clutching the talisman with both hands, he stood and tried to make a run for it. He wasn't sure where he was—or when—and would have preferred to get his bearings before shifting again, but he wouldn't have that luxury. After taking only a step or two, another shot rang out. Unlike the other bullets that pierced the darkness and nothing more, this one found its mark.

The bullet caught him in the right shoulder, and it felt like he'd been hit with a baseball bat. The pain was local, burning, and intense. Had it been a shotgun blast, he may have died right then and there.

He dropped to his knees, knowing that without medical attention, he'd likely bleed to death. With three people chasing him in unfamiliar territory, at least one of them with a gun, he felt his only hope of survival was to shift out of that timeline.

His right arm was almost completely numb. The talisman felt heavy, and he was afraid of dropping it, so he supported it with his left. With all the reserve strength he could muster, he tried twisting it. Yet with very little strength in his right hand, he couldn't get the sections to move. He attempted to twist it again, but his fingertips were wet from blood that had run down from his shoulder, and they just slid along the edges. After wiping his right hand on his shirt, he tried one more time. Nothing.

"There he is!" a man with a gruff voice yelled from behind.

"Hold him 'til I get there!" another called from further back.

Time was running out—they were closing in. Trying for what would likely be the very last time, Taylor squeezed the talisman edges with all his might until his fingers ached. He gave it a good twist. He didn't know if it turned enough, or even at all. He had to make sure he shifted before the men got there. With no weapon, he was a sitting duck, and there was no way that he was going to give up the talisman.

The world became a thick, inky shroud. He was dizzy, and he felt nauseous. The symptoms were worse than the other times that he had shifted, but neither his forehead nor shoulder hurt any longer, and that was a relief.

Suddenly it was light out, and the world once again revealed itself. Midday, perhaps. He quickly looked back. No one was in pursuit. He shook his head, confused. He couldn't understand why he was not traveling backward through his own timeline: college, high school, elementary school, childhood. For some reason, he was shifting on a path unknown to him.

Ordinarily, Taylor didn't frighten easily. Even

when the guy with the rifle was shooting at him, he was concerned, but not frightened. Traveling a different, previously uncharted, timeline, however, was terrifying. The thought made his skin crawl.

There was no sign of the men, their tents, or their wagons. He sighed. The fact that he was still on the island and not somewhere in Chicago at an earlier time of his life, however, was disturbing. How he hated time travel!

The ground was rocky and sandy. The landscape was generally flat until gradually sloping upward with more trees, jagged rocks, and thick shrubs. To the west, where the patch of sandy ground turned around a bend, the slope was at a greater incline. The groundcover was denser with larger and more numerous boulders. Further west and to the south, he could hear crashing waves. The air was muggy and his clothes clung. The smell of seaweed and stale sulfur filled the air. A swarm of pesky gnats wasted no time in greeting him by buzzing around his eyes and ears.

He recognized the sights, sounds, and smells as the area that he had excavated with Rutherford and his colleagues two years ago, but now it looked significantly different. Then, the area had been barren, devoid of beach grass and yucca. It was now covered with wild plants. The ground where he stood was relatively level, more so than he remembered. There were no stakes, string lines, or other cast-off supplies usually left by forgetful or careless archaeologists. Groves of trees crowded the sloping hills behind him. The area seemed untouched.

The sun was nearly overhead, around noon he guessed. The heat seared his face and neck. Much too warm for a suit and tie. With a jolt, Taylor realized he was wearing the clothes that he had been wearing when he killed John Shaw in the Moline woods, not the work clothes he wore when he was on the group dig with Rutherford and the others. Probably because he hadn't lived through this timeline before. It was as good a guess as any. He shrugged off the jacket, threw it over his shoulder, and loosened the tie.

The tree line became denser as the path wound inland. It was the direction back to Saint William, the port where they had gotten their gear for the dig. Only now, the path looked overgrown and dangerous. To the west, where the path narrowed and rounded a bend, the area was rocky and nearly covered in thick plant growth. To the south, a fair distance beyond the area where they had dug as a group, the ground sloped gently downward toward the rocky shore of the ocean with thorny blackberry bushes, various cacti, and creeping buttercup with yellow flowers. Traveling in that direction would be difficult if not impossible. To the north, the ground sloped upward. Not a severe incline but undoubtedly difficult with loose gravel underfoot all the way to the top, some two hundred yards to the crest.

None of the directions looked particularly appealing, but Taylor couldn't stay where he was. He needed food, water, shelter, and a way back to Chicago. The sooner the better.

Damn that Shaw for dragging him into this time travel crap! He vowed that if he got a chance to kill Shaw again, he'd make sure to torture the bastard first in retaliation for this detour.

Wiping the sweat off his brow, he headed in the only logical direction—east, toward Saint William and civilization.

He had only gotten a few hundred yards before the flat sandy ground morphed into a forest of trees and thick brambles. If there had ever been a path through there, it had long been overgrown. He tried to traverse it anyway, hoping that it would open up and lead directly into Saint William.

After walking for an hour, Taylor stopped and sat on a fallen tree to rest and assess the situation. It didn't seem like he'd gotten very far. The path had never appeared, and the woods looked even denser in the direction he was headed. At this rate, by the time he got to Saint William, if he got there at all, it would be long past dark. And who knows what animals lurked in the woods, waiting for some unsuspecting sap to come wandering through.

This was stupid. He knew that if he were to try to trek through an unknown forest, he would have to get an earlier start. And if he were to even hope to get back to the clearing where he started from, he had to go back before he was so completely turned around that he couldn't find the return route.

Taylor stood and started back the way that he'd come. *Damn that Shaw!*

An hour later, after stepping over rocks, surface roots, and fallen tree branches, the sky was once again visible through the thick canopy. A slight breeze cooled his face and cheered him slightly. At least he wouldn't be stuck in the middle of some woods in the dark of night.

He emerged from the woods into the familiar flat and sandy area where he had first arrived. The sun was more than halfway to the horizon. It was the right decision to return. There was no way that he would have made it to Saint William with no transportation and no path.

Taylor gazed up the slope, searching for any signs of civilization. Perhaps at the crest he could see if there was a better path, or *any* path for that matter.

He started up the incline. It was gradual at first. A modest ten percent grade, then sloping more dramatically. It was like climbing a staircase one stair at a time, and then two, and then three. His thighs and calves ached from having trekked fruitlessly through the woods.

Each step was now more taxing than the last. He panted, trying to catch his breath as he pushed himself onward, trying to get to the top of the hill. It was a cruel reminder that he wasn't in as good of shape as he thought. The loose gravel and rock prevented a good foothold, making the climb all the more difficult. Several times, he lost his footing and fell to his knees. He didn't dare look, but he was sure that they were skinned raw.

It took a good hour to climb to the top of the hill, past the trees and around the boulders and bushes. Once at the top he bent over, resting his hands on top of his sore knees. Looking out over the hills and valleys that unfolded before him, there was nothing but trees, bushes, and dense groundcover plants. The area was blanketed with various hues of green, along with intermittent patches of white, red, and yellow from wild flora.

In the distance, where Saint William should have been, was just dense forest extending all the way to the opposite shore. The shops, the café, the marina, the smattering of modest tin-roofed, multicolored homes were all gone. Where there should be docks, boats, and a fair-sized village was just a thin line of empty beach.

Turning around to get a panoramic view, he saw no signs of civilization in any direction. He was on Antigua all right. He recognized the shape of the island.

"Hello!" he yelled. "Is there anyone out there?! Can anyone *hear* me?!"

No answer. The only response was a few birds squawking their displeasure at having been disturbed. Taylor's frustration from trudging through the trees and up the hill quickly turned to hopelessness. He lowered himself to the ground, sitting on a grassy patch, and shook his head. The talisman had sent him back to Antigua before it had been inhabited. How long ago was that? A few hundred years? A thousand or more? It was hard to believe that the situation could have gotten any worse. He didn't have a clue what to do next.

Pulling up his pant legs, he examined his bruised knees. As expected, they were scraped raw and oozing blood. They weren't serious injuries, just annoying. Still, it would be nice to get some antiseptic and gauze bandages. If only he wasn't stuck on some fucking island!

The sun began to set. He still had no food, water, or shelter. There was, however, one thing that he *did* have—the talisman. He felt it through the fabric of his pants. It was reassuring to still be in possession of it, despite the fact that it was precisely the reason he was in this predicament in the first place. It might not be much, but it was still his best hope of getting home.

As he examined it in his hands, careful not to twist the sides, Taylor watched the sunlight accentuate the different-sized bumps on one side. He pictured the other half, the missing component Shaw confessed to, fitting on top. But how did the talisman make time-shifting possible? And why had it brought him *here* of all places?

For a long moment, he debated with himself whether his situation was dire enough to time-shift again and take his chances. Ideally, he would be able to travel in the opposite direction and just go home, but the stupid thing didn't permit that. Not yet anyway.

His feeling of hopelessness morphed into fury at the thought of being stranded on Antigua. He had to fight the urge to throw the damned thing deep into the woods as punishment for sending him there. Common sense prevailed, and the feeling passed. Like it or not, the talisman was a lifeline.

A new thought occurred to him. What if the talisman had sent him to the island not because it followed the timeline of *his* life, but the timeline of its own? Of course! That made sense. It came from the island originally, and when he shifted, that's where they returned. Which could only mean one thing—that the other half had to still be in the cave. If it was, he had a ticket home!

Undeterred by his utter fatigue, Taylor jumped up, shoving the talisman back into his pocket. He started back down the hill. The gravel beneath his feet gave way and he fell down several times, but he didn't care.

He now had something that he thought had been lost to him—hope.

Sweat poured off his head. The heat and humidity had irritated him all the way up the hill, but he hardly noticed them on the way down.

When he reached the bottom of the hill, the sun was near the horizon. The temperature had cooled a degree or two. It would be dark soon. His goal was to find the other half of the talisman and be home for dinner. His heart pounded, now more from anticipation than stress or exhaustion.

Taylor hurried as fast as he could to where they had dug a few months ago … or really, years *from* now. He would have run if his aching legs would have allowed. It was all he could do to walk quickly.

When he was fairly certain he was standing at his original dig site, he looked up and down the sandy flat. The path bent to the west, where Shaw said that Rutherford told him to dig and where they had found the talisman.

He walked around the bend, just beyond where the rest of the group would have been digging. At the base of the hill, where the ground leveled out, was a thick clump of shrubs and thorny blackberry vines surrounded by large boulders and slabs of rock. The vines looked to be growing right out of solid stone.

The patch of flat sand faded away past that, disappearing into thick woods. A lot had changed on the island since the last time he was there. While it was possible that the cave Shaw had referred to was further on, Taylor had a feeling that it was close. At least he hoped it was. He wasn't looking forward to scrounging for food or spending one more minute on the island than was absolutely necessary.

Using both hands, he started pulling vines away from the rock surface. The thorns on the vines snagged his sleeves and tore his fingers. He jerked his hands back, cursing his stupidity. Now, using his jacket to protect his hands, he pulled the vines aside.

He was elated to confirm that it was not solid rock underneath. Instead, the vines and foliage had hidden a recessed area in the hillside. A natural rock formation creating a small underground cave.

He wished that he had a flashlight, a lantern, or even a lighter, but he was inadequately prepared for spelunking. He pulled more vines aside. Doing so permitted just enough waning sunlight into the hollow. What he thought was a 'cave' was nothing more than a shallow depression in the rock. Barely three or four feet deep and five or six feet wide, best that he could tell. It *had* to be the area where the talisman was found.

Taylor stepped cautiously through the narrow opening. Immediately, he began feeling around the sandy bottom. His hands were still sensitive from the thorn pricks. The gritty sand and pebbles irritated the raw skin, but he ignored the pain.

He expected to feel the other half of the talisman at any moment or, at the very least, the skeleton that had been there. He felt neither. Just sand, gravel, moss, and small twigs.

If there *had* been anything there, it was long gone. A feeling of dread enveloped him. But then he had a thought. He had gone backward in time. Either the talisman halves weren't there yet, or this wasn't the right spot.

Darkness was covering the island. If this wasn't the right cave, he would have to go looking for it at first light. If this *was* the correct hole, there was no way of knowing how long he would have to wait before the talisman halves would be deposited there. It could be days, years, or decades. His heart sank.

Survival on a deserted island was going to be difficult. Escape even more so. With no knowledge of raft building, fire starting, hunting, or any other skills necessary for life in the wilderness, he knew that his chances of long-term survival were dismal.

As he sat in the hole contemplating his dire situation and options, the sun set completely. Darkness swallowed the island. Using his jacket for protection again, he pulled the blackberry vines back across the mouth of the cave. He would worry about food and escape tomorrow, but tonight, at least, he was safe and had shelter from the elements.

Reclined in the dark recess of the shallow cave, simmering in a stew of depression, self-pity, and fear, Taylor once again wished that he had kept the Smith & Wesson after shooting that worthless cow-kicker John Shaw. It would have come in handy to hunt for game, protect himself from predators, or to end his own life if it didn't seem like it was a life worth living. Damn his poor planning!

He contemplated whether to use the talisman to go even further back in time. Fear of the unknown kept him from trying. What would he find, dinosaurs? No thanks, he decided. Things were bad enough.

The temperature was dropping, the cave was damp and musty, and he began to shiver. He knew it would be a long and uncomfortable night.

Curled up on his side, his knees to his chest, Taylor fell asleep clutching the talisman. He didn't feel the warm tears roll over his cheeks or hear them hit the soft soil beneath him. Nor did he hear the venomous fer-de-lance slither through the blackberry bush and into the hole.

The bite was quick and painful. No one heard him scream.

37

FOR THE NINTH EVENING IN A ROW, it was hot, muggy, and he couldn't sleep. The wind was blowing, but it didn't help much to cool off an otherwise sweltering day. Every evening on the island was the same. The wind beat against the small tent sides, shaking the poles and keeping him awake. Just one more day, and they could go home. John Shaw couldn't wait.

It wasn't that he didn't enjoy the opportunity to go on an actual archaeological dig with Professor Rutherford, it was just that he hadn't expected it to be so tiring and fruitless. After spending day after day on his side or stomach scratching away at the soil, he could have used a good night's sleep. It was only wishful thinking.

It didn't help that they had come up empty-handed thus far. Traveling all the way from Chicago to the island of Antigua was a hardship by itself. The frustration of not having much to show for it just exacerbated the situation.

John sat up, swinging his legs over the edge of the cot. Sleep was not coming any time soon. The wind caused the canvas to beat out an erratic rhythm on the tent poles. It was unnerving the first few nights, but he'd become accustomed to it. Now, it was almost melodic. Still, he sat there trembling. He was anxious to go home, it's true, but he had a sense of impending … something. Something he couldn't explain.

He reached over and grabbed his canteen. He took a sip and swished the water around his mouth. It was warm but moistened his lips and throat.

He sat there thinking. Besides being the last day on the island, it felt like it would be significant for another reason, although he had no idea what that might be. Perhaps they would make a significant discovery. Frankly, even a *small* one would make them all feel productive. Perhaps that would explain his feeling of anxiousness. Or not.

It would be more than a half hour before he felt relaxed enough to lie back down to try and sleep.

38

SUNRISE. ALL FIVE RESEARCH ASSISTANTS—
John Shaw, Louis Hectle, Harrison Bennett, Hannah
Miller, and Taylor Jennings—awoke with the clanging
sound of Professor Rutherford beating a ladle on a steel
pan.

"Up and out, people!" the professor shouted. "Up
and out. A quick breakfast before we attack our destiny.
There are worlds to discover. Secrets to reveal. Let's
look sharp!"

John smiled and dressed quickly. He admired the
professor's optimism. It was refreshing, especially after
his restless night. Perhaps there might be a reason to
celebrate after all.

After finishing breakfast, the students half-heartedly
carried their picks and brushes to their respective dig areas.
If the day was anything like the others, there wouldn't
be much to celebrate. It hardly seemed worth the effort.

They were mentally taxed and ready to call it quits. It was a long journey home.

Rutherford sidled up to John. "Come with me," he said quietly.

"Yes, sir."

John stood, grabbed his tools, and walked toward the dig areas. Without realizing it, his gait slowed. He was suddenly awash with a strong feeling of déjà vu. Taken the *same* steps. Said the *same* words. Felt the *same* way. The hair on the back of his neck rose as he tried to shake off the unsettling feeling.

John stopped before getting to the bend in the path. He didn't know why. His stomach knotted up and every synapse was firing, telling him not to go further. His mind was so entangled with his internal debate that he hadn't heard Hannah Miller come up behind him.

"John, what's wrong?" she asked.

John spun around.

"You don't look so good."

Taylor, overhearing, piped in, "He can't help it, that's the way he always looks!"

John looked at Hannah. The concern on her face was evident and sincere. Then, he looked past her to Taylor, bent over his own dig area, laughing at his perceived wit.

"What is it?" Hannah asked. She put her hand on John's arm, ready to steady him if he was suffering from heat exhaustion, a common condition that the professor had warned them about many times.

"Something about Taylor," he said softly.

"I know. He's kind of a jerk."

John shook his head. "No, it's something else. As if … ."

He stopped. There were no words to describe what he felt because he didn't know *how* he felt. If there *were* words, however, he was certainly willing to say them to *her*.

Other than the professor, Hannah was the only person he truly respected in the group. She was one of few people he knew who was always kind and sincere. She had an honest, caring, loving side that had shown through no matter the place or situation. They had classes together, but they had never really spent much time talking to each other. Never in depth, anyway. John was shy, and she always seemed … out of his league.

Now, standing on the sandy excavation site of Antigua, reaching out to him, she seemed approachable. Over the past year, he'd spent too much time thinking about why she *wouldn't* be interested in him and far too little time thinking that she may. He didn't want to let another opportunity pass by.

"Hannah, I've been thinking. When we get back, I would very much like to have dinner with you."

She smiled. Without hesitation she answered, "That would be nice."

"Coming, young Shaw?" the professor called from around the bend.

John looked toward where the professor had gone and then back to Hannah. He would have rather stayed right there, continuing their conversation, but he had an obligation.

Just as he was about to leave, he asked, "Does

anything seem … different to you?"

It was an odd question, she thought. The fact that John took a bold step to ask her out to dinner was different. Somehow, she suspected, that wasn't what he meant.

"Different? How?"

He shook his head, feeling foolish. "I don't know. It's weird. It feels like we've … ." Then he stopped.

"We've what?"

Looking her straight in the eye, he continued. "Like we've done this before."

The professor called out, "Shaw!"

He turned and ran to catch up with the professor, who was quickly losing his patience. When John rounded the bend, he wasn't at all surprised to see the professor surveying the area at the base of the hill. He was holding his hat and wiping his face with a handkerchief. John expected as much.

"I have a feeling. Let's try here," the professor said.

Ordinarily, John would never question the professor's decisions, but the tingle on the back of his neck signaled danger. It wasn't rational, but just like the ominous feeling of entering a dark alley in the dead of night, he felt that something threatening was lurking.

"Right in this area," the professor said, sweeping his arm in a wide arc.

"Why here?" John asked politely. "Why now?"

Rutherford put his hat back on. "Just a feeling," he said, smiling. "That's all."

John decided not to try and convince the professor that *his* feeling was the one to follow. He could offer nothing substantial to back it up. Nevertheless, danger was imminent. He was sure of it.

The professor hurried off to check on the others. John immediately began to stake and run a string line. For the rest of the day, he scraped away inches of compacted sandy soil and brushed away everything he loosened. With every pick of his hammer, he expected to make a discovery. Not because the professor had a 'feeling' that they would. He *knew* that he would.

Other than short snack breaks, and occasional sips of water, John worked tirelessly at his plot. The professor checked on him occasionally but spent most of his time supervising and assisting the others. John had a feeling that for some reason the professor did not want to draw undue attention to the new dig area.

Late in the afternoon, alone and out of sight of the others, John took a break and leaned back on his heels. Wiping his face with his hanky, he stared straight ahead at the sloping hillside in front of him. A sense of déjà vu or impending danger or whatever it was rang out like church bells at high noon. Whatever danger was to befall him was, somehow, intrinsically linked to that hillside.

He stood and looked down the path. No one was coming. He turned his attention from the dig at ground level and started to scrape away some of the soil at the base of the hill where it rose from the flat. The gravel and sand started to fall away from where he scraped, some of it inward. His hands began to tremble.

With minimal effort, the blade of the shovel pushed into the soil at the base of the hill. Checking over his shoulder to make sure that he was still alone, John started pulling material away. There was an opening. The more he pulled, the larger the opening became. It was a miniature cave that had been covered up by plant growth and gravel that had cascaded from up the hill.

For a reason he couldn't explain, he knew it would be there. Even more surprising was that he knew it wouldn't be empty.

The sun was setting. Long shadows covered the dig area. The professor would certainly be back soon to check on his progress. He had to hurry.

Just enough remaining sunlight pierced the surface opening to show a glint of something at the bottom of the hole. Although the reflective object appeared to be only coin-sized, he suspected that it was larger and partially buried. He drew a deep breath. He felt a mixed sense of relief and trepidation. *Relief* that at last there seemed to be an actual object of which to be afraid. *Trepidation* because the fear remained.

Along with the object was a human skeleton, slightly covered with sand and browning from age. Like the object, he had expected it to be there.

He crouched. This was just the sort of discovery to make the trip worthwhile. Yet, he had a strong feeling that the object should never be revealed. It was as if he had uncovered a cursed tablet of an ancient pharaoh inside a sacred tomb. This was no tablet, however. It was no tomb. And he was fairly certain that the skeleton was not some pharaoh. Nevertheless, the object seemed just as cursed. John knew what he had to do.

Minutes later, Professor Rutherford came around the bend to check on John's progress. He was still hopeful, but time was running out.

"Any luck, young Shaw?" he asked, before noticing that the boy was not in the designated dig area. "What the … ?"

He looked down the path and back again. Nothing. The sound of tumbling gravel drew his attention up the hillside. There, about twenty feet up, was John. The boy was struggling to climb the steep gravel embankment and not making very much progress. His feet were slipping out from under him, causing rock and sand to cascade down in waves. It looked to be deliberate—but he couldn't be sure.

The mini avalanche of loose gravel tumbling down the hill landed at the base of the hill, right in front of the new dig area where John was supposed to be working.

"Shaw! What the blazes are you doing up there? Have you lost your mind? Come down here!"

John heard the professor's command but continued to stamp his feet on the gravel. Another wave of aggregate tumbled down.

"Did you hear me, Shaw? Come down here at once!"

This time, John did not hesitate. Turning, he slid on his backside for the remainder of the descent, bringing a wave of loose rock with him. When he reached the bottom of the hill, the professor grabbed him by the shoulder.

"What in in the world were you doing up there, boy?"

"Professor," John tried to explain. "There's

something wrong here. Something that shouldn't be. I can't explain. I just know that … ."

Before he could continue, Rutherford noticed that some of the rock and gravel that had slid down the hill was now disappearing at the base. He watched for a moment and saw a hole appear. He'd come just in time. A minute or two later and the rockslide would have filled up the hole and he would never have known that it was there.

"What have we here?!" he asked. "Have we found something?"

John felt awful. If he had been a little faster, or had discovered the hole just a little sooner, he could have filled it in.

"Shovel," Rutherford demanded, his arm extended.

John handed the shovel and stepped back, waiting.

Using the shovel blade, Rutherford pulled material away from the opening. His smile grew with every inch further exposed. When the opening was about a yard wide, he leaned in, nearly falling headfirst into it. He then ran his fingers through the sand and gravel at the bottom of the hole.

For what seemed like an eternity, John waited for the professor to emerge. He wasn't sure how he would explain his actions of trying to cover up what he had discovered. He just knew it was the right thing to do.

Rutherford pushed himself out of the hole. He brushed the sand off his hands and stood up.

"Well, that was disappointing," he said.

"Professor?"

Rutherford took a deep breath. "I can't say that I

understand what you were doing, or why you were away from your post, but since it's the last day, I suppose I can't get too upset."

John was confused. "In the hole. You found … ."

"Nothing," Rutherford interrupted. "Not a damned thing."

Disappointed, the professor brushed himself off and started back toward the main dig area. "Give yourself another half hour. If you don't come up with anything, start breaking down. We have a long trip ahead of us tomorrow."

"Yes, sir."

John waited until the professor rounded the bend and was out of sight. He then jumped toward the opening of the hole and peered in. The skeleton was gone!

Thinking that the gravel he'd kicked down must have covered it up, he leaned into the hole and felt around for the remains. There weren't any. A human skeleton, brown with age, had been there minutes earlier. He was sure of it. Now, there wasn't so much as a knuckle.

He wondered if he was suffering from heat exhaustion, as Hannah probably suspected. Perhaps hallucinating. If he hadn't snatched the gold puck-like object from the hole and stuck it in his pocket before the professor arrived, he might have been convinced of that.

A half hour later, he removed the string line and pulled up the stakes. While the other students did the same for their areas, he packed his tools in one of the pickup trucks and went quickly to his tent. He wanted some time alone to examine the gold object and contemplate why he felt it necessary to keep it from the professor.

Something about the object indicated that it was best if no one knew about it. He sat on the edge of his cot. The hard wooden frame dug into the back of his legs, and he stared at the shiny object.

Maybe greed was the reason he wanted to keep this thing a secret. No, John decided, he had no interest in monetary gain. For the selfish satisfaction of the discovery then. No, he was a student on a quest for education and truth, nothing more. He would have been just as thrilled if any of his classmates had found something.

But this thing, this … talisman, was not just 'something,' it was something more. He just didn't know what. It felt like he *expected* to find it and that he should know what it was.

Talisman.

As he examined the gold puck, he rolled the word around in his head, then spoke it softly, "talisman." The name fit, although he couldn't fathom why.

It had weight to it. He wouldn't have been surprised if it was solid gold. Probably worth a lot of money, but John suspected there was more to it than that. The bumps on one side, for instance. They looked to have some meaning or purpose. Like it was half of a whole. Like there should be another piece, a piece with recessed bumps … .

Wait a minute, he thought, gazing away. Why did *that* seem familiar? Recessed bumps? A second half?

Odd that he should think that, but it seemed logical. Equally odd was the fact that the skeleton itself seemed familiar. As if he had seen it before or should know to whom the bones belonged.

His temples started to throb, and he shook his head. This was crazy thinking. As a student of archaeology, he was being trained to discover clues and assemble a picture. In this case, however, pictures were starting to come to him with very few clues. Whirlwind images flying around like a spinning centrifuge with scarcely enough detail to make any of them out. He didn't need to decipher them, however, to know that they were significant. They were trying to tell him something. Something that he should already know.

John's earlier feeling of danger had given way to something more sinister. Death. But whose? No doubt the person who is now a skeleton … or *was*, since the skeleton had mysteriously disappeared. Obviously. But it felt like the talisman was an integral piece to the puzzle. John remembered the way the skeleton had been clutching the thing.

"What's so special about you, little fella?" he asked softly, gazing at the talisman in his hand.

Another wave of familiarity washed over him. He'd heard those words before … or had *said* them.

The hair on the back of his neck stood up. This was no imaginary déjà vu experience. No closely related events with similar undertones. This was all too familiar. The centrifuge was slowing, images floating to the surface, a picture being formed. He was *remembering*.

The talisman was familiar because he'd seen it before. Possessed it, even.

It belonged to him … or did, once before. He

scratched his chin. Before, *what*?

Before it was *taken* from him, he realized. Taken by the person who had been the skeleton!

John stood with a start, bumping his head on one of the tent crossbars, although he hardly noticed. The snapshots in his mind, the puzzle pieces, had all aligned and the picture it formed was now crystal clear. They were no longer faded images distorted with doubt and paranoia but a memory as sharp as if he had just experienced it.

It was all there now. Professor Rutherford handing him the talisman back in Chicago with a warning. The professor's suicide. Getting attacked in the hallway. His ransacked dorm room. Dropping out of the university. Working at the school in Moline. And then … then … Taylor. Taylor had visited him. They went for a ride. He was shot. Twice. Then … nothing. No memory after that.

The thought frightened him. He shook his head. This was no memory at all. This was something that was *going* to happen. He felt it to be right. He *knew* it to be right.

As strange and bizarre as it might seem, John knew without question that the talisman had something to do with time travel. Backward. Only backward. Taylor must have taken the talisman, shifted backward, and died. Fell into the hole and broke his neck, perhaps. Or maybe just starved to death. Now, centuries or millennia later, when they all went to the island to dig the site, he came across Taylor's skeleton still with the talisman.

John wanted to pace, but there was no room

in the tent. Instead, he sat. And then stood again. Adrenaline pumped through him. Thoughts were clearer than he had expected, and he wanted to remember them all.

"John, are you coming for dinner?" Hannah called from somewhere near the stone fire pit where they cooked all their meals. It would be a later-than-normal dinner, since it was their last day on the island, and they had excavated longer than usual. The sun was setting quickly.

"Leave him alone. He's probably got a sheep in there," Taylor said, deliberately loud.

Taylor.

There was nothing to like about Taylor. His constant teasing and sarcastic manners were annoying. His off-color comments involving so-called farm humor were offensive. Knowing what would happen in the future made John resent him all the more. The longer he thought about it, the angrier he became.

After returning the talisman to his pocket, he quickly unzipped the tent flap and hurried outside to the campfire.

He stood at the edge of the circle while everyone else ate freshly cooked stew and cornbread. He stared at the man who would cause him so much trouble in about three months. John clenched his teeth.

Taylor sat up and stared back. "What are you looking at, plowboy?"

Although tempted to fight his nemesis, John resisted the urge. No one would have understood why. The events that might warrant retaliation hadn't happened yet. If he acted on impulse now, everyone would think that *he* was the antagonist, not Taylor.

Hannah stood up from the log she'd been sitting on and handed him a bowl of steaming stew and a spoon.

"You all right?" she asked, softly.

He was so distracted thinking about what he was going to have to do to protect himself from Taylor in the coming months that he didn't hear what she said.

"John?"

He snapped out of his thoughts. She had the same concerned expression as when he was about to go around the bend to the professor's new dig site. It bothered him to think that in the future he would cause her anguish. How had he missed the opportunity to get to know her better when he had the chance?

The opportunity presented itself on a different timeline inside the professor's office, he remembered. Shortly after that, however, he was on the run trying to protect the talisman. He wasn't about to let another chance pass.

He took the bowl from her hand, leaned forward, and kissed her. She did not lean away. It was not a lingering kiss but one that made its point.

Hannah seemed a little surprised. John had never made any advances toward her in the past, unlike Taylor, who had made numerous attempts to win her affection. Her eyes widened but she didn't mind the kiss. In fact, she moved closer, closed her eyes, and kissed him in return. This time, the kiss was planted with authority.

Some catcalls were raised by Louis and Harrison. Taylor said nothing.

"Okay, okay," Professor Rutherford said, returning from his tent after hearing the commotion by the fire. They were too close to going home for him to worry about being a chaperone now.

"Better than a sheep, eh Opie?" Taylor asked, snidely.

John turned toward Taylor. Hannah continued to grip his arm. She knew that there was something between the two men. Something that had been brewing for some time, but she didn't want to see it escalate. She certainly didn't want anything to happen to John.

John stopped, looked at Hannah, and smiled. She smiled back. It was a reassuring smile that left little doubt that they would pick up where they left off when they got back to Chicago. In this timeline, they had created a spark. Fanned a flame. And if he had anything to say about it, they would build a bonfire.

There was still, however, the issue of Taylor.

Sooner or later John knew that he would have to confront the man who would try to kill him and steal the talisman. He wondered if he should take the offensive and attack first, or whether he should be defensive and protect himself when the attack *does* happen. Knowing what was going to happen would certainly give him the advantage.

"It's water under the bridge," Hannah said, walking away from the circle. She hoped that John would follow. He did, and they stopped.

"What do you mean?" he asked.

"You shouldn't let him bother you. You know how he is. There are just some things that will never change."

She's probably right, John thought. The universe is probably locked into some twisted loop, like a Möbius strip. They'll go back to Chicago, Taylor will rob him, he'll go back in time and die on the island, and the whole thing will start again. It was a sobering thought. His heart sank.

John nodded, reassuring her that he wasn't going to do something stupid. But his thoughts were elsewhere.

He started walking toward the pickup trucks. The sun was setting quickly. The air cooled. Gravel crunched with each footstep. Hannah walked alongside. She wasn't sure he wanted company but wasn't willing to abandon that brief romantic interlude that they'd begun a moment earlier. She hoped that there would be a closing comment, or perhaps another kiss.

They were halfway to the trucks. A good thirty yards from the other students and out of earshot. John stopped suddenly and wheeled around to face the direction from which had just come, his eyes wide.

"Things *did* change!" he exclaimed.

"What do you mean?"

"The skeleton. It was there, and then it was gone. It changed."

"You lost me," she admitted.

"Tell me. Did we uncover anything while here on the island?"

She frowned and shook her head. "Nothing of any significance. You know that."

He started pacing, rubbing his chin. He did his best thinking while moving.

"The skeleton was there in the first timeline," he

muttered to himself as he tried to put these new pieces together. "Everyone commented on it. This time when I found it, it disappeared minutes later. Why?"

Hannah hadn't moved, hadn't flinched. She watched and waited, her eyebrows drawn together. John obviously had something on his mind and needed a moment.

Suddenly, he stopped and threw his arms in the air. "Of course!"

This timeline was different because he had kept the talisman instead of giving it to the professor. By keeping it, he started down a timeline that protected it successfully from Taylor. If Taylor never takes ownership of it in the future, then he can't shift backward and die with it in the hole. That's why the skeleton disappeared. Because Taylor never shifted backward!

A sense of relief washed over John, the likes of which he had never felt before. As if an unidentified albatross had been lifted from his shoulders. He remembered the stress and anxiety he felt in the future with the other timeline. Now, he felt free of that. Cleansed. He sighed deeply and smiled.

John realized that there was still the obligation to keep the talisman a secret and safe, but the disappearing skeleton was proof that he could achieve that goal. From Taylor, at least.

John turned to Hannah and threw his arms around her, beaming. "Things can be different. They *are* different!"

She had no idea what he was spouting off about, but he now seemed happy. Less tense. She returned the smile and put her arms around him. "I could have told you that things were different."

He nodded. "Things are going to be all right. I can feel it."

"I could have told you *that* too."

She rested her cheek on his chest, and they held each other tightly. She closed her eyes, hoping that this was just the beginning of a long future together. From the sound of his pounding heart, she knew it would be.

The air was starting to chill. But they remained warm in each other's arms. Neither wanted the moment to end.

The archaeological expedition to Antigua was nearing its conclusion. The next day, the students would finish the last of their packing, tear down their tents, and start their long journey home.

As difficult as it was the past ten days working on a hot, humid, remote island, John felt that his challenge had only just begun. Nevertheless, he was optimistic. He knew that as long as he secured the talisman, kept it secret and away from everyone, including himself, there would only be one present—the one they were currently in.

And the future? Well, the future would stay right where it belonged. Unknown and always ahead of them.

Epilogue

FIVE YEARS LATER

"How's it coming?" Hannah asked, as she came down the stairs.

"Almost done," John answered, standing back to admire his work.

He had just applied the second coat of paint on the basement wall. It was the last in a series of necessary house projects. Next was to decorate the nursery.

Hannah moved next to her husband and slipped her arm around his waist. John put his arm around her shoulders.

"It looks wonderful. You're a real Rembrandt."

John smiled, turned and kissed her. "It's just a wall," he said.

She smiled. "Yes, but it's *our* wall. In *our* house."

John smiled and nodded.

Hannah put her hand on her enlarged belly. "And you finished just in time for the baby."

"Ah, yes, the baby," he said. "How time flies. It wasn't all that long ago we were college students. Now look at us. Married with a child on the way."

"And a house of our own. That *you* built!"

"It wasn't easy, or fast," he said, "but we got it done."

"It was mostly you, but I helped too. A little, at least. With all the experience you gained working at George Washington Elementary, you made it look easy! And in such a short time!"

John gave his wife a squeeze of appreciation.

He never told her *how* he had acquired all that experience. Her knowledge of the talisman and its secrets was left in a different timeline. He didn't like keeping a secret from Hannah, but it was for her safety, and that of their child, that he did not revisit the subject.

Had he told her about the talisman in *this* timeline, she may have had doubts about stowing it between the walls of the house they had just finished building.

No, he didn't believe that there should be secrets in a marriage, with the exception of this one thing.

"You'd better get cleaned up. We're going by the neighbor's for their barbecue, remember? And I still have to make the pasta salad!"

"I'll be right there," John answered.

"I love you," she called out as she started up the stairs.

"Love you more!"

He waited until she was on the main floor and

out of earshot. Then, he put his palm on the wall, not only to see if it was dry, but also to see if the talisman was emitting any sound, hum, or vibration. The paint had dried, and there was no clue the talisman was there.

With his hand still on the wall, he thought back to the note he'd written. The one he included with the talisman which he placed in the hollow of a cinderblock, behind thick plasterboard:

> *TO WHOM IT MAY CONCERN,*
> *Although I have taken extraordinary*
> *care to see that this ... thing ... not be found,*
> *you have somehow come across it,*
> *nevertheless. Take my advice and return this*
> *note and the item to the place you have found it*
> *and leave it there. Or, if you must, move it*
> *to a more secure location. Just remove it*
> *from your existence. Forget—if you can—*
> *that you ever came across it. And whatever*
> *you do, resist the temptation to tinker with*
> *it or give it away. Trust me, you will be*
> *better off without it. We all will.*
> *John Shaw*

John sighed and removed his hand. At last, the talisman was securely hidden, just as he had promised Professor Rutherford in a previous timeline. No one knew it was there. No one would ever stumble upon it. It was safe at last.

He only wished that he could tell the professor that he had secured the talisman. How he had taken the responsibility of protecting it seriously. John felt that the professor would have been proud, or at least, satisfied.

Alas, that conversation would never happen. Not only was the professor serving time in prison for stealing items that belonged to the university, but he knew nothing of the talisman in *this* timeline.

John took a deep breath and smiled as he headed upstairs to get ready for the barbecue.

With a wife he adored and the promise of a baby on the way, he couldn't wait to find out what the future held—just like everyone else.

ABOUT THE AUTHOR

Tom Catalano is the author of numerous books of fiction and poetry. Some titles are for adults, while others are suitable for teens, pre-teens, and children. He likes to say that he has a book for every member of the family.

His novels and short stories are generally urban science fiction and psychological suspense, while others are slice-of-life with feel-good themes. He takes improbable situations and makes them seem possible. Several of his short stories have won science fiction contests.

His rhyming poems take a lighthearted look at everyday events, while his sentimental poems are heart-warming reflections of people, places, and events. They have appeared in newspapers and magazines throughout North America.

Tom is originally from the Chicago suburbs and graduated from Aurora University. He has read his work at bookstores, libraries, schools, churches, and community events across the country. He has been interviewed on television several times and his books are available worldwide.

# # #

OTHER BOOKS BY TOM CATALANO:

- **The Edge of Imagination**
Eleven short stories of urban science fiction and psychological suspense. Ordinary people put in extraordinary situations with unexpected endings. If you like *The Twilight Zone*, you'll love these stories! 176 pgs, paperback. Adults-older teens. (ISBN 978-1-882646-10-4)

- **Tall Tales & Short Stories**
Thirteen short stories of psychological suspense, mystery, light romance, and comedy. Stories that will make you smile and/or keep you guessing until the end. 176 pgs, paperback. Adults-older teens.
(ISBN 978-1-882646-16-6)

- **Nicholas, The Santa Story**
The rhyming story of how Nicholas chose to become Santa after hearing the voice of God and visiting Baby Jesus. An original heartwarming story that connects the birth of Jesus with the secular traditions of the holiday using historical fiction. Very popular with grandparents, parents, and children. 44 pgs, hardcover, fully illustrated. All ages. (ISBN 978-1-882646-12-8)

More books on next page!

OTHER BOOKS BY TOM CATALANO:

- **Funny Rhymes About Life!**
  Amusing rhymes on everyday subjects that adults can relate to, like love, marriage, getting older, feeling lazy, unexpected events, telemarketers, honey-do projects, stink breath, and much more! 92 pgs, paperback. Adults. (ISBN 978-1-882646-13-5)

- **Witty Words of Wisdom**
  150 original funny, clever, inspiring, or thought-provoking nuggets of wit and wisdom. Samples: *"I'm not lazy. I'm selectively productive." "Getting older is just nature's way of seasoning to taste." "I did not grow up. I was raised."* 96 pgs, paperback. Adults-teens. (ISBN 978-1-882646-11-1)

- **Poems For His Glory**
  Expect to feel God's presence while reading these faith-inspiring rhyming poems (i.e. *Hope, Heaven, A Cross To Bear, Repaid*). Many positive reviews by faith leaders of various religious denominations. Co-written by Emma Catalano. 96 pgs, paperback. Families. (ISBN 978-1-882646-09-8)

OTHER BOOKS BY TOM CATALANO:

- **Rhyme & Reason**
The author's first book. A wide range of subjects, emotions, and humor. Includes: *A Child's Christmas*, *Work Dreams*, *Las Vegas Vacation of Mine*, *Wanderlust*, and *Pearanoid*. 96 pgs. Adults-teens. (ISBN 978-1-882646-07-4)

- **Poetry 'N Motion**
Rhyming poems to make you laugh and feel good. Includes touching poems on Christmas, love, family, and more. 96 pgs. Adults-teens. (ISBN 978-1-882646-03-6)

- **Verse Things First**
Fun rhyming poems to tickle your funny bone, have you feeling good, and touch you. Many poems about Christmas, love, and family. Very popular. 96 pgs. Adults-teens. (ISBN 978-1-882646-43-2)

- **I Dig Mud & Yellow Blood**
Funny and touching rhyming poems about Caterpillar (the heavy equipment manufacturer), Cat dealers, and the people who use construction equipment. 48 pgs, paperback. Adults-teens. (ISBN 978-1-882646-91-3)

More books on next page!

OTHER BOOKS BY TOM CATALANO:

- **Rhymes For Teens**
Rhyming poems that don't take themselves too seriously. Will have pre-teens, teens (and adults!) smiling and feeling good. Includes: *Wishes For Dishes, Stinky Feet, Me Me Me, I Dreamt I Was You, Phew!, and more.* 80 pgs. Pre-teens, teens, adults. (ISBN 978-1-882646-48-7)

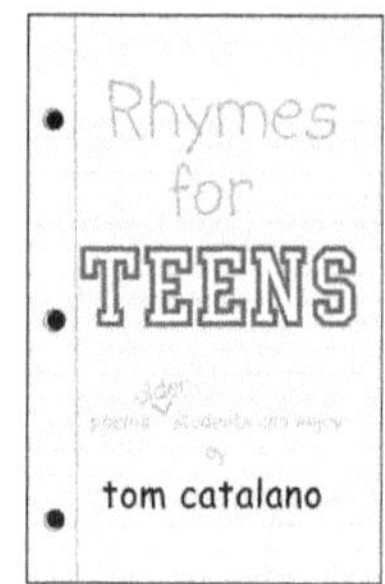

- **Jelly In My Belly**
Silly, funny, and touching rhyming poems that will have children, pre-teens, and teens smiling and laughing. Includes: *How To Make A Friend, Anudder Peanut Butter, Bitter Batter, The Wish List.* 48 pgs. Children. (ISBN 978-1-882646-02-9)

- **Rhymes For Kids!**
Chock full of silly and feel-good rhyming poems that kids will enjoy. Read them aloud and smile! Includes: *I Wish I Was A Pizza, Bubble Trouble, All God's Critters, Christmas Rap, My Friend Mary-Jean*, and the popular *Cute Little Birdie.* 48 pgs. Children. (ISBN 978-1-882646-05-0)

Order from your favorite bookseller, Amazon.com, and tomcatalano.com

www.ingramcontent.com/pod-product-compliance
Lightning Source LLC
Chambersburg PA
CBHW040515170726
48295CB00012B/211